Marion Ettlinger

About the Author

ADAM BRAVER is the author of *Divine Sarah* and *Mr. Lincoln's Wars*, a selection of the Barnes & Noble Discover New Writers program and Border's Original Voices series. *Crows over the Wheatfield* was a 2006 Book Sense Pick. His work has appeared in *Daedalus*, *Cimarron Review*, *Post Road*, and the *Pittsburgh Quarterly*. He teaches creative writing at Roger Williams University in Bristol, Rhode Island.

OTHER BOOKS
BY ADAM BRAVER

Divine Sarah

Mr. Lincoln's Wars

CROWS *over the* WHEATFIELD

Adam Braver

HARPER PERENNIAL

NEW YORK • LONDON • TORONTO • SYDNEY

HARPER ● PERENNIAL

Portions of this book have appeared in different form in *Daedalus*.

A hardcover edition of this book was published in 2006 by William Morrow, an imprint of HarperCollins Publishers.

FIRST HARPER PERENNIAL EDITION PUBLISHED 2007.

Designed by Susan Yang

The Library of Congress has catalogued the hardcover edition as follows:

Braver, Adam.

    Crows over the wheatfield : a novel / Adam Braver.—1st ed.
      p. cm.
    ISBN: 978-0-06-078232-0 (acid-free paper)
    ISBN-10: 0-06-078232-3 (acid-free paper)
    1. Women college teachers—Fiction. 2. Traffic accidents—Fiction.
   3. Providence (R.I.)—Fiction. 4. Psychological fiction. I. Title.

PS3602.R39C76 2006
813'.6—dc22

                         2006043818

ISBN: 978-0-06-078233-7 (pbk.)
ISBN-10: 0-06-078233-1 (pbk.)

07 08 09 10 11 ❖/RRD 10 9 8 7 6 5 4 3 2 1

To

Henry Ferris

and

Nat Sobel

People usually escape from their troubles into the future; they draw an imaginary line across the path of time, a line beyond which their current troubles will cease to exist.

— Milan Kundera,
THE UNBEARABLE LIGHTNESS OF BEING

PART ONE

October,

November,

January

Late October

I t was amazing how different the world appeared once shifted
back an hour. How altered the towns along Route 111 looked
at 5:30 P.M., now that the hands of the clocks had been maneu-
vered. The storefronts of the smaller villages that usually were
filled by darkness and northern decay were gleaming tonight. Lit
up on the insides, they shone through normal working hours, almost festively alive. And this illusion seemed to work on pedestrians, as more people cluttered the sidewalks, creating the myth that
there was life after dark in these forgotten little coastal towns—all
you needed to do was turn back the clocks.

Claire's commute home from campus usually concluded with
the veil of dusk over her Providence driveway. If she was quick
enough, Claire could leash up her one-year-old dog, Cocoa, and
walk the length of her street until she was at the top of the hill.
From there she could watch the sun drop into the other half of the

world. Perhaps it was the result of finding herself alone again, but she needed the nightly ritual to wring out her psyche.

The first night of standard time each October was always disorienting. Coming out of the classroom, she saw the night pouring through the sky, reminding her of the same power and explosion of Van Gogh's form against a brilliantly conceived dawn. And, for a moment, she understood Vincent's momentary lapses of lucidity, of how strange and blinding the natural world must have seemed—one that only bold brushstrokes could tame. (She thought to make a note of that for her class, and possibly for her newest book project.)

The drive down 111 was in near total darkness, without even the moon as a night-light. She trailed red brake lights that cast a fiery hue over the night. Traffic was snarled per usual at the town of Carver. These roads had never been built with the expectation that they would be traveled by the hordes of commuters that had extended the city into every outreach of the region. And poor Carver, so fragile and all alone, with little to show but a Dunkin' Donuts, a hobby shop, a string of stagnant antique shops, and a hidden work center for retarded adults, had become the epicenter of the coastal traffic. After winding around the waterfronts, the major shortcuts and minor routes all collided in Carver for a straight path out to the freeway. A final ten-mile-per-hour crawl that stretched along past once glorious houses that now sat fearfully exposed at the roadside.

Clouds had darkened the edges of the horizon, giving a strange dual dimension to the blackened sky. In an odd moment of prewinter fury, a flock of black-winged birds whipped the sky, swooning to the left, with a sudden awkward turn to the right, as though lost and trying to rediscover their way south. They looked equally frozen at the merge, shadowed against the brilliance of the still glistening bay that paralleled 111.

Claire looked over to her left at the houses that had stood for nearly two centuries. For seven years she had been commuting this road from the university, yet she was noticing them for the first time. Perhaps separating from Richard had really opened new sights for her. There was a red Colonial, its lit-up windows sparkling and winking back at the drivers. Beside it a little shack that must have housed generations of New England fisherman who trolled for quahogs or lobsters. And how different this all must have looked, four generations ago. These homes originally built with northeastern reserve, where heavily trafficked routes did not belly up to their front lawns, where seclusion was their protection from the changing world. Claire squinted to read the historical plaque by the red Colonial's door, but couldn't quite make out the name of the original owners. She thought she might have seen the name WILLIAMS, and then wondered if the Williamses could have ever imagined that this is what would happen to their lovely home. The pride of their workmanship set three blocks from the bay, isolation that must have afforded them a view into the sweetly infinite horizon. This implied paradise now sat along the backed-up roadway, one block from a Shell gas station, a block the other way from a Blockbuster video, and directly across the street from a fried chicken stand that also made donuts and tacos.

The traffic started to move a little, enough that Claire dragged the stick of her nearly new Honda Accord into second. The other side was running remarkably faster, as those residents heading into the village were unfazed by the darkness at this earlier hour. It was their road and their night. Yet, as suddenly as she found her side moving, she was just as quickly stepping on the brake.

Just hold tight, Cocoa. Hold tight.

On the front lawn of the red Colonial stood a young boy, maybe ten, maybe younger (perhaps older, it is hard to tell in these days of adult fashions for children). Yellow light squared off every available window of the red Colonial, yet still there was a strange emptiness to the house behind him. Had he been there before, and just been obscured by her thoughts? He postured with one hand on his hip and the other clutching a skateboard. His expression looked somewhat puzzled, as though his pupils were in a permanent state of refraction from trying to adjust to the new night. Claire witnessed a certain disappointment in him. His hour of play before dinner had been cheated from him; the daylight stolen, replaced by a stream of unforgiving cars with burning headlights. She watched the decision process. He sized up the elements, weighing the possible against the impossible, dislocating risk from consequence. But mostly she saw the defiance of righteousness, of a boy's decision to refuse to have his right to play taken. He threw down the skateboard, stepped aboard, bent his knees, and clumsily sailed it off the lawn toward the narrow strip of crumpled sidewalk that 111 bordered. The leaves broke under his wheels. In near darkness, on a deteriorated sidewalk, the boy was barely in control of the board as the cars sailed beside him.

Clouds began to overtake the sky, making the early evening seem darker. From the Honda there was no skating noise, just the cool breeze of cars beating down the opposing lane, some still without headlights, not fully accepting the dusk. She should have said something to the boy. She was convincing herself that this was not the neglect of TV-obsessed parents who had told their son to go outside and play until dinner is ready. Perhaps he was the latchkey child of working parents who were jammed up by the traffic right now. She briefly looked away from the inching bumper ahead to study the boy's face, looking for something.

Hold tight, Cocoa.

Claire leaned forward to turn up the radio. This section of road was always brutal on the airwaves. The final ten minutes of this hour's *All Things Considered* was supposed to be a story about the changing role of the museum, questioning whether it was driving the culture of art or merely responding to the demands of its consumers and donor bases. She tried to edge the car forward a bit, hoping another few feet would be enough to clear the static.

Traffic had barely moved. The skateboarding boy reappeared beside her, moving carelessly closer to the street's edge. His board flipped up, out from under his awkward feet. The nose and front wheels touched on the macadam as he stupidly reached out for it, his head seconds away from a speeding Pepsi truck that was too large and in too much of a hurry to be on 111 at rush hour. Claire screamed for the boy to look out, but her voice was lost to the roar of the truck's diesel engine. She was a little glad that she was not heard, as she might have distracted the boy and caused him to freeze in place, making the chance of an accident that much more inevitable. But, predictably, the boy still did not leave the area.

The southbound traffic had opened up a little more, and the cars were flying by faster. Each fender took the slight curve in front of the red Colonial with a little more daring. Either undaunted by the boy in front, or more than likely not seeing him at all.

Hold tight, Cocoa. I'll be home for you soon.

It was nearing the top of the hour, and the local affiliate announced the weather, saddening her with the news that the temperatures were beginning their annual descent. A typical NPR segue, a collaboration between a steel drum and an acoustic guitar, gave way to Robert Siegel's introduction of the museum story. Claire smiled when she heard that Maggie Harrison, a friend and colleague, would be the focus of the piece. It was nice to hear Maggie's voice again, reminding her that she needed to call Maggie's husband, Bill, who was editing her latest book, to give him a status report. Claire listened in carefully. The seriousness of Maggie's voice made her laugh, mostly from the memory of how unserious they had been together at the Worcester Marriott's bar after a day of conference papers delivered at Clark last year. It hadn't been that long after Richard had moved out, and Claire, having felt very alone and very friendless, had welcomed the late nights and forgetting, even if it was for only a three-day weekend. Still, Claire could recognize the professional Maggie in the interview—the passion rising in her voice when pressed to a defense against high-powered commerce that was trying to co-opt the essence of art, in collusion with the overall assault on high culture. She listened with interest until a wave of static hijacked the station with the distant cadence of mariachi music. Many a radio story had been lost over this quarter mile of Carver road.

Just ahead, on a side street to her right, an older black Delta 88 started to nose its way out onto Route 111, the chrome trim stripped from the door, with one nub dangling near the rear shank. Claire was not a newcomer to Rhode Island, but she had never really gotten used to the driving practice of swinging into oncoming traffic. Sometimes Claire went out of her way to speed up in order to prevent the cars from butting in to the stream.

Letting cars pull out in front of you was a custom here. The real locals said it was bred from courtesy. The oncoming driver was supposed to recognize the plight of the stranded turner and hit the brakes. Then he was to give a slight wave of the hand and let the motorist proceed to turn left in front of everybody, instead of waiting for the natural break in the traffic. The practice yielded two negative results. One was all the near accidents that were caused by the sudden, unexpected braking of a car on a straightaway, the other was the danger from cars such as this one that just expected the stopping as a formality, and then pulled out into traffic anyway, nearly causing as many accidents.

From the moment she first moved to Rhode Island, Claire was determined not to be part of that system. She incurred the wrathful stares of those whom she bypassed on her right—only vaguely spared verbal abuses when they saw her Rhode Island license plates. The practice may have been a holdover from a simpler time. But these two-hundred-year-old roads had since become complex arteries of traffic that carried people all over the region.

Claire tapped at the buttons of the radio, hoping to tune in the story on a side frequency. She really wanted to hear Maggie finish her interview. If worse came to worse, Claire could always flip over to the FM side to try to find WBUR in Boston, although by the time she found it, the story would probably be over.

The car in the facing traffic followed the regional custom by stopping cold in the road, jamming up all the autos behind it. Claire could see its conductor's hand beginning to wave on a Delta

88. Another case of the illusion of order leading to disorder. The Delta 88 began to edge out. It hesitated, unsure of what Claire might do. She herself was uncertain. At this point, there was no reason not to let the car go. The whole highway had come to a complete halt for it. The chaos had already formed into sequence, and in a ridiculous turn, Claire, by not participating, would now be the one causing the dysfunction. The stage was set. Everything in place. The pedestrians stood poised, ready to cross through the street, as though there magically appeared crosswalks and orange reflector-vested guards. In this one flicker of time, Claire saw herself on a moral precipice, as though stopping would promote an errant system and make her an accomplice to every roadside danger on Route 111. To complicate things, the traffic ahead had broken open. If she stopped, Claire risked missing the break and getting stuck at the red light ahead.

There was surprise in the eyes of the Delta 88's driver when Claire did not appear to be slowing down (and in fact even speeding up in order to make the light—and get back into range of NPR). In that moment, Claire saw the woman's heavily mascaraed eyes. They were painted and pronounced. She imagined the makeup had been carefully applied—thicker at the bottom, thinned at the top, accented by an unusual spike that collided with the outside corner of the eyes. Hardened and desperate. A woman who had been beaten down by dreams and fists. Reduced to a helplessness that seethed in anger, where her only sense of power was when she could control a two-ton piece of steel and blast it uncompromisingly into the road, using this antediluvian New England driving tradition to engage in a ridiculous battle against class, nosing its way into the roadway, the thoughts almost emanating out the windshield that *no 2001 Accord EX is going to tell me how to drive.* Claire practically heard it while the woman inched forward with testosterone machismo. Claire should have just braked and given the woman one moment, a small victory in a lifetime of defeats, but she would not let herself be bullied.

As she stepped on the gas, Claire tried to tell that to the woman through a firm but empathetic gaze. The Delta 88 woman threw up her middle finger, and shouted, "Bitch" as she slammed on her brakes, causing the Delta 88 to jerk to a halt, rocking back and forth on overloaded springs.

Claire looked straight ahead, consciously trying to ignore her. As the radio signal began to strengthen, Claire reached over to adjust the dial back to its regular setting.

Somebody screamed from the sidewalk. Claire looked up to see the boy frozen in place, his head and shoulders squared clearly in front of her windshield.

And for a moment it is a still photograph.

The boy is looking directly at her with an expression free from fear. He is oddly at ease. And as Claire looks at his face, she has the sudden realization that this is a face she will never forget. This face will emerge from the shadows when she closes her eyes at night.

She sees his red hair, colored by a particular shade of Scot orange, cropped close to the head, with defined lines shaved up over the perfectly symmetric ears. The top is left tousled, although not shaggy enough to incur a parent's wrath. His thin nose points with purpose but seems oddly small for the roundness of his face. Slightly chapped lips are set apart with a little space, void of expression. And she wishes she could see his smile. Not seeing his teeth will always leave the image incomplete. She is fully aware of how dramatically a smile can alter the way a person looks. Warmth, charm, bitterness, devilishness. They all reveal themselves in the smile. And in the eyes, as well. A pair of blue irises as pure as a new marble looks back at her, too young to have to witness the sadness of the world.

For one last second they look at each other.

Just stare.

Claire never heard the thump of the car. Later she won't remember slamming the brakes, nor recall how her car ended up parked along the side of the road, only a vague memory of hearing Maggie's voice fading. The air bags never deployed; the collision was that subtle. Her head throbbed. And she found herself fearfully banging at the car door. A temporary memory loss at how to open the goddamn thing. She fumbled for the handle while kicking instinctively at the base. Her mind and nerves operated with no central thought commands, as though she was fighting defensively for her life. She couldn't get out of this Japanese suit of armor. Even for a moment. Just to see if the boy was all right.

A man cupped his hands against the window on the driver's door. He leaned in close, peering, his breath fogging a near perfect circle. Claire looked at him and called out, "Get me out of here. Please."

He looked kindly in his long black overcoat, with the wind blowing his salt-and-pepper hair. He sported a cropped gray beard, not too unlike Freud's, but without the scholarly authority. "If you could just open up the lock for me," he said. The last word wavered slightly at the end, the point when emotion is finally allowed to supplant bravery. "Can you do it, miss? . . . Paramedics are on their way. On their way. I called . . . Two times, I called. They are on their . . . They said they're on the way."

Claire froze in place. For the life of her, she could not remember where the lock was. She fumbled her hands around. She closed her eyes once, and then opened them again, hoping that the freshness would bring everything back into perspective. Somehow, her brain was unable to command her hands to reach for the door.

Traffic was stopped in all directions. Constant footsteps patted circles around her. Claire heard crying. She heard panic. But mostly what she heard was a strange silence, one in which all the sound waves were thickly coated in plastic, bouncing off one another mutedly. In the distance the ambulance howl cried from Billington, winding its way through the cars that clogged the highway. She knew the boy must be lying in the street somewhere near the edge of her front tire. She needed to get out to save him. But she could not find the goddamn lock.

The passenger door swung open, letting in a wave of excitement. Claire turned to see the man from outside kneeling in the neighboring seat. "Did you hit your head?" His voice was a little thinner than it had seemed from outside the car. "Is your head all right?" he asked with a nervous whisper.

"What happened to the boy?" Her voice did not sound as her own, rather some implanted response mechanism programmed for unfortunate circumstances. Television had trained her well.

The man looked down. "The ambulance is on its way."

"I tried to tell him to be careful. I tried . . ."

"He skated out in front. No regard for . . . We all saw it. From across the street. My office window. It was slow motion that happened in a second . . . We all . . . Yelled, but not . . . We all saw."

"I tried . . ."

"No business being there. No. None at all. Pure recklessness."

"I even yelled out once."

"The ambulance is on the way."

Claire closed her eyes. Her head was going to explode. She tried to speak calmly through modulated words. "I can't seem to manage to open my door." It didn't strike her as funny, but she thought that she might start laughing at any moment. Maybe at irony. Or at the sadness of pure helplessness. "I can't remember how to open the damn door."

The man looked at her.

"Can you just help me out of here?"

"Maybe you should just wait until the police get here. They know what to do with these things." The man nestled into the passenger's seat. His muddy shoes stepped on the papers, further jostling them in his effort to avoid them. He closed the door, insulating the chaos. "I'll sit with you until help comes." He must have had children, and been through the worst emergency room scares. "Police are on their way . . . Probably best if you just stay put."

"I yelled out once. And that car kept coming at me. They all do it, although it's totally reckless. Kept coming . . . What else could I have . . . ?"

"I hear the sirens coming closer now. Traffic is backed up. Deep."

"I think that I should get out. Can you help me get out? I could help the boy."

"They'll be here any minute."

Claire lifted her head and turned to look at him. Outside the headlights cut through the darkness, etching fine ivory beams only broken by drivers who had jumped out of their cars, rushing to figure out the right thing to do. The scene seemed to become more festive as the red and yellow lights of the emergency vehicles finally approached. Claire looked at the strange man sitting in her front seat. She began to repeat that she had tried to warn the boy, and then interrupted herself by finally flipping the door handle, again only to find it locked.

The man placed his hand on her back. It might have been comforting, but it left her feeling oddly violated. He was kind. Kinder than she would know how to be in this situation. "You don't need to stay," she said. "You don't need to protect me. I'll be okay. Fine. If you could just help me open the—"

"The police are arriving now. They'll need to talk with you, I'm sure."

"Just tell me that he's alive . . ."

"And the paramedics will check your . . . It's okay, I'm just across the street . . . I work across . . . The accounting agency . . . I can . . ."

"Just help me out of here."

Outside the groans and rumbles of fire trucks and ambulances shook the ground. Their lighthouse beams swirling colored fingers of light. The urgency accelerated, as she felt the presence of authority and control.

The man opened the passenger door. "Over here," he shouted toward the paramedics. "Over here." He left one leg in the car, his weight on the ball of his other foot while his hand pressed against the ceiling.

"Please just help me out. Someone," Claire muttered, aware that she was only speaking to herself.

A paramedic scooted the man to the side and slipped into the warmed seat beside her. He introduced himself as Jim. Asked her name, and she told him. He asked how she was doing. His voice sounded a little casual given the potential, an obviously intended psychology to alleviate panic. "I'm all right," she answered. "How is the boy?"

"I need to take a look at your head. These kinds of accidents can sneak an injury up on you. Let me take a look now, Claire."

"No," she said. "I am fine. Please tell me about the—"

"In just a minute I will come around to the other side and help you out." He spoke as though she had suffered a brain trauma. He barely looked older than most of her students, with the same simple, clean-cut look. "We have to have you stand. Can you do that for me, Claire? Stand? First, please look my way. You can hear me, right?"

Before she could protest, he was pulling down on her eyelid, blinding her with a penlight. She didn't object. What else could she do? "Good," Jim spoke as he worked. "Look up." Then he peered into the other one. "Looking good . . . If there was any jarring, things can seem momentarily disoriented for some time. But not to worry."

Jim reached across her and popped open the lock. Her sight was blurred and burning brightly.

When he opened her door from the outside, Jim stood with his red toolbox in hand, the accounting Samaritan behind him. Behind both of them, Claire could see the wall of people carefully arranged by the police officers finally on the scene. Yellow tape was being strapped around the perimeter. The lighting was all very strange. A pitched dark that falsely dazzled under the artifice of generated lights, turning the loneliness of tragedy into pure man-made brilliance.

Jim bent down and squeezed around her knee. "A little tender," he said. "Do you remember hitting anything?"

Claire shook her head, no.

"Can you stretch it out for me?"

She tried, but it was a little stiff.

"Can you stand on it, Claire?"

The paramedic lifted her by the upper arm. At the true moment of finally being freed from the car, she suddenly felt afraid. She did not want to let go of the steering wheel. As he pulled her up, planted her on both feet, she looked down to avoid the scene. And there, before she could avert her eyes from the emergency team huddle, Claire saw a patch of the boy's red hair against the black macadam. She witnessed the control of the paramedics, responding with ease, reaching into their boxes for needles and apparatuses, their postures calm but their hands beginning to shake.

Claire felt her chest pump. It became almost impossible to swallow, as though her throat was rebelliously constricting, while her body became obsessed with getting air.

She kept staring at the red hair.

Her hearing started to diminish until all she could hear was a loud pounding sound, as if mallets beat her eardrums. The paramedic was talking at her, but it wouldn't matter. She couldn't hear him anyway. Her head started to feel light. She finally drew her eyes away fast enough to see Jim strapping an oxygen mask to her face. She ripped it off instinctively and turned her head to vomit against the side of the Accord.

Claire retreated to her car. She sat with the door open, an olive green blanket wrapped around her like a cape. The scene played on as if it were a television show that she had seen a million times. Various police asked quick questions as though she had already read the script. Administered the Breathalyzer. Rerouted the traffic. Their postures, the modulation of their voices, and their formalities were all comfortably familiar. Claire was thankful that she knew the show. She knew how to answer the questions. What to expect, and what was expected of her. At least something seemed normal. She had been cleared by the paramedics assigned to her, who walked away empty-handed—only advising her to see a doctor if the pain in her leg persisted. She promised she would.

Twice she had tried to go over to the boy, but both times had been stopped by police officers. They took her registration, her license, and her insurance card. An officer named Almeida asked her routine questions as he organized the documents—how fast was she traveling? When did she first notice the boy? And as though he already knew the answers, he walked away without excusing himself to radio in her documents from the patrol car.

Claire stood up, tugging the blanket around her waist. The paramedics were hovered by the left headlight of her car, forming a half circle that revealed nothing other than their backs. Silver camera flashes exploded from the front bumper. Another officer marked off white lines while measuring them. And the traffic, by now backed up all the way to Newport, crept around the police barricade, each driver trying to steal a look without appearing obvious. Claire tried to muster the strength to stand on her tiptoes to look over the medics for the red hair. Inching herself forward, she was stopped by a police officer who was out of uniform but still bearing the official-ness of the uniform. He did not introduce himself but instead handed her his card. She didn't look at it. "Been a rough night for you, Miss Andrews."

She nodded, her hearing still muffled. How odd all these strangers knew her by name.

He stood between her and the boy.

"Some good news for you. Your blood alcohol level has registered zero . . ."

". . . I rarely drink during the week."

"But I do have a few things I need to go over with you, like how fast you were going, what led up to the moment of impact. Those kinds of questions."

"I just answered those for Mr. Almeida . . . He has my driver's license in his car."

"I realize that, Miss Andrews, but I am with the traffic investigation unit. Please bear with me."

She leaned to peer over at the boy. The cop swayed with her, blocking her view.

"These things have to be done procedurally. You can imagine all the lawyers and insurance investigators that will be looking over these reports." It was strange that he seemed to be apologizing. "This is all in your best interest."

They stood beside the car. Inches away from the boy, as the voices of the paramedics began to rise. Then one of them ran desperately back to the truck where he grabbed a plastic bag, ripped it open with his teeth, and discarded the plastic shard on the pavement. A sense of panic seemed to rise from the spot of highway in front of her car. The wind came up cold and heavy, having traveled across the bay. At first it stung Claire's ankles, almost having snapped at them, but then it felt like it had wrapped itself around her calves and thighs. The nameless investigator continued to ask questions in a modulated voice that she sensed held a trace of sympathy. It was a strange universe that they inhabited, where the dramas of each world seemed so separate, as though they were going on miles apart. Each time Claire tried to look over at the boy, the investigator moved in her way and asked another question. She played along. One more minute of camaraderie before she would walk away and live this evening alone for the rest of her life.

The boy was carried into the ambulance. Claire only saw the rise of his small frame formed under the thick blanket. She strained to see if it covered his face, but the investigator blocked her off. All she saw was the boy's streak of red hair blended into the siren's light. Then the ambulance pushed its way through the remaining snarl of traffic, en route to deliver the boy to the emergency room at Children's Hospital in Providence.

She stepped to the side and looked to where the boy had lain. It was just a black stain, no different from the refuse of leaking oil. Darkened by its fresh dampness, the spot would soon fade into the macadam.

The investigator looked over his shoulder, seemingly startled by the siren's light, then slipped his notepad into his pocket. He coughed for her attention. "Is it best to reach you at home or at the university?"

"Either way . . . Either way you can find me."

The fire trucks began to pull away, along with the extra police units. Claire felt her chest lighten, sensing the stripping away of sound that would leave her alone in silence. In a way, wishing this moment would never have to end.

"I almost forgot to ask," the investigator said. "Did you know the boy? I only ask because with these small towns one never knows."

She shook her head, no. At least she didn't think so.

"My advice to you is to stay away from the parents. Fight the urge for apology. For remorse. When the world goes crazy, the people in it do too. Best to just keep looking forward, and figure out what you need to figure out in your own way."

Claire didn't think she could stand any longer. Her knee was stiffening, and all the strength was draining from her body. She reached out to shake his hand. "Thank you," she said. For a second he was supporting her full weight.

"We'll be in touch." The investigator momentarily looked away, and then walked off, barking out a directive to a uniform to measure the distance from the curb to the current location of the car one more time.

From her car, Claire watched the investigation begin to wrap up. The traffic had been reduced to the remnants of those few who slowed down to take in the details. The camera flashes still bounced off the Accord's bumper, where, almost eerily, the car appeared to have only lost a front turning light. They flashed off the police-marked road. Off each angle of the intersection. All the questions had been asked. The witnesses queried, except the Delta 88 woman, who had driven off rather quickly after the impact, certainly never once considering her own culpability. Claire was told not to worry. The witnesses corroborated her story. There was nothing she could have done. Could have been anyone. It was not her fault. It was just down to procedure now. She nodded her head, thanking him as he spoke, and stretched her leg out a little bit to loosen the knee, dabbing it with the compress that the paramedic had left behind.

With each passing moment the night grew quieter. The branches looked like bones that had grown petrified and spindly, reaching out helplessly from the arched backs of the trees. The leaves, weeks past dried and fallen, had been swept into thoughtful piles house by house, passively fearing the wind. The crows had departed long ago. Bored from disinterest, and pulled by instinct, they had winged off much more stealthily than they had entered.

Officer Almeida told Claire that she was welcome to leave. There were still some loose ends to be tied, but they didn't need her anymore at this juncture. He had her contact information. She should expect a follow-up call with the questions that they may have neglected to ask on the scene. But, for now, he understood that she must be exhausted and bewildered. "Is there someone you would like to call before you leave?" he offered. "I'm no psychiatrist, but sometimes it is best not to be home alone."

She started to shake her head, no. Thinking for one moment that she might just crawl into the backseat, curl up with her jacket laid over her, and sleep until the morning sun forced her to leave. And for now, Claire regretted that she had Cocoa. That dog sitting home alone was the only reason she had to force herself back into her car. But the officer was right. This was no night to be alone. "Thank you," she said. She nodded, and took the cell phone that Almeida offered, pulling it through the open window.

It was in times of crises when she wished her parents were still living. Since her separation from Richard, Claire had had to manage completely alone again. Yes, she made polite conversation with her colleagues, followed up on invitations to various social events, but she kept all her friends at a distance. She had needed to discover who she was, without the expectations of who she had been. In truth, she couldn't think of a single person whom she could say remained a close friend from the days before and during her marriage. Maybe that was the sacrifice of her work. Or perhaps she had dedicated too much of her time to Richard. And now, not more than six months after she had given the speech that they needed to stop depending on each other in order to get a better gauge on where they stood, she held the cell phone, folded and miniature, almost delicate in her palms, trying to remember Richard's Cambridge studio number. Finally, she found one of Richard's business cards that he had left in her glove box.

It took total command of her concentration to make her finger dial the number. It was as though she had no body, her physicality gone numb and useless, almost ghostlike, where her thoughts only floated freely, with little connection to the physical world around her. She touched each number slowly, watching her hands as though they belonged to somebody else.

Richard answered on the first ring, probably engaged in the critical moment of a drawing, and too distressed by the phone's intrusiveness to do anything other than pick it up to make it stop. "Hello."

He was the type who needed notice. You could count on an uncomfortable silence if last-minute tasks were dropped on him. He was an artist who sat diligently at his easel most every day, a set of colored pencils in his hand, sketching fairly standard illustrations of the superficial muscles of the face. Mostly, he worked on order for the Harvard medical school. When he wasn't in his Cambridge studio, Richard was at the bottom levels of buildings, watching bodies being autopsied for a firsthand view of the subjects. His work was precise, capturing the essence of photography, with little call for an aesthetic value—somehow even a step beyond realism. The only goal was to capture the subject, void of any symbolic representation. He was the last of a dying breed—refusing to follow many of his colleagues into the digital world. He wouldn't make the move to airbrush or acrylics, instead using Verithin pencils as his only tool. Claire always had felt a little sadness for Richard. He had been blessed with remarkable skills, the gift to take in something with his eyes and then see through it with his hands. But because he disregarded his imaginative talents, his art would never be anything other than his vocation. He had abandoned a sense of interpreting the world, satisfied with just reporting on it.

"Richard." Claire couldn't say any more. She didn't know what to say. They don't show this scene in the movies.

"Claire? This is a surprise. . . . Can I call you back in about five minutes? I'm struggling with getting this one stupid tendon right. It looks like a piece of machinery right now. Five minutes?"

She hesitated out of instinct, almost ready to agree. "I can't." That was almost painful to say. Her body stiffened with the realization that she was reaching out to the person who two years ago, in a privately contrived existential panic, had tried to push her away; but despite his almost immediate recantation, the damage had lingered for another year until she sadly, but defiantly, had declared the trial separation.

"Where are you?"

"It's too much right now." Speaking any more than a single sentence would crush her.

"Are you okay?"

"Please come to the house tonight. Can you?"

"Claire . . . I don't know about . . ."

"You need to."

"The 93 traffic will be unbearable. I don't know when——"

"I need you to come now."

Richard sounded antsy. Maybe concerned, maybe bothered. "All right," he said. "I'll leave now. Maybe the Mass. Pike will be . . . Can you just tell me . . . Where are . . . ?"

"I can't believe it is even real . . . It's too horrible."

There was a pause, and then he said, "Okay."

She folded the phone in half, not sure if that had hung it up. When Claire looked around, and only she and Almeida were still there, the haunting vacancy of the scene began to make the accident devastatingly more real. She started to realize how impossible the drive home might be.

Almeida stared into the Accord on occasion as he finished his survey. He wrote down a few notes, and then started up his car, probably to let it warm. The gray exhaust blew straight and hard, almost solid looking. He left his door open and walked over to Claire. "That's all I have," he said.

"Thank you, officer." She returned his phone to him.

"You going to be all right going home?"

She lied, *yes*.

"I can follow you if you would like."

"I'll be fine."

"And you're sure there will be someone to meet you at home."

She nodded.

"Because," be continued, "a person should not be alone following an incident like this. The mind can play funny tricks on itself. I've seen a lot of this. Also saw it in the Gulf War. A couple of soldiers in my unit were involved in friendly fire. Knew the men they had eliminated by name. Held themselves in silence. Wouldn't talk to a soul. They could only stand to look at each other, until they could no longer stand to even look at themselves. But you don't need to know about that. All I'm saying is that you shouldn't be alone at a time like this. Know what I mean? Now I am just going to wait in my car until you're ready to go. Just going to be waiting, is all."

"Thank you, officer. I appreciate your concern." She rolled up her window, and watched him walk off to his patrol car, holstering his flashlight. Once inside the car, he turned on the map light, reached over to the passenger's seat, and picked up a steel clipboard and made a quick note. He spoke into the radio, and then switched off the light. All she saw was the blank expression of his rear lights in the total darkness, surrounded by invisible chalk lines and multicolored plastic shards.

She slipped the key into the ignition and slowly turned it, expecting a brutal growl from the engine. Instead, she was greeted with the usual soft hum. She sat for a few minutes while the motor turned, letting it warm, acutely aware of the unconsciousness of machinery. Almost amazed that something so powerful and brutal would have no sense of right and wrong. She sat and listened to the engine purr.

Claire placed her palms on the steering wheel without gripping too hard. The three pedals on the floor initially looked confusing, and she had to tell her left foot to engage the clutch at the same moment that she pushed the gearshift into first. Her right foot steadied on the gas pedal, waiting for the command. She was still afraid to go. She would have to shift again, but she did not want to have to take two hands off the wheel while she drove. Ever.

She knew that Cocoa sat waiting at home. One minute scampering by the door when an engine sound came close, and then leaving disappointedly for the kitchen or couch when the suspect car continued on. The brown lab probably was lying in front of the door on the Pottery Barn runner that had once looked so elegant in the catalog, but between Cocoa's homesteading and the seasonal muds, its untimely wear had returned the foyer to the same helpless shape. By now, Cocoa was undoubtedly fast asleep, unaware that night had prematurely fallen, as her stomach gurgled in hunger, and her bowels built up unconsciously. She welcomed the companionship, but in truth that was secondary. When the house was dark and empty, Cocoa's main concern had to be filling and emptying her stomach. "Don't worry," Claire said out loud. "I'm almost home."

Claire closed her eyes and sucked in a deep breath. Whatever the reason, Cocoa did need her. And Claire needed to go home. On the exhalation she would press on the gas, no matter how much strength it took. She pulled forward without noticing the stain. It had already blended into the story of Route 111.

❧   ❧   ❧

IT WAS AS THOUGH IT was her first time behind the wheel. A fifteen-and-a-half-year-old in driver's training, never having driven before, awed by the power and size of the automobile. And by its potential destructiveness. The car was the thing songs were made of. The means of the great escape from the boredom and mundanity of high school and adolescence. The deliverance from all the petty meanderings of midwestern towns like Dayton, Ohio, where escape only seemed otherwise possible if you could jump through the silver screen. But once behind a set of wheels, there was nothing holding you back other than your own cowardice. But when a young Claire had sat in the driver's training car, with an awkward but nasty man beside her with his foot jauntily tapping on the instructor's brake, she felt physically diminished. It was as though she were four years old, reaching up at a steering wheel that was three times her size, her eyes barely peering over the dashboard. The car had seemed cavernous, as though she were driving a house, and she had felt both awe and hopelessness at controlling the vehicle, understanding the power of the car, and leaving her to wonder if she would ever have the means to escape Dayton. Now as she drove down Route 111 toward Interstate 195, she held on to the wheel for dear life. Once again, submissive to the authority of the machinery. Especially so, now that it had shown what it was capable of.

Route 111 was quiet, the dim lights pasted against roadside windows recalling a time when this was not a trafficked byway, but instead a neighborhood road. A pasture of clouds rolled along the sky, sometimes moving just enough to reveal the speckled stars and knife-slit moon. She drove forty miles per hour down a road that she rarely clocked in at less than sixty-five at this time of night. Each shadow that fell across the lane caused her to lift her foot off the gas, ready to slam down on the brake. Claire gripped the steering wheel tightly like a novice cowgirl clutching the reins of a wild horse.

It felt almost impossible to focus on anything. She made a list in her head of what would need to be done, trying to reduce the aftermath down to a task in order to keep some sense of control over her body. Contact her insurance company. A lawyer.

There had already been too much to do.

Richard would help. And she would accept, even though his willingness to care for her would potentially annoy her. Claire was still not fully cleansed of the tension that had built up over the final year before he moved out; because lest anybody forget, despite what all future chroniclers of their legacy will write in future volumes, it was Richard who began the formal dissolution of the marriage. He was the one who stood in the house two years ago to recite a speech that sounded so rehearsed he might have taped it: that he felt this intense need to be alone, and that he couldn't quite define why, that it wasn't her, or her and him, but rather that maybe he was just someone who needed a life of solitude. She had been too shocked to call bullshit on him. To note his refusal to entertain the idea that the definition of a crisis suggests a transitory dilemma seeking a methodical solution, not destruction. In the coming days Richard would act as though he had not made that speech. In fact, he would further declare his love for Claire, as though there had been no shadows cast. But that conversation never left Claire's mind. She always thought of the words as being bullshit, but the very fact that they could be expressed at all had nagged at her. The fragility of the relationship gnawed. A cracked drinking glass that is still used daily but never discarded out of sentiment. She had started to question every difference between them, examine every pore, from the way they hung their towels to the differences of aesthetics to his abandonment of fine arts. She had watched that crack splinter until it was she who awoke one morning, holding the glass in her hand, and decided to throw it into the trash before the inevitable break and subsequent shatter. It would reduce the chances of blood. One can't live in a world without trust.

How could this have happened?

If she had just let the Delta 88 go.

Or looked at the road instead of reading those brash lips.

Or even just let the radio alone.

Or not been in the car on a road where a boy stupidly decides to run out into traffic.

For all the multitudes of split-second decisions that could have altered the fatal moment, she knew she would visit and revisit every single one of them for the rest of her life.

She saw the boy in the shadows of every tree along the interstate. Winging his arms out for balance, gazing at the quiet road before him. His reddish hair sat atop a firm jaw that seemed unusually square-shaped for such a young boy, and his eyes shone a sky-ish blue that lit the night. Put altogether, he still carried the genes of original New England settlers, a growing rarity for the region. His posture stood firm and confidant, no doubt the carbon copy of his father's, before fading into a row of roadside shrubs.

The Accord traveled smoothly down I-95, as though it had no past. Claire released her foot from the gas, slowing the car down. There was no hurry.

Richard would not be at her house yet. By the time he actually shut down his office, walked over to his car, and worked his way into the I-93 traffic, it would be at least another hour before he reached Providence. Then he would come in through the door, beat up and abused by the commute, immediately launching into a battle story about a driver who tormented him the entire trip down, and how he ended up getting off in Pawtucket to get away from that asshole, adding another fifteen minutes of stop-and-go driving to the trip. Once he calmed down about that, he surely would catapult into his analysis of an NPR story about something involving the government. Then he would say that he was sorry, that he commanded the moment and talked only about himself again—how was she? He would walk over to Claire, place a hand on each of her shoulders and kiss her lightly on each cheek, as if all was normal. It was a routine that her husband, the self-proclaimed iconoclast, would be horrified to know that he had followed ever since the separation.

Claire didn't know how she would tell Richard. She could greet him at the door with her face glazed by the tears that she worried would explode the moment that she saw him. Or she could listen to his introduction per usual, and then tell her story as commonplace as all the others that she did in the usual allotted moment, following the pattern they had developed over the years. Claire could not picture the words to the narrative rising through her chest, nor the sounds coming from her mouth. It was not her story yet. She had no emotional ownership over the events, and she scarcely felt that she would know the story anymore than one of the members of the crowd that huddled behind that police line. She was deeply involved and distant at once. She wondered if she would connect into the accident when she told Richard. If the mere expression of the words would create tangible symbols that were tactile and full of life.

Instantly, Richard would ask a million questions. He would act the role of the inquisitor, following the path that all men must take, where facts always outmuscle emotion. Claire would answer every question exactly the same—*I don't know*. He would want to know how this happened and who did what. And all she could ever tell him was that she didn't know. If he did ask anything about the boy, Claire would be able to describe the skateboarder as though look-

ing at a portrait on the wall, with the precision to detail that tran-
scended technique. But any moments leading up to seeing his face
before the windshield were just randomly edited scenes.

She changed lanes for no real reason, other than to try to keep
command over the car. She did not look in the mirror. Instead she
twisted her shoulders and head.

Instinctively taking the Gano Street exit, Claire drove along
the road that bisected the Seekonk River and the sloping edges of
Fox Point toward her home in the more coveted Blackstone edge of
the East Side. The right side of the road had an odd mixture of industrial shops and artisan stands, while the left harbored the
spillover of Colonials and triple-deckers from the denser hill
above. Ahead on the right, the still new-looking Dunkin' Donuts,
built to replicate the neighborhood's style, with its faux steepled
Victorian architecture, sat lit up against the dark night. She was
tempted to pull over and order a coffee regular, and sit hovered
over the steaming cup the way lonely people do. She would sip
down her joe, and stare out the window until Richard was sure to
arrive. But Claire continued to drive, thinking that hot coffee is impossible to drink but cold coffee is unbearable to taste. How most
things are only right when in perfect balance.

Halloween decorations had begun to appear on the block, but
nothing too sophisticated at this early point of the week. A few
jack-o'-lanterns populated the porches. An occasional paper skele-
ton in the window. Pulled cotton had been strewn up the porch pillars. Her East Side neighborhood was very competitive about the
holiday, with the expectation of mandatory participation. Failure
to participate could taint you for the rest of the year, thereby vio-
lating the New England ethic of privacy behind closed doors. She

would have to ask Richard to manage this—she just couldn't imagine who else to turn to. He could go to the CVS for all the requisite supplies to maintain a respectable Halloween home, and then over to pick up the luminaria supplies at the Wallers' house. Richard could handle Steve and Janet Waller without betraying Claire or explaining his sudden domestic reemergence. He would limit the topics to his own work as a medical illustrator. The Wallers, filled with Ivy League envy, were most fascinated by the ongoing but separate relationship he had with Harvard. For a while, at least, he was going to have to block the light so Claire could hide in the shadow.

She pulled into the narrow driveway, leaving enough room for Richard to get his car in. The motion light nailed high up off the attic announced her by flooding the entire length of the driveway. It did not feel intrusive, but rather like the warmth of a winter sun. If Claire looked up, she knew that she would see Cocoa nosing her snout at the window, looking out curiously anxious. Claire stared straight ahead into the dark backyard, where premature layers of night hid the manicured sense of order. She didn't want to leave the car. Her house would feel too normal. It might tell her that the events of this night actually had happened.

Claire butted at the door with her shoulder. She had her notes tucked carefully under the arm. She had left the student work on the floor of the Accord. The door was resistant, something she quickly realized was due to Cocoa's body block, fueled by excitement. "Come on, girl," Claire said, "just let me in."

The dog jumped on her, landing two paws against her waist. The notes nearly tumbled from Claire's grip. "Just hold tight, would you. Now that's my girl."

Claire pushed past the excitable dog, threw her coat onto the couch, and dropped her notes on the coffee table in front of the television. The front page of this morning's paper still sat folded on the table. Next to it sat her quarter-filled coffee mug. The remote had guiltily taken precedence over all reading materials, cordoning off a worthy but not pressing stack of mail that had been there for days. The lamp glowed perfectly, switched on by the timer an hour ago, giving the house a warming feeling. As though surrounded by a yellow rope and a DO NOT TOUCH sign, the dining room was as she had left it, almost since the day Richard had moved out.

Cocoa danced at her heels, occasionally leaping in clumsy acrobatics, with a quiet but present whine. "I know, girl," Claire said. "I know."

The lab dutifully followed her into the kitchen. The granite counters were void of any sign of life, save for the sponge streak that ran diagonally from the sink to the tall black coffeemaker, a hastened attempt at cleaning when she had already been ten minutes behind schedule this morning. The Amana range that had come with the house was dull and white, with little personality other than the cagey pepper grains that remained uncleaned near the base of the gas exhaler. The matching refrigerator also appeared slow and tired, its energy-sucking groan nightly increasing in volume. She recently had seriously been considering finally redoing this outdated kitchen. She was going to modernize. Maybe buy industrial appliances, naked and stripped in stark gray, a postmodern counterweight to the antiquity of the kitchen's original 1930s cabinets. Replace the counters at the same time. It was all being planned from the moment they had first looked at the house.

A project that never became more than a plan. The truth was that other things took precedence. As her time became more and more limited, Claire needed to make choices about how to use it, and frankly her writing, teaching, and self were going to come first. When she seriously considered the idea of the remodel, it seemed that the kitchen didn't look so bad. It was spacious and filled with character. The appliances were just that—big utilitarian steel creatures whose values should not be confused with aestheticism. But still it always had felt terminally unfinished.

She walked over to the miniature garbage can in the far corner of the kitchen. It reached midcalf and was modeled after the old-fashioned alley cans with the corrugated metal ridges along the sides, and knight's shield lid. Inside she stored Cocoa's kibbles, which were served as both breakfast and dinner. At the time it had seemed excessive to purchase an expensive adornment for her dog, a Restoration Hardware tchotchke at best. But then Cocoa had begun to help herself to the bag of food that Claire kept neatly folded over in the far corner beside the radiator. The chow would spill across the tiles, with Cocoa inevitably knocking bits of food under the stove and into hidden places that would not be revealed for weeks at a time, until she was unexplainably on her belly, pawing and pawing ferociously into the unreachable crevices. It had reminded her of every dirty dish that Richard had left in the sink in those last days, a harmless thing really, but one that she had focused on. His inability to notice the sloppy effect it had on the house drove her crazy. And she hadn't said anything, instead watched him dump plates into the sink, getting angrier and angrier when he didn't see how much it bothered her.

Cocoa appeared satisfied. Following a flurry of quick leaps, she settled down in front of her bowl, her snout digging its way through, chewing as though she had not eaten in days.

Claire moved out of the kitchen and stopped in the hallway. She inhaled the house, taking in all the smells that defined her home: the lavender scent perfuming from the bathroom, the lingering mustiness that worked its way up from the basement. The strange concoction of unidentifiable aromas that had found homes in her kitchen to create a single unique kitchen smell. The house reeked throughout of a metallic-infused wood odor, one that had come with the previous owner, something Claire had attributed to historic layers of lead paint slapped against the walls. It never changed. Some seasons brought variations of the odorous themes, but it was as constant as Cocoa's needs to eat and be loved.

Her life had changed tonight. She might have been wrapped in layers of confusion and questions, but she was lucid enough to know that starting two hours ago she would be viewing a different world for the rest of her life. You don't just run a kid over on his skateboard and expect to keep on schedule. Fault or no fault. She had walked into her home a different person than when she had left, yet the house had remained unchanged. There was no comfort. And would she have felt better about it if the house had been robbed and bruised of spirit, even by something as mundane as Cocoa chewing up the couch or pissing on the bed? Anything to suggest that the world had changed with her—not just left her alone in it.

Claire leaned against the wall, bracing her hands along the cool plaster. She slipped slightly but pushed her palms in for balance. Cocoa looked up from her bowl, her erected ears turned quizzically toward the noise, but then returned to the comfort of her meal. Claire closed her eyes, wishing that she had the ability to fall asleep standing up. A weak light faded across her eyelids. The sound of Cocoa's crunching drifted off into the distance. She felt in between, with the past still firmly behind her, but the future still forming itself. And in that moment she watched a shape begin to form. Her heart beat as she recalled the face of the boy. They looked at each other for a moment. She knew why he was there. If Claire had been religious she would have prayed.

Cocoa startled in the way that dogs supposedly do in the presence of ghosts, causing Claire to jump. Cocoa ran to the door in an apprehensive jog, beginning to form a bark as the doorbell rang. Claire shook her head and inhaled. She pulled down on her blouse, straightening it at the waist, thinking that she could never wear this shirt again. She walked with a quick stride through the living room to the front door, cautioning Cocoa from howling out a full-fledged bark. "Don't worry, it's only Richard, girl. Don't get excited. He's just come to visit." The dog, having moved into the house after Richard vacated it, still had not developed an instinctual trust of the man she had replaced. Getting a dog had been a discussion for them early in their marriage. Richard had not wanted any animals, arguing that he and Claire were too busy with their lives, they were not even home enough to give a dog the required attention. Although she disagreed, Claire did not push the point. She didn't even bother to continue the conversation. But the minute Richard had moved out, she drove out to the humane society and adopted Cocoa, who, on that first night, had slept at Claire's feet, anxious but trusting.

Under the yellow porch light her husband looked drawn, with road-weary eyes. The collar of his overcoat was partially turned

in, tucked between his shirt and the shoulder of his silvery sport-
coat, part of the late 1970s–early 1980s Richard Andrews collection. He was the type who never looked fully prepared, always a bit
disheveled, with chunks of silvery hair emerging in odd directions.
Even his clean-shaven face left the impression of a day-old beard,
or a sloppy shave at best. But people rarely noticed this. He had a
handsomeness that was pure and honest, and oddly striking.
Richard's appeal did not rely on aloofness or confidence, but rather
on a lack of awareness.

In the mudroom, Richard reached for her hands. His fingers
were still stained by colored lead. He had not stopped to wash
them. Against all her plans, Claire fell into his arms, burying her
cheek into his chest. His jacket was still cold from outside. She
sobbed without tears, to the point that it became difficult to
breathe.

"What is it?" Richard asked.

Claire shook her head, no. Her cheeks burned against his coat.

"Let's sit down." He guided her into the living room with her
arms still hugged around him. They almost stumbled onto the
couch. She knew that she had to tell him what happened. It
shouldn't be so difficult to say *I accidentally hit a boy who stupidly
ran in front of the car*, but she feared her voice would turn this oth-
erly experience into something tangible.

Claire scooted down and lay her head against the center pillow,
staring up at the ceiling. She kicked her socked feet up on the arm
of the couch. Richard leaned over and brushed her hair from her
eyes, hiding some of the emerging gray.

"You sounded so upset on the phone," he said.

She closed her eyes, wishing she didn't find comfort in him.

"You spend so much time trying to imagine yourself with a different life."

He pushed another loose strand of hair aside.

"It's just a blink of the eye, Richard. And you have to look fast."

Richard stopped for a moment. "Claire, you need to tell me what happened. When you called, you sounded terrible."

"I didn't look, Richard."

"I don't understand."

"I didn't look in time."

Richard took her hands, without requesting an explanation. It occurred to her that she could ask him to go. Bend the truth, and tell him that she is all right, and she is glad that he came, but really, it was all an overreaction, and she is fine now. Letting down her guard left her more vulnerable, and she was afraid of what that could mean with Richard.

She let go of his grip and draped her hand to the floor, where Cocoa sympathetically licked her briny fingers. And then she tried to tell him what she remembered of the story. But it was like somebody cut the sound or something, because she had no auditory recollection. In fact, she didn't remember any sounds until the accountant was insisting that she was hurt, and working his way into her car. And that's what happened. She didn't know what else was going to happen now. That's what she was getting at. That's what she meant. That's what she was trying to say.

Richard knew better than to offer greeting card words. "Do you know what happened to the boy?" He spoke clinically.

"I don't know anything. I don't know his name. I don't know his age. I don't know a fucking thing. If I hadn't seen that patch of red hair on the asphalt . . ." She swallowed back tears. "But, actually, I do think I know what happened. I do think . . ."

"This will all be okay," Richard said. "We will get through this. It will all be okay. We will get through this." And he repeated that one more time with a little more emphasis, enough that spoke to the fear in his voice, while the way he said *we* was as comforting as it was frightening.

He would stay the night.

He would be there as long as she needed him.

What choice did she have?

❦   ❦   ❦

RICHARD SLEPT HEAVILY TO THE television sound track. In the living room, leaned into the corner of the couch, his body sunk deep into the pillows. He rarely snored but often made unintelligible mumbling sounds and rhythmic lip smackings when thoroughly exhausted. He had declared that he would stay in the guest room for the next few days through Halloween, and tried to insist that Claire cancel her classes for the week, but she had refused. She felt the need to keep in motion, fearing that even the slightest pause for breath would cause what was left of her whole world to break down. She told him he should just go back home. But he wouldn't. Even as she said it, she knew he wouldn't.

Claire leaned into the opposite corner of the couch, not ready to face the aloneness of her bedroom yet. She tucked her hands under her cheek and closed her eyes in the pretense of sleep. The police officers had been tight-lipped at the crash sight, trying not to betray any news on the boy's condition. But maybe it was the way they had averted their eyes when she asked, or maybe it was an intangible sense, but Claire was almost certain that the boy had died. Everything at that scene had felt too still. Almost breathlike.

Between Richard's sleep noises, Cocoa was engaged in some of her own. It must have been some harrowing dog dream that had her scratching at the floor and reflexively calling out muted miniature barks.

Suddenly Claire couldn't breathe. It was as though the automated systems of her body had been shut off. The old air sat trapped in her lungs, stale and heavy, unable to be exhaled. She tried to talk her lungs into action, afraid that she might drown in her own breath, finally instructing her body to bellow out the spent oxygen and, with careful instructions, inhale a fresh supply. Her head was light. For a split second nothing was familiar in the room.

Cocoa jerked her head up, her eyes alarmingly awake. She rose to her feet and stood by the door. "Okay," Claire whispered. She slipped on her clogs before leashing up the dog. She walked tentatively. "We can both use the fresh air."

In 1888, a year before he painted Starry Night, *Vincent van Gogh fired up a gas jet one September evening in Arles and painted* The Starry Night *over the Rhone. It had occurred to him that the only way to capture the true essence of night was to stand within the subject, by, as he wrote, "going out at night to paint the stars." It is very easy to imagine Vincent standing alone in the dark, leaning in to his canvas as the gas jets hiss beside him, fully understanding that only under the "harsh gold of the gas" could the beauty of darkness emerge. He grips the brush tightly, smearing the paints on in a heavy impasto, watching the lovers that haunt the foreground, equally en-*

tranced by the notion of the poets' symbolic reverence of the starlit night. Gauguin will not arrive for another month, if he actually comes at all. Vincent looks out at the southern sky as though it is his only friend. It has become impossible to count on others. Sometimes a man's only companion is the world in which he lives.

Cocoa squatted on the grass, and then sniffed around the driveway. She rubbed her snout against the side of Claire's car, where student papers still lay scattered on the passenger's mat, strange and quiet witnesses to the events of the night.

Claire looked up at the moonless sky. It seemed impossible that the sun would rise by morning, where she would be in her corner of the McGee building, leading a second-year graduate seminar called the Psychology of the Painting, counting on students to use Hegel and Heidegger as a counter to various charges of formalism and postmodernism. And they will look to her as they always have, perhaps intrinsically aware that something is different about Dr. Andrews. *Slightly off*, they will murmur. *She doesn't seem right.* All without the understanding that the Dr. Andrews that they once knew, they will never know again.

Cocoa's leash had gone slack as she nestled her snout beside Claire's leg. All the lights on the street were turned out, revealing a starlit sky. The world felt like Claire's alone. She had witnessed the fragility of life tonight. She had seen the instant when a life changes. When a worldview is shifted by chance. It did not leave her with a fatalistic feeling. Nor did it leave her overcome with the ironist's joie de vivre that would command her to enjoy and appreciate the life that surrounded her.

Claire brought Cocoa back into the house and unleashed her. The dog immediately dashed into the living room and settled onto the rug in front of Richard, who was deep asleep, his long, narrow back rising and falling in contented sighs. She unfolded a chenille blanket and spread it over him, pulling it up just below his chin. She put her hand just above his mouth, feeling his breath.

She sat at the kitchen table for much of the night. She thought about the boy. She tried to piece together all the minutes and moments. She wondered if she would become a different person, somehow healed of all her quirks and defects. Or more likely it would add another one much greater than all the others.

She reminded herself to breathe.

Maybe horrible situations don't change you.

Maybe they are waiting for you.

Late November

Having Richard in the guest room was the only sense of true life in her house. The room was tucked away on the second floor, nearly hidden, with its own staircase down to the kitchen, probably having been a servant's quarters when such things were acceptable. But in the days since the accident, and the confirmation that the boy had died well before the ambulance ever reached Providence, Richard had made the room into a temporary work studio, only occasionally rushing up to Cambridge to meet with clients, but being certain to be present for his wife when she arrived home from work.

He had set his easel against the window, allowing only the best light to seep over the top. Clipped to the side was an elbow lamp gone crooked at the joint, held in place by a temporary bandage of duct tape. Between the easel and the twin bed where he slept, Richard had unfolded a cheap card table and covered it with an old white sheet. The Verithin pencils lay side by side in a disrupted color pattern whose logic Richard couldn't explain, but one that made instinctual sense to his grabbing hands, probably not too different from Christopher Sholes's intuitive fingers, which had laid out the *QWERTY* keyboard more than 130 years ago. There appeared to be a disproportionate number of erasers and sharpeners to pencils. Richard had learned over the years that it was best practice to always have those items accessible. One didn't want to lose momentum in a search for tools. Pads of paper leaned against the table legs, while rejected sketches lay balled up all along the wood floor. The wastebasket sat curiously empty of even the earliest drafts. Some promising sketches were taped to the walls. But only the occasional rendering would ever be recognized as the prototype for a finished drawing that would eventually end up in some fourth-year medical student's textbook on the muscles of the face.

In the month since the accident, Claire couldn't have managed without Richard. She may never have been sure that she could trust him with love, but she could rely on his loyalty. He still believed they eventually would come back together, either stubbornly or naively unwilling to acknowledge that his slip of words, or *stupid moment of crisis*, was that damaging. Regardless, without any implication of contrivance or manipulation, Richard had been taking care of all the details. He had taken her down to the police station to sign the necessary forms, putting his arm around her to shield her from view of anybody they might happen to know. He had inspected the front of the car when she refused to look at it, and made the arrangements with her insurance company to replace the dented bumper and the crushed right side lights. A damage that wasn't as severe as what it represented.

Richard had even delayed a deadline in order to sit with Claire at a meeting with Ron Bernard, the FreedomSafe Insurance attorney, for a preliminary discussion about what the company thought might turn into a protracted legal battle. Bernard never moved from behind his desk, keeping his hands flat on the top, as though emblematic of his honesty. "As the cliché goes," he had said, "you've got your good news, and you have got your bad news."

Claire had wanted to fold into herself at that moment. The accident was a week and a half ago, and what she really wanted Bernard to tell her was whether she would ever be able to sleep through the night again. Instead she watched him talk to Richard. Bernard's face was wide but not fat. She imagined that his cheeks might have been thinner at one point, but had broadened with age, taking his features along with the expansion. The only true symmetrical justice was the narrow goatee that slid along the nasallabial folds past the corners of his lips, shaping his face into a sharp point.

"I am going to be perfectly straight with you," Bernard said, still addressing Richard. "The family of the victim will be seeking a wrongful death suit."

"And that means . . . ?" Richard asked.

Bernard shrugged his shoulders. "It means what it means. They will try to prove that your wife here was negligent, somehow at fault, and then try to sue accordingly. They'll go after FreedomSafe for the maximum coverage that your wife has, and possibly some of her personal assets if they can prove they deserve more."

Ron Bernard had yet to mention Claire by name. Nor even by her proper title.

"So we just sit here and wait?" Richard asked.

"Here is where we are: the state of Rhode Island has what they call a Comparative Negligence Standard. Simply put, someone like your wife only pays the percentage of what she is responsible for. Meaning, if she is fifty percent responsible for the accident, then she pays fifty percent of the damages. Ten percent, then ten percent. And let the games begin. The family's lawyer will set out to prove that your wife was one hundred percent responsible, while we try to take it as low as we can. Usually, after a couple of years, we settle in the middle, either by jury or by arbitration."

Claire finally spoke. She barely recognized her own voice buried in a raspy whisper. "He skated right out in front of me, and I should have . . . Or maybe I shouldn't have . . . But he skated *right* out in front." It sickened her to say that much.

"That's important," Bernard replied. "And the good news is that the police report backs that up as a so-called dart out. Now we'll have our adjuster out there investigating, trying to put together the case. And of course the plaintiffs will have their own investigation going on, hoping to dig up details that place blame on you. From the police report, they know that you were not speeding. But who knows, perhaps you were talking on the cell phone."

"She doesn't even have one."

"Maybe so, but those are the kinds of assumptions they'll be looking to uncover. They will try to make the case that somehow your wife was not driving in a safe enough manner to prevent the accident. Just think of anything imaginable, and know that they will be investigating it. How often you have a drink after work. If you are always rushing home. Road rage. Your mood that day. They'll seek out the witnesses. People you know, and people you have never heard of. Meanwhile, we'll be portraying a responsible and sympathetic defendant who has unfairly been held accountable for circumstances beyond her control, especially based on a juvenile's failure to use reasonable care—even calling his parents into question for leaving him alone out there to play along the roadway at night. As you can imagine, emotions will run high following a tragedy of this nature."

Claire wished they would stop playing lawyer tricks. A boy had lost his life because of her car. She knew that no judgment could ever take that away.

"Is there anything you can think of, Mrs. Andrews? On your behalf, we have the accountant who witnessed the accident. He certainly corroborates your version and the police report. But we still need to anticipate any other potential accounts that the family may project as damaging. The worst thing for us is to get caught by surprise."

"Caught by surprise," she murmured.

"Pardon?"

"Nothing," she said. "Nothing."

"Number one rule," Bernard stated. For the first time he lifted his palms off the desktop. He clapped them together and held a prayer form. He pulled the heels to his chest, rotating all ten fingers until they pointed at Claire. "Anybody calls you, you tell them to talk to me. Besides your husband here, the only person you talk with about this accident is the assigned insurance adjuster, who still better be talking to me first. Otherwise, all communication is through this office. Believe me, the plaintiffs' team will have their own investigators out there. The upright ones seek my permission to contact you. The scumbags ride renegade, trying to run up their commission. So, please, remember the number one rule."

Claire and Richard nodded.

"And it is . . . ?"

Richard recited it back.

Ron Bernard looked over to Claire. He rested his palms on the desk pad again. His veins bulged aqua blue. "You just have to go on now. Not be involved. We will look out for you. Lead your life as normal. And know that we are working for your best interests."

She should have felt relieved.

          ❦   ❦   ❦

CLAIRE SPENT THE FOLLOWING TWO and a half weeks after that meeting trying to find ways to reconfigure her routine. Returning to her classes so quickly did give her a pretense of normalcy, although her mind, fogged over in displacement and medication, struggled to keep engaged. Her manuscript had sat on the living room table, exactly where she had placed it following the accident, a relic from another life. She still was not sleeping well. The antianxiety medication that Dr. Heddeman had given her had helped to calm her during the day but did little to clear her mind at night. The doctor had offered something more potent for sleep, but Claire had refused him, already fearful of the chemicals and changes currently refiguring her body.

She drove a new route to campus that added twenty minutes. It was prettier. She crossed over bays in Massachusetts, and then trailed Rhode Island harbors, where the late fall air sharpened the sea caps. She would never travel Route 111 again. She did not even allow herself to know the boy's name. It had not been listed on the initial accident report, as the details had still been thin at the time (and his status as a minor also kept him anonymous). Ron Bernard had only referred to the family as the plaintiffs. There had been one mention in the shore's weekly newspaper, but it had read as a police bulletin, with no names attached. And if anybody at the university knew, they were not letting her know. In a way it was better. Without a name he was not fully defined.

§ § §

RICHARD HAD JUST COME DOWNSTAIRS as Claire came through the door. It was exactly one month to the day of the accident, although neither had that in mind. Cocoa was dancing at his heels, confusedly blocking Richard off while urging him to the door with a constant whine. "I think she has to go out," Richard said. "I told her to wait until you got home. Begged her to hold it in." He leaned over, trying to snap the leash to her collar. "One thing I don't want to do is pick up dog crap with a plastic bag. And especially act like it is nothing. Goddamn neighborhood is full of people who have the world at their disposal, yet they will walk around with a bag of shit in their hands. Dangling and flipping it around their wrists like it's a keepsake." Cocoa twisted her head away. Richard tried to steady her neck once more, while he pulled back on the metal clasp. "And they'll sit there and talk with you. Carry on a whole conversation with the bag in their hand. Stinking the place up worse than a campground toilet. I'll tell you who the worst are—Steve and Janet Waller. They stand there talking at you about people stringing up Christmas lights before the Thanksgiving table has been cleared, and all the other offenses of the neighborhood, while they are literally stinking out the streets. Goddamn crazy, I tell you."

"Well, I'm home," Claire said as Richard handed her the leash. "Come on, girl," she said, and set down her satchel. It fell over with a slam. Papers slid out the open pouch, pouring, as though they were being manufactured on the spot. "Damn it," she said.

Cocoa jumped.

Still holding the leash, Claire bent over and tried to stack the papers back in their proper order. Her hands forcefully laid the pages one by one on top of each other. She neatly patted the sides, pushing them back into her bag.

"Claire!" Richard yelled out.

"What . . . ?"

Cocoa was starting to squat, her hind legs tightened together as her front paws braced into the floor. Her snout pointed upward as she stared off in vacant concentration.

"Cocoa!" Claire said. She pulled on the leash, snapping the dog from her fecal spell, and managed to tug her out through the front door just in time. "Son of a bitch," Claire called out from the porch. "Richard, get me a bag, would you? Or just bring any of the pages from my manuscript on the coffee table. They'll work just as well. Shit for shit."

Claire walked across the house, letting the plastic bag lead her at arm's length toward the kitchen. There, she stepped on the pedal where the lid popped up, and then dropped the bag into the silver cylinder. She leaned back against the counter and placed her hands over her face. She should have been crying, but she wasn't.

"What is it?" Richard asked.

"What do you think, *what is it*?"

"Claire?"

And she stood and looked at him, her hands on her hips, grinding her teeth. "Nothing is right, Richard . . . Did you really think everything could just be normal? That it's all *what's for dinner* and dog shit and neighbors?"

"Claire, nothing is . . . But we are getting through this . . ."

"Which *we're* is it, Richard? When do you wake up and decide you need to be alone? Maybe after the legal business is over? Or after I sleep a full night?"

"Let's not confuse things, okay? I understand that everything is off—"

"You know what? I don't even know why you're here. Why you . . . Never mind. Never mind, Richard. I need to not have this conversation right now. I am sorry that I started it, but . . . Okay, Richard? Can we not have this conversation right now?"

His hands dug into his pockets. He looked afraid to speak.

Claire closed her eyes and saw that woman who, two years ago, had been sitting on the couch when Richard had made his "alone" speech. And she could see the woman's expression, horrified and wounded at once, and already swirling into a place of aloneness. Twisting her wedding ring, and trying to cut the skin with her diamond. Trying to piece this all together, make sense of her husband's sudden outburst not really being so sudden. Maybe it started with the time he showed off a new drawing of a neck, and made the seemingly harmless comment that they were as different as the bulging blue veins and red arteries. Or maybe it was when he began staying nights in Cambridge following work at Harvard, and not because he was having an affair (no, that would be too easy), but because he needed to be away from home for a while. Or maybe it was the phantom gut pains that drove him out of bed and onto the couch. Or maybe. Or maybe. That woman had sat digging the corner of the diamond into her finger while Richard had made a declaration of nonlove to her, barely able to hear him; too busy trying to reconstruct every moment of history to understand how all her expectations came crashing down so easily. Never stopping for one second to consider that she might have been part of letting all this happen. Or more precisely: what had come between them *was* them.

Richard looked uncomfortable. He swallowed once, and then wiped his hands against his pants.

"What?" she said. "Why do you look like that? I didn't mean to make you . . ."

"Now don't get alarmed."

"Is that like passing the scene of a disaster and saying, *Don't look?*"

"Ron Bernard called earlier."

"I don't know if I want to know."

"An investigator for the family is going to call you. Ron has given the okay on this. The investigator knows the questions he's allowed to ask."

"Does Bernard even know him?"

"All he said was that the investigator sounded strictly professional. Bernard knows the firm he works for."

"But he doesn't know him?"

Richard looked down to the message pad to decipher his handwriting. "The man's name is Trevor McCarthy, from DiMallo Law Offices. Apparently he has been talking with some witnesses on the scene, and just needs to have you corroborate a few details. Something about the car that pulled out in front of you."

She could see that large angry face screaming out from the

Delta 88, throwing up a middle finger and yelling out to Claire, as though finally gathering enough strength to burst through all the shit that the world had piled on top of her.

"Okay?" Richard said. "Remember, Trevor McCarthy. Di-Mallo Law Offices. All Ron Bernard asked is that you take careful notes of the conversation, and then report it back to him . . . He said that if this is the best they can do, then the case looks good. FreedomSafe is not paying out on anything that it doesn't rightly owe . . . It's going to be all right. Okay?"

Claire clenched her fists, and inhaled. She nodded that she understood. She sadly exhaled.

Richard cleared his throat. Even he must have been aware of the almost casual nature in which they discussed the case, as though this whole nightmare was something tangible that could be fixed by the righteousness of the law.

And when they should have hugged, she turned away, desperate to be held, but unwilling to risk it.

WEDNESDAY

Her book.

Still only a manuscript.

Sitting untouched in her living room.

Her book.

The big breakthrough, leaving behind the university presses for a major house. Bringing Van Gogh theory to the masses. An expansion of a short paper she had delivered at the Art History, Aesthetics, Visual Studies Conference at Clark University. A clinical dissection that juxtaposed the assumptions of Vincent's life at the time he painted *Crows over the Wheatfield*. She had taken each object of importance from the work and assigned it to a specific real-life moment, tossing in a little self-molded Freudian psychology for spice. From there, she had looked at the structure of the painting (citing Roger Fry's theories on "plastic form"), and put forth the question as to whether this painting was nothing other than form, or if indeed it exercised an "object-presenting experience" that overtook the subject of a wheat field. Only understanding what Van Gogh saw and thought could answer what the painting represented—unless of course it was a scenic wheat field and nothing else. She felt that so far it had the precision of a clinician, reading as though every other word had the subliminal *Ph.D.* watermarked behind it. The tone of the book fit perfectly into the canon of aesthetic discourse, underscoring one of the great ironies of art criticism—how dispassionately one can talk about passion. Although her editor, Bill Harrison, felt good about the book, Claire felt like a true failure. She had become too far lost in analysis and theory. All she really had wanted to do was walk in Vincent's shoes hard enough to feel that last step where he stops firmly, lifts the pistol to his chest, aims it imprecisely but just precise enough, and then works out the final piece of courage to squeeze the trigger.

❦   ❦   ❦

SHE SAT AT HER OFFICE desk, weight perched on her right elbow, with a hand placed on the telephone receiver. She needed to call Bill to let him know where the book stood, which was in fact nowhere further than it was last time she had spoken with him. She hoped Bill wouldn't ask for details about how she was rethinking the conclusion. She had no answers. Was there even a beginning? At one point, the other evening, she had picked up the manuscript, neatly stacked with a thick rubber band around it, thinking she was going to resume work on it, imagining that she had some semblance of direction back in her life. But as she looked over the first page, reading the words as though struggling over an assigned textbook, Claire quickly returned the page to the stack, double binding it until the rubber band had no snap left in it. The book didn't even make sense anymore. *Aesthetic philosophy. Interpretative values and definitions. Critical monists*, coupled with *phenomenology* and its philosophical and theoretical trends, and on and on and on. Just the regular art history/aesthetics bullshit. In truth, there was not a goddamn thing in there about the painting.

As she dialed the phone, Claire looked up at the poster of *Crows over the Wheatfield* that hung over her desk. Claire had never had it framed, instead keeping it under plastic wrap in the corner of her office, exactly as it was when she had brought it back from Auverssur-Oise several years ago. She had always planned to have it framed, but had grown used to it balancing the corner of the room. Finally, about a year ago, she borrowed some thumbtacks and a hammer from the maintenance guys and tacked it to the plaster. Now the painting looked down on her. The portrait of the wheat field under the ominous crow-filled sky. Sometimes Claire saw the three paths flowing away into the expanse of possibilities. Other times, she saw them racing forward, converging wildly on the same unseen point in the foreground. How could she possibly write with any authority about the painting when she didn't even know what she saw in it anymore?

She was surprised to hear Maggie Harrison answer Bill's office phone. That voice on the radio had lingered with Claire since the accident, as though Maggie herself had been witness to the horrible event. "It's Claire," she said. "I am sorry, I thought I was calling Bill at his office. Did I mix the numbers and call your home? Isn't this his office?"

"It is indeed. But my word," she said. Her southern accent contrasted the erudite New York diction that she'd used on *All Things Considered*. "I'll be darned if the world is not one big series of coincidences. This is not hyperbolic flattery in the least, but I was just talking about you to Bill. How strange is that? I just stopped in on my way down to the campus, and I had been prepping for a section on the influence of nineteenth-century Japanese art, and I remembered your book about Van Gogh and the Japanese woodcuts, and . . . And how are you? It's been a while since we've heard from you. How *are* you?"

She paused. Since telling Richard the details that evening of the accident, Claire realized that she had not told anyone else about it. And how does one tell such a thing? Is it possible to know the right combination of words that convey the depth of the situation, yet still sound reassuring? She should have practiced. Said it aloud at least once. Because she stumbled with "You see," and then "What I am trying to say is . . ."

"Claire, is something wrong?"

"It was an accident, Maggie." She tried to sound as unaffected as possible. "I was in an accident."

"Oh good lord, Claire. Are you okay?"

"I hit a boy, Maggie. I hit a boy with my car." It was eerie how easily that came out. Her stomach tightened, holding in air, as her head seemed to float. The words were easy. Like listening to somebody else's voice.

"Oh my word. Claire . . . I don't know what to—"

"You don't have to."

"But you know we are here . . ."

"It's okay, Maggie. I didn't call to burden . . . I just wanted to let Bill know about the book. Why I have been behind . . . But that the book is . . ."

"You shouldn't have to be worrying about . . . Let me get him for you . . . Bill! Bill, honey! . . . You can't be thinking about such a thing at a time like—"

"It's okay, Maggie."

"Bill!"

And it was strange this sudden power to cause people to feel uncomfortable. It was apparent when she saw her neighbors out on the street, the Wallers smiling falsely, and then ducking into their car to avoid conversation. Passing half-familiar faces at the ATM machine. At the coffeehouse. Who knew what they understood, but they all submitted to her, waiting for her cue on how to react, shifting and darting until she gave some indication. Maybe that was what Richard had felt like when he had stood above her on the couch, talking about not being in love anymore. He had only managed to find the strength to continue his speech through the weakness of her reaction.

"Claire?" Bill took the phone. "What has happened? What is going on?"

"I was in an accident." The second time was even easier. "I was just telling Maggie."

"And there was a boy involved? Is that what Maggie said?"

"I told her, yes."

"Oh, I wished you would have called us sooner. We would have come right up to be with you. Would have dropped everything . . . I mean, do you need a lawyer? What can we do for you? What can we . . . ? Do you know what happened to the boy? How is he doing?"

Claire looked back up to the painting, at the point where the three roads came together in the foreground. "He died, Bill," she said matter-of-factly. How else could she say it? "He died."

"Oh, Jesus Christ. Jesus Christ. Oh, Claire."

And oddly enough she found herself in the position of comforting him. Perhaps that was akin to the power she had sensed, the same way she had had to comfort Richard when they first separated. Still, she did not know what to say to Bill; those were words that nobody really knows, a sentence whose construction is impossible. "Don't worry," was all she spoke. "Don't worry, Bill."

He told her obviously not to be concerned about the book right now. To take care of herself. The book can wait, of course. That is of no concern.

"But it is a concern."

"Believe me, it can wait. Put it aside for now. Please, Claire."

"I don't know if I can put it aside until I know what I am putting aside." She laughed at her own remark. She could tell this made Bill uncomfortable. That was not her intent. "I know you care," she said. "I know you do. It's like I am seeing the painting for the first time . . . In fact, I am looking at *Crows* right now, and it looks different, Bill. That's all I am saying is that it looks different. And that's what I want to understand. How, for the first time, it looks different. Not why we should all see it the same, but how I, or anyone, can see it different. That's all I'm saying, Bill. I know you care. I know you do. And that's all I'm saying."

Before he hung up, he reiterated that he was not telling her what to do, because who was he to say what to do in a situation such as this, but he did want her to know that she should not feel any pressure from him on this book. But do know that he is always there professionally, and that he and Maggie are always there for her.

When Claire hung up, she stared at the phone for a few minutes, thinking that actually the call could have been more awkward. That was not a relief. Just an impossible observation.

❦   ❦   ❦

It was not a matter of her being secretive. Nor was it really an issue of privacy. For most of her life Claire had tried to keep her worlds contained. She thought of it as a matter of dignity. Nobody at the university had known when she and Richard had split. In fact, when word leaked out, her colleagues were surprised at how decent and mannered she looked. Claire had not given the expected distress signals, leading people to comment that either she had ice in her veins, was a pillar of intellect and reason, or was the greatest actress of their generation. She had been losing and misplacing things. Keys. Sunglasses. Notes. Messages. She attributed it to a general lack of sleep, and overall exhaustion. It should only be natural, given the circumstances. But what if it never passed? That is what scared her. That she would live this way forever. That this is who she is.

Claire adapted to a new way of negotiating the campus. She would stay at her desk until the half-hour mark, when classes were populated and other faculty and administrators had retreated to their offices. That was when she would leave. Walking the winding concrete paths that terraced the lawns, only flanked by the grinding leaf mulchers trying to keep one step ahead of autumn. She would move briskly toward her car, almost certain to be alone at that hour, but still keeping her head down in case she passed a colleague. It still wasn't clear what the campus knew (or didn't know) about her story, but Claire was certain that they at least suspected something. It was in the way that they looked at her, with both sympathy and suspicion. And with hardly a word being passed, she would sense uneasiness about them, causing an almost visible tension that was only severed by cursory exit lines. As if suddenly they had all become strangers. There were no past references anymore. Only a muddy present that was impossible to see through.

¤   ¤   ¤

WHILE WAITING FOR THE HALF-HOUR mark, Claire read through a student paper intending to establish Van Gogh's state of mind around the time he painted *Crows*. The student, Tatiana, had studied the people whom Vincent engaged with in Auvers, trying to establish a psychological profile of the painter based on documented encounters. Tatiana's report was well written and researched, although it suffered from the same lack of originality that nearly all papers on this subject shared; namely, it focused only on Vincent's relationship with Dr. Gachet—friend, physician, and amateur painter—and, for the contemporary psychologist, father figure. Claire skimmed most of the paper, already familiar with the anecdotes and usual citations, looking for Tatiana's analysis. She was nearly at the end of the paper, the point where the Van

Gogh–Gachet relationship mysteriously dissolves, when she was stopped by the oft-cited quote from one of Vincent's letters to his brother, Theo, in which Van Gogh writes that they should not count on Dr. Gachet because he is as at least as sick as Vincent. "Now when one blind man leads another blind man," he concludes to Theo, "don't they both fall in the ditch?"

Claire looked back up to the painting. The crows fluttering in and out in soundless fury. A breeze pulling the wheat stalks to the right. The streak of black clouds overhead that smudged down into blue sky. In it she witnessed the terror of Vincent in the fields. It occurred to her that maybe Vincent didn't *just* kill himself. Dr. Gachet had cultivated and then somehow betrayed his trust, and perhaps that had been more than Vincent could take. After all, hadn't Vincent, in those final days, told Theo about how much he still loved art and life? Gachet must have said something drastic to change the relationship. And when Vincent saw that Gachet was not who he thought he was, he must have felt so lost. Claire could only imagine Vincent marching around in those wheat fields with nowhere to go, the paths converging down on him, either to lead him forward, or send him back.

She glanced at the clock, not quite at the half-hour mark, and startled when the phone rang. Tatiana's paper dropped to the floor. Claire reached down to grab it. She didn't catch the phone in time, which was just as well.

Playing back the recording, Claire heard an unfamiliar voice introduce itself as Trevor McCarthy from DiMallo Law Offices. He addressed her as Mrs. Andrews and said that he needed to talk with her about the accident. He asked her to call back at her earliest convenience, and said that he only required about five to ten minutes of her time. He just needed to confirm some details from her perspective. He left his number with the area code first, which struck her odd, as it was clearly local. That detail distracted her just enough to miss the final two numbers. She needed to listen to the message again, to pick up the missing digits. But she decided against it. She didn't know what she would possibly say other than the fact that she had hit a boy on Route 111 a month ago and then he died.

Claire gathered up her papers hastily. And she wished that she could live in a world where she could travel unseen instead of one where she feared that all eyes were watching her, whispering behind her back in assumptions and accusations. Even her own office wasn't safe anymore.

She moved quickly toward the parking lot, making a quick left when she saw her dean near the administration building, his back turned in conversation. Claire skirted across the lawn on a treaded path, where the trees were bare, like sadly misshapen arms shamed without strength. And in them, their simplicity was their beauty, their resolve to stand defenseless against the elements. Still they stood proud, their mangled branches witnessing the events that had passed under them.

♜   ♜   ♜

CLAIRE GOT HOME IN THE early afternoon and saw immediately that Richard looked terrible. His eyes were glassy, and his shoulders slumped forward in exhaustion. There were two streaks of missed whiskers on his left cheek. He was wearing the same T-shirt he had gone to sleep in last night, only this afternoon it was smudged with pencil colors, a smear of rainbow. Living in their old house in Providence had to be hard on him. Richard had been very reluctant to let go of their relationship—never fully grasping how two years of distance followed by a tiny atom bomb could lead to the final destruction of a marriage. As though trying to show his trustworthiness and honor, he hadn't stayed in the Providence house a minute past the day they had separated; instead he headed straight to Cambridge. He had kept in contact with Claire, almost as though they had been in early stages of courtship, just hampered by geography. He had sent her scribbles and pictures, and they talked on the phone about the silly things that happened to them. He would drop everything for her when she needed it, while struggling to maintain his distance, both physically and emotionally. And it was only in the occasional late-night phone call, his voice desperate and aching, when he would again ask her why they were separated, and each time Claire would struggle with her explanation of trust, because the power of the emotion was far greater than the definition of the word. Richard stopped asking. He returned to daily accounts, and casual conversation. It seemed to be the only way he could keep order for himself. And then last May, Claire told him that she needed to sever all communication, she needed space away to figure out how everything in their marriage had reached this point, and where it could go, if anywhere. Richard had been silent on the phone. And that was the last time they had spoken until she had called him from Route 111.

Claire knew it was difficult for him to be so attentive while back in this house. Still, despite any awkwardness, Claire was glad she could count on him, and, she sensed, Richard was glad to be counted on. No matter the toll it might take on him.

Claire told him he look tired.

He said, "It's just been a hard illustration, is all . . . The one that I'm working on," he reminded her. "It seems impossible."

"Maybe you should take a break from it. Let it sit."

"If I had the time. But they want the goddamn thing by Friday. And it's such a simple drawing. *Levator labii*. Two muscles that descend off the nose. But I can't seem to bring any presence to them. Any life. I swear I've done this illustration a dozen times. Maybe that's the problem. Too many times."

"It will come. You have two days. Just use the time."

"Spoken like a critic. It's hard for me to focus these days, Claire, with everything that's happened, and . . ."

She looked down, fully understanding the unspoken part of the sentence. She might have said something about how these matters will work themselves out, but wouldn't that sound strange coming from her? She pursed her lips and swallowed, not feeling nearly as awkward as he looked.

Richard said, "Which reminds me . . ." He looked over toward the phone. "Trevor McCarthy called today. He's the one who—"

"I'm surprised you picked up the phone."

"I thought it was my client."

"Well, you shouldn't be giving out the number."

"Either way," Richard said, "you have to call him." He threw his hands up. "You can't just expect something that difficult to go away just because you want it to."

They stared at each other for a moment.

Richard wiped his hands on his shirt, smearing the colors even more. He looked to the floor, and then, sensing his wife's thoughts, he reached over and took her hand. He placed it between both of his and squeezed down with reassuring force. "Everything is heading in the right direction, okay?" He looked away. "Trust me."

She slipped her hand out, tempted to hug him, or even just touch his shoulders. But still afraid.

His stare cavernously peeked out; wrinkled lines fell down his cheeks like totem markers. He looked so much like his father, had his father not been terrorized by a restless anxiety that turned nasty. Both men had a kind of worn beauty, where a gentle feature among the rugged parts seems so sadly profound. But Richard had tried his best to distinguish himself from his father in every way— forever distancing himself from the old man's proud ignorance.

Claire turned away toward the window. "You better finish your drawing," she said as she watched a blackbird land on the sill. "Friday always comes too soon."

THURSDAY

Neither Richard nor Cocoa was downstairs. Claire had sat an extra hour in the office, staring up at the *Crows* poster, afraid to go outside until some community event being held on the library quad broke up. Somewhere out there was the boy's family. They were not permitted any contact with each other. Ron Bernard had made that rule number two. But she knew the parents would not be able to resist saying something if they passed her at the post office door or saw her coming out of the Coffee Hut. They surely knew who she was and had probably looked her up on the university Web site. Despite what they had agreed, how could the parents just hold their heads up and pass by her? And no matter what Bernard had said, how could she have stopped herself from publicly confessing her guilt under their grieving eyes?

It was strange to walk into an empty house. She couldn't imagine Richard taking Cocoa for a walk around the East Side; it was too cold now. And if humaneness had forced Richard to take Cocoa out for her own relief, he would never have strolled beyond the front yard.

She inhaled the stillness of the living room, and it made her wonder about the boy's family, the permanent quiet in their house.

"Claire?" Richard called from upstairs. She heard Cocoa's claws slipping and sliding on the wood floors above. Claire smiled for the first time in the past month, thinking of Cocoa sleeping at Richard's feet as he worked. They were quite an unlikely pair to find each other's company. The recluse and the needy. "Claire?" he called again. "That you down there? Claire?"

Claire started up the staircase. She stopped to look back at the clock in the living room, still in the habit of checking for the half-hour mark.

"Claire?" His tone sounded worried.

"Of course it is me, Richard," she said coming down the hall-way. "Who else would it—"

"I know you don't want to me pick up the phone . . ."

She stopped in the hallway. "Why? Who called? Is it that Mc-Carthy who called again? Who called?"

"It is just that there were four calls in a row where the person hung up. And then a fifth one came, and I picked up the phone, and I answered it *What do you want?* Then there was a long pause, fol-lowed by a hang up." Richard then changed the tone of his voice, as though remembering his role was to calm. "It spooked me is all. That's all I mean to say. I just got a little spooked."

Standing in the doorway of Richard's room, Claire was stopped by the illustration on the easel. The human face stripped of its significance. All the skin and beauty peeled away. It was nothing but a series of interlocking muscles, strands that were deepened by shades of red, and selectively shadowed by thin, almost invisible, black lines. The face turned slightly to the right, posed with the same mysterious inevitabilities of the Dutch masters; the hollow eye sockets conveyed the sad expressiveness of the great self-portraits. The upper half of the neck twisted delicately, bringing the front two muscles forward in prominence. Through his simple drawing, Richard had managed to capture the elusive combination of vulnerability and strength—reduced it right down to the musculature.

Claire said, "That is truly striking." She stepped into the room. "The essence . . . You can see the whole human body in there. It really is amazing, Richard."

"I never thought you would say that about one of my drawings again."

"I didn't think I would either. . . . Something is different about this one. The technique is much more dramatic, but you can see the irony."

"It probably is context." Richard was shaking his head. "I'm sure that the room frames it differently. It is really not much different from what I usually do."

"It is truly wonderful." Her eyes watered. She looked once more at the drawing, taken in by its raw emotion. She really wanted to hug Richard, but she did not want to make too much out of the moment.

He said, "I am sorry. I hope I didn't scare you when you came in. I hope I haven't worried you. You know, regarding the phone calls, I mean. It was just a reaction. Nothing more than a reaction."

Claire placed her palms against her face, and let them slide down her cheeks.

❦   ❦   ❦

LATER THAT NIGHT, CLAIRE CLIMBED into her bed. She thought of Richard lying in his upstairs, hands laced behind his head, watching the shadows on the ceiling. And the room was right above hers, and if she really thought about it, it was only the spatial height that was distancing them. She was volleyed between his vulnerabilities and his need to protect, thankfully separated by a ceiling, where she could then roll over and fall asleep with the comfort of him, but wake up with the safety of being alone.

FRIDAY

On the last day before winter break, Claire sat in her office with the door shut. Lit by the blue light of the computer screen, she stared at a stack of ungraded quizzes she had given weeks ago. Apparently the students had forgotten about them too. The telephone ringer was off, and the e-mail was shut down. Hasty footsteps made their way toward her office. She sat braced until she heard the retreat. Turning around, she saw it was just an assignment that had been slid under the door. Her fright had managed to reduce her to an agoraphobic state, paralyzed by the thought of seeing her colleagues scattering for the holidays, imagining what they might see if they got a good look at her.

Now with the traffic she would not be home until 4:30 P.M.

Richard was going back to Cambridge for a full week to try to wrap up an obligation to a group of cardiologists who were trying to deliver their manuscript by Christmas. He hoped he could be back for Christmas eve, but he didn't want to commit. Claire had managed to tell him that she was fine, saying that it is probably more odd for us to spend Christmas together than it is for us to spend it apart. Still, she was hoping for the chance to see Richard before he left. They didn't talk about it at breakfast, but she didn't think he would go before five.

All three roads on the *Crows* print seemed to be coming right at her, led by the swarm of crows. They winged toward her with a vulturelike curiosity. One of the three roads was bound to hold the promise of salvation. The others were lures, tempting resolve and stability, but really booby-trapped with pitfalls and false glories. She could see how Vincent must have felt when he returned to that wheat field only weeks after painting it, gun in hand, staring out at those three paths. Lost in a moment where instinct no longer matters. Where you can no longer trust the trustworthy. How hopeless he must have felt standing there. Standing there, the familiar pattern of the wheat fields having changed since he had painted them weeks earlier. They were bleak and stark, somebody else's portrait now. There was no safe exit before the paths in front of him. And with all the genius that manifested itself into his right hand, the only thing it could do under the circumstance was will his index finger to squeeze the trigger.

❦   ❦   ❦

By 4:24 P.M., Claire worked up the courage to leave.

❦   ❦   ❦

She pulled out of the K lot, winding up the campus road to-ward Bay Road. The cars heading out for the Christmas break moved slowly. But it was more than the holiday rush. The drivers crawled with voyeuristic stares toward the roadside. Whatever was jamming things up appeared to be taking place at the traffic light. Only three cars made the left with the arrow, while a single car barely had managed the right turn.

Normally the students were edging around one another, trying to cut in from the side lots, but this line coming out of the west side of campus had an unusual solemnity. Claire inched along in the stream, pumping her brakes, pulling herself in time with the bumper of the lead car. She kept an uneasy, vigilant watch ahead, and to the sides, looking for an opening. She really wanted to see Richard before he left.

Rounding the bend, Claire noticed everybody at the stoplight looking to the right-hand corner. She couldn't see what lay ahead. It appeared that the drivers were struggling to read something. Creeping closer up the street, Claire could see the head and torso of someone standing over the hill. A sandwich board was draped around her neck. She appeared to be from Central America, with strikingly Indian features. She was short and stocky, wearing a white dress with full-length sleeves. She could have been ten, or she could have been one hundred. As Claire edged up, she guessed her to be closer to eight years old. The girl held her expressionless face still, not from boredom, but as though directed to maintain an angelic presence.

Claire couldn't breathe. Her heartbeat seemed to be fading. She went cold and dizzy when the girl's full body finally came into view. It was as though the accident had just replayed itself again. A large pixilated photo of the boy stretched down the length of this girl's body. It was a school picture, shot from the shoulders up. He was dressed in a white oxford shirt, with his head cocked and feigning a smile at the photographer's insistence. Scrawled in black marker across the top read, REMEMBER RONNIE KENNEALY. Below, in giant red marker was the word JUSTICE, each letter written in broad, thick letters.

Claire looked at the picture, and then at the girl. She was clearly a hired hand, bearing no obvious relation to the boy, neither physically nor emotionally. But still the girl had affected a funereal stare that was sadly peaceful.

Any trace of strength that Claire had gained was quickly drained away. She felt herself being surrounded by lawyers, by the family, by the reactions of strangers. Now she was stuck at this intersection with the face of the boy looking down on her. And, worse yet, he now had a name. He was Ronnie, son of the Kennealys. The only truth left was that her bumper had taken his life.

The light changed to green. Turning with the cold breeze that swept off the bay, the girl turned away from Claire, taking Ronnie's stare with her. Claire sat still. The drivers behind her grew impatient for her to move. At first, there was polite horn beeping. Longer blows quickly followed. Soon all the cars down the line leaned on their horns, sounding off in the sad and furied expression of a wake.

Still Claire couldn't move.

The boy now named Ronnie refused to look at her.

She sat helpless, until finally she pressed on the gas pedal and moved ahead.

♦ ♦ ♦

THAT EVENING RICHARD GOT THE full story from Ron Bernard. He then called Claire from Cambridge to give her all the details. Bernard had known that Ronnie Kennealy was the son of Carver resident and small business owner Dave Kennealy and his wife, Mary Ann. But what had taken Bernard nearly a month to track was that Dave Kennealy was more than a townie riffraff who restored antique bathtubs by the sweat of his own hands and that of a single laborer named Renaldo. Or that Mary Ann was another mousy Carver woman in her husband's shadow, not ever making eye contact in accordance with her awkward graces. Bernard (still relatively new to the region after transferring from the New London office, and not as versed in local lore) had learned that Dave Kennealy was in fact the son of Fletcher Kennealy, a figure who had made a legal career out of protecting every public and private business dealing that came out of city hall, and then some. There wasn't a power broker in this state that hadn't been indebted to him at some point. Manipulating the press. Sleazy investigators. Fletcher Kennealy once had been the city attorney, and in that role protected many officials from the kind of scandals and accusations that had made Rhode Island politics notorious. He hadn't stayed long in that job, but once in the private sector he represented many of the Smith Hill officials who had left the capital. In his heyday, Kennealy was known for being quietly powerful, the wizard behind the curtain. In an age where mass media was still finding its footing, Kennealy had pioneered the confluence of the political agenda with the local news's need for scandal. His quiet machinations had been considered to be the fuel that kept the political machine moving. But in spite of the illusion of immortality that infects the powerful, Kennealy's power and reputation had died with the power brokers he once represented. Nearing his mid-eighties, he was rarely seen. Even the family scandals that had been East Side parlor talk had vanished. His children had dissociated themselves from him, hoping they could establish an identity purified of their father's polluted past.

Although Dave Kennealy may have eschewed the family reputation to work with his hands in the quiet of Carver, when his own boy was brutally killed, he appeared ready to stand battle alongside the family mantle.

Word had it that Dave Kennealy was cashing in all his family chits to make certain this case was the biggest story to hit Rhode Island in years. Based on what Ron Bernard learned about the history of Kennealy political tactics, the family would ensure that the story was all over the TV news, and a regular feature of the *Providence Herald*—with the goal of showing the world that this was no accident, in order to influence future proceedings. Despite their legal team's denials, today's incident with the girl clearly was the first move. As a fellow attorney had told him, "Fletcher Kennealy would stab his hand into the center of the earth, and grab the axis and yank it out to stop the world from turning." It's going to be best to lay low for a while, Bernard recommended. "Tell your wife to stay out of the bright lights. Is there anywhere she can go for a few weeks? Far away?"

Claire paused when Richard finished. Cradling the receiver with her neck and shoulder, she opened the medicine bottle and swallowed a single antianxiety pill with no water. She said, "Maybe I should go to France. Get back to the book."

"I don't think Bernard meant to go that far."

"Does it make a difference?"

Richard was quiet. He breathed heavily into the phone. "I suppose it doesn't make a difference. He did say far away. Let's check with him to make sure, I guess." He was quiet again. "I guess," he said.

She could hear the city noises of Cambridge through Richard's phone. The Red Line rumbling down its tracks. Horns and shouts. Slamming doors and sirens. The ringing of Salvation Army bells in front of the store below his window.

It reminded her of how far away he was.

Late December to Mid-January

Christmas 1888 must have been Vincent van Gogh's lowest and most comforting moment. On December 23, he had sliced off a portion of ear in the ultimate act of devastation born from disappointment. But ten months earlier, on February 20, Vincent believed his arrival in Arles was the beginning of good things to come. Charmed by the light and the culture of this southern village, the painter quickly had tried to commandeer his presence in the South into the beginning of a movement. He worked hard at cajoling other painters to make the trip down to join him in inaugurating the Studio of the South. *After much persuasion, Paul Gauguin had agreed to come to live in Vincent's so-called Yellow House as the movement's leader. (That relationship has been analyzed through both anecdotal evidence and scholarly conjecture, most notably by Maggie Harrison—reference her work,* The Passion of the Yellow House, *a book based on her interpretations of both artists' work at the time, in conjunction with commentary from leading psychoanalysts—although hope- lessly biased in favor of Gauguin!)*

And there can be no doubt that Vincent's adulation for Gauguin began to rival his own passion for painting. Vincent had been overjoyed with the expectation of Gauguin's arrival. He had decorated the Yellow House for him, stating that he was "preparing the prettier room upstairs, which I shall try to make as much as possible like the boudoir of a really artistic woman." *He must have been giddy with excitement when Gauguin arrived, romanticized by the drama of art, and no doubt physically attracted to the elder's rugged stature. Maggie Harrison wrote of homoerotic tendencies in* The Pas- sion of the Yellow House, *and that Vincent's behavior sug- gested that of a doting wife, more than a cohort. Poor Vincent, disappointed by his own concoctions for intimacy and compan- ionship, always felt rejected by Gauguin. On that December 23 night, Gauguin led Vincent through the narrow Arles lanes in pursuit of prostitutes. Maggie Harrison's book makes much of this incident, suggesting that the love-struck had helped the ob- ject of his affection seek others. Accounts of the evening vary (with Gauguin's later recollection being the most dramatic— and the most discounted), but either way, Van Gogh ended the evening furious with Gauguin, and with a portion of his left ear missing and delivered to a prostitute named Rachel, per- haps as a gesture of camaraderie, a sad toast to the emotional ignorance of coveted men who will enter your life but will never share it. With a bandage held tight to his ear, Vincent was led home by the postman, where he promptly thanked the letter car- rier before sending him away. Vincent would then have walked past Gauguin's pretty room, already emptied, as the idol had left town, terrified by Van Gogh's violence—and not wanting to risk further association. But, even in a state of shock, Vincent was not surprised by his friend's absence, he knew that incompatibility had come between them, or more succinctly, in his own words:* "Gauguin was not happy with the little yellow house where we work, and especially with me."

Vincent lay down in his bed, the blood flowing from his ear, as he drifted in and out of consciousness. The expectations had been more than unfulfilled—they had been destroyed. And as he lay there feeling the blood oddly cool against his neck, he must have hoped that it would all drain out at once, cleansing him of this life. It was the heartbreak of the adolescent. The letdown of the dreamer. A life that had seemed so perfectly beautiful had just as suddenly revealed its hideous scars. There is no question that as he allowed himself to drift out of consciousness, Van Gogh hoped that he would never wake again.

Theo was at the bedside when Vincent awoke in the hospital. Following the postman's advice, a policeman named Roberts had checked in on Vincent in the Yellow House and subsequently rushed the wounded painter to the hospital, where his dutiful brother was summoned from a celebratory weekend after announcing his engagement to the future Johanna van Gogh. In seeing his brother, Vincent felt a rush of comfort.

The swirling out-of-control night now seemed distant when he looked at Theo's reassuring stare. Theo likely did not ask Vincent what had happened with Gauguin, the prostitute, or the ear; only told him that he had made arrangements with Johanna to stay with Vincent until the ear had healed. They discussed heading north to Auvers. Vincent felt hopeful with this discussion, saying that recent events convinced him that this all necessitated a return to the North. Theo agreed, but from a more methodical viewpoint. It would be best if Vincent kept to himself for a while, to draw on a new inspiration to bring some sense of solemnity to him. (Meanwhile, Theo would look into this doctor up in Auvers for whom Cézanne had been so enthusiastic.) The two brothers celebrated Christmas in the hospital room. They talked of family and art. Every day until January 7, Vincent would ask Theo to tell him again about how good the North would be for him. And each time Theo reassured him, there was no past for Vincent. Only a future.

Claire told Richard that Cocoa needed plenty of attention while she was overseas. Real attention. He couldn't just feed her and then toss her out the back door twice a day to shit. Her dog had come to expect a certain level of companionship, and it was nothing short of cruel to expect her to live the same ornamental life as a goldfish. She had made a list for caring for the lab, one that was separate from the caring of the house. In return, Claire allowed Richard to convert the upstairs bedroom into a studio. He could move his bedding into their old room. It was not a life intended to replicate their past, but rather to preserve her current one until she returned. No assumptions were made.

After last month's placard stunt, Ron Bernard had encouraged the idea of a research trip to France. While he needed Claire to be on call, Bernard believed that being away for a brief time actually made for good strategy, given the public exploits of the Kennealys. Three weeks at the most, with a tightly scheduled itinerary. It would temporarily free her from the open scrutiny and allow her to continue her work. He had also seen her going abroad as a public relations counterattack—demonstrating the responsible scholar engaged in her work, not the lunatic shut-in who is afraid to show her face out of guilt.

Claire had agreed reluctantly, knowing it meant that she would need to face her book again, trying to find the meaning in something she didn't quite see anymore. But getting out of Rhode Island did seem appealing. Any errand outside the house was stressful. Anybody could be the Kennealys. Or witnesses. Or investigators. She had started sending Richard to the grocery store, to the gas station, and for all other needs. Since classes ended, Claire had only left the house once to go to campus at the behest of her dean, Bruce Wright, on the Monday following the placard incident. Bruce Wright had called her into his office, suggesting that she consider a semester off, "perhaps to research," he said grudgingly. Bruce was always irritated by Claire and her fellow faculty members who had gained prominence in their fields, and exercised it when needed. More than twenty years ago, Bruce had chosen to go into administration as his way of expressing his scholarly devotion, and ever since, he had become very defensive over his position. Bruce made constant reference to the fallacy of social Darwinism, forever citing that it was not the strongest and brightest who survived and prospered, but rather those who gained recognition, and then resorted to self-promotion. He knew scores of mathematicians who engaged in critical research, yet as far as university administrations were concerned, such scholars were always overshadowed by those who were getting favorable book reviews in the *New York Times* or NSF grants. It was a speech that

Claire had heard many times before and was prepared to hear again. He had taken off his glasses in his per usual dramatic form, landing them on his desk, letting the steel frames ring throughout the room. "I understand that this is rather late in the year to be having this conversation, but—"

"These are exigent circumstances."

Bruce had looked down, presuming to acknowledge the unspoken. Not a single person on that campus had mentioned anything to Claire about the accident, even though the sandwich board incident had caused quite a stir. A photograph had ended up in both the student newspaper and the shore paper. And to make matters worse, without knowing of Claire's involvement, the multicultural studies department had taped the photo from the news clipping to their office door; it was not clear if it stood as a representation of heroism or exploitation.

"Claire, you must understand . . . What I mean to say is that . . ." Bruce put his glasses back on. "I think, given the recent events of the last month, that the provost's office is in agreement that a semester sabbatical serves the mutual interest of the university and your own work." Bruce stood up, still refusing to speak the obvious. He clapped his hands together, as though the meeting was over. "The university believes in trying to support our faculty in whatever ways it can."

Bruce had put his hand out to Claire. She politely shook it. He tried to make eye contact with her but kept looking down at the tops of his shoes. "Please don't forget to fill out the necessary paperwork. Julie can help you, if you need it." He still wouldn't let go of her hand. "This will be good for you."

She had slid her hand out from his grip. "Thank you, Bruce."

Q   Q   Q

CLAIRE MADE PLANS TO LEAVE after Christmas. Somehow it seemed better to spend Christmas alone in Providence than in France. At least Cocoa would be by her side. As it turned out, Richard had finished his project by Christmas eve, but Claire told him just to stay in Cambridge. She ended up sitting desperately alone through Christmas eve and Christmas day, stroking Cocoa's head and unwrapping a giant dog biscuit for her dog. Last year, she and Richard had spent the first Christmas of their separation together, both too terrified to risk it alone. But this was the first one on her own. She felt it was the only way to assess the future with any clarity.

Q   Q   Q

BY THE FIRST OF THE year, the loose ends for the trip had been tied together surprisingly smoothly. Maggie Harrison had offered to help Claire organize the trip, while her husband, Bill, maintained a poorly disguised glee that Claire was getting back into the book. In her last phone call, she had told him some of her ideas about the complicity of Gachet in Vincent's death, and how that might be tied into the painting. Bill said it sounded intriguing, and that he knew Maggie had never trusted Gachet much either for some reason. He hoped Claire found something on the trip that helped forward that theory. It sounded as though it could make for a good book.

Ron Bernard had one lone condition: Claire needed to meet Trevor McCarthy in Bernard's office before she left. For Bernard, it would mollify his nagging concern that the Kennealy team would try to say publicly that Claire had left the country to avoid answering questions. Even a brief meeting would show that she was being fully cooperative, willing to halt her illustrious career to *get to the bottom of the truth*. They scheduled the meeting on the day before she was set to leave. Then, at least, they could shut the door on Trevor McCarthy.

Claire's tickets were bought. The itinerary set. She would return to Auvers-sur-Oise, grounding herself among the familiar streets and sooted air, now replicated with modern conventions and layers of trampled dreams. Maybe she would rediscover *Crows over the Wheatfield*. At least uncover some of its truths.

MONDAY

It seems as though no matters of public interest are ever private nor without hyperbole. Yet somehow they live on to tell the tale. Following the ear incident, Le Forum Républicain, *the local Arles newspaper, reported it as such:* "Last Sunday at half past eleven, a local painter named Vincent van Gogh, a native of Holland, appeared at the maison de tolerance n. 1, asked for a girl named Rachel, and handed her his ear with these words: 'Keep this object carefully.' Then he disappeared. The police, informed of these happenings, which could be attributed only to an unfortunate maniac, looked the next morning for this individual, whom they found in his bed with barely a sign of life."

One would assume that Theo kept this article from his brother's attention. In the matter of one short week, the private demons had become the public scrutiny.

⚜   ⚜   ⚜

THEY ALL FACED RON BERNARD'S desk. Claire and Richard paired off to the right, with Trevor McCarthy seated on the left. Amazingly, he looked just as she had pictured him. Early thirties. Close-cropped hair, spiked with scented gel. Disproportionately short legs anchored his stocky body. There was nothing pleasant about his face, just the blank demeanor of a school yard wall pocked by the imprints from dodgeball games. He sat with his legs crossed, arms folded, and bouncing his left leg in annoyingly stilted rhythms.

Eschewing formality, Bernard leaned into his desk. The edge cut into his gut. "I swear to God, Trevor, you relay to Jack Di-Mallo that another bullshit stunt like last month's at the college will have me screaming of ethics charges in every newspaper. You tell him that."

"DiMallo swears that he has no knowledge of, nor was he involved with, the girl holding the sign. Believe me, Ron, you know he would never encourage that. Jack DiMallo play by the rules."

Bernard laughed. "But from what I hear, his clients are . . . Goddamn, inflicting emotional distress on my client and poisoning a jury pool in one fell swoop. Bravo. Brilliant. Tell DiMallo I doff my cap to him. But, I repeat, if there is a next time I will . . . So help me." Claire figured Bernard's outburst was for her benefit. She appreciated watching McCarthy shift in his chair. "Now let's get on with this, shall we. I understand that Mrs. Andrews has obligations."

McCarthy spoke quickly. A pedestrian had come forward to

say that an older black car had been trying to work its way into the traffic, and that there may have been something of a battle between the drivers. The witness believed it caused just enough distraction to encourage the accident. McCarthy wasn't looking for Claire's version, only if she remembered such a car, and, if she did, could she provide a description. He was trying to track down the driver of the black car and reminded Claire that the testimony could be beneficial to her.

Claire stared at McCarthy until she forced his eyes to the floor. "What do I say?" she asked Bernard.

He answered, "The truth."

"There were many cars," she spoke. "Old and new. The road was traffic. All traffic."

"Let me rephrase this: can you help me locate the model of a black car that might have been involved?"

She looked beyond McCarthy, out the window. The moist gray clouds thickened in striated layers, starting to lighten, as though contemplating snow.

McCarthy pushed himself to the edge of his chair. His cheeks reddened. He looked to Ron Bernard. "Tell her she needs to be forthright. She needs to be forthright. Can you tell her that? She just can't be—Forthright, can you tell her that?"

Claire tingled in nervousness. Her head went light in the reflex of anticipation and fear.

Richard and Bernard looked to each other. McCarthy's legs opened a bit wider, and he tapped his foot faster. A thread dangled from the hem of his chinos.

"Look, Mrs. Andrews," Bernard said. "Just know that nothing

that you say here will incriminate you. In fact, it can only help the case. It is best to have everything corroborated." He tried to give a gentle smile.

Claire bit down on her lip, shaking her head. Only recently had she been able to get through a whole day without reliving the guilt every damn minute, and here she was drawn right back into it. There was no way that anybody in this room was going to ever believe that she didn't record and memorize every detail of that night, right down to nuance of smell and touch. What she knew now was only the aftermath. Like looking at your own bloodied fist with no explanation for what came before.

"Claire," Richard said.

"What do you want me to say?"

"The car," McCarthy said. "I told you about it already. I told you, the car."

"The car?"

"I told you, the car. Didn't you hear me tell you about the car? I told her about the car. Explicitly."

"I don't know."

"About the car? Is that what you are saying? You don't know anything about the car. I need to get this straight. I need to report correctly." McCarthy pulled down on his tie, trying to drag the shortened tip to its properly appointed position at the belt. "You don't know anything about the car, you are telling me."

"My car," she said.

McCarthy looked at Bernard. "Her car? What's she talking about, her car?"

"My car is all I know, and I barely remember that. But there is nothing different that you would have . . . No reason to expect . . . He *just* shouldn't have been . . . And if you think that you are going to sit here and pin this on . . . Well, then you can stop."

"Oh, I can stop?"

"Yes, you can stop. You just sit there and try to fill in the blank with whatever crap that you—"

Bernard jumped in. "Mrs. Andrews, I think it is best of you . . ." He was still seated behind his desk, with McCarthy frozen in place.

Claire took Richard's hand and pulled him from his seat. "I won't just sit here and . . ."

Richard tried to resist, but as she stood she kept him in tow, tugging him reluctantly toward the door.

She swallowed, hoping to push air down into her queasy lungs.

When Van Gogh finally was released from the hospital and back in Arles, he went through a furious period of painting. The self-portraits, with gauze wrapped around his head to bandage the left ear, suggest what the townspeople might have seen when he would venture from the studio. Imagine the monster from the newspaper article standing before you on a Romanesque street, frail and distraught, with little patches of dried blood still staining the bandage. This was too much for a populace still enchanted by superstition and myth. It took only a month before Vincent broke down again. An episode that was so publicly violent that the citizens of the village petitioned to have the painter imprisoned in a hospital cell. Writing of being held under "lock and key and with keepers, looking out a window at township of people here cowardly enough to join together against one man, and that man ill," *he must have been relieved when finally Theo, in conjunction with a local minister, arranged for Vincent to go to the sanitarium in Saint-Rémy for a true recovery. It was one step farther north. Away from the daily haranguing outside the hospital cell window, the publicly made allusions in the newspaper, and the curious onlookers that passed through the halls, staring at him as though they had paid admission. The move into the sanitarium in Saint-Rémy had felt liberating. And more importantly, one more gate to pass through en route to a free and healthy life in the North.*

Claire lay in her bed. She could hear Richard creaking upstairs. Tomorrow, when he would be in her bed, she would be in one overseas. Within the week, a bond would be formed between Richard and Cocoa that would make the dog forget all about Claire.

Her plane would not leave until two o'clock tomorrow afternoon, still giving her most of the morning for last-minute details. But, for some reason, she was restless, tossing and turning, rolling over to look at the clock.

The light coming through the window looked strange. She could not make out the hands on the clock, but she knew the hour was well before sunrise. An odd yellow glow washed over the curtains, striking in its luminescence, but still lacking the power of the sun. She tried closing her eyes, even dragging a pillow over her head, but she could still sense the glow.

Claire had been a junior in college when she had first traveled to France. Even then she was ambitious to learn more about Van Gogh than he knew about himself. She had gone south, walked the tree-lined streets of Saint-Rémy, weaving under the knotted olives, planning to make her way up to St. Paul's Asylum, and then into the wheat fields, where she waited for night to fall, so she could see the stars and sky exactly as Vincent had when he painted them. The surrounding light had stopped her. Its subtle glow called forth all the colors and forms, in a pure composition of magnificence. Claire had imagined Vincent being so struck by the light and its complementing elements that he must have felt as though he had found his aesthetic paradise. But, slowly, as the elegance of the figures were revealed to him, so too must have been the imperfections. This great gift of light also would be his tormentor. Vincent quickly would realize that his own form was being revealed. The flaws and deficiencies shining bright, radiating his angry sadness. At the time, Claire had been certain that's what he had experienced, because she too had felt it; struck still by the most vividly haunting beauty one could imagine. She had never known so much self-loathing in all her life. It began with a superficial dissection of her body and mind. Then it slowly penetrated her soul. She had gone back to the hotel room that night, afraid to sleep. At dusk she took the earliest train back to Paris, where she retreated into the safety of the museums and libraries, as she would for the next nineteen years of her life.

Claire still felt the threat of the painter's light. It scared her to think that she could move on. Could anybody other than a sociopath inflict such a horror and still eat breakfast the next morning when the sun rose?

TUESDAY

The phone rang as Claire closed the front door, not locking it as she left. It is frightening how simple it is to leave once you make the decision. She felt no nostalgia for the postholiday Providence streets. Piles of dirty snow were shoved up against the corners. Next to nearly every trash can was a tattered Christmas tree with receding needles and stray tinsel, surrounded by smashed cartons and remnants of wrapping paper held by Scotch tape, waving like flags in the winter breeze. Green recycling bins filled with champagne bottles weighted down flattened pizza boxes. She had been the invalided observer for the holiday season, shut in behind closed curtains and off-the-hook telephones. She was glad to see the holidays organized and waiting for waste management to dispose of them. And she was glad to be swept away ahead of them.

Richard drove her to the airport. He commented that it was strange that she was taking only one suitcase; she usually overpacked even for the shortest conference. They quickly agreed that for three weeks it didn't really matter, because even two more suitcases of clothing would not be enough.

Every address. Every phone number. And along with those, Richard wanted every detail that altered the itinerary. She agreed to call, having decided against taking her laptop because she got too flustered with figuring out the dial-up modems, and she was forever losing those European adaptors. He would be on an airplane the minute she needed him. "Where did I go wrong?" Claire said. "At thirty-nine I finally have a knight in shining armor. He is chivalrous. He is smart. He is handsome. He is my estranged husband," causing Richard to belt out his faux lounge rendition of "That's What Friends Are For." He held the syllabic space between *are* and *for* in aching dramatics until they both erupted into a laughter that relieved all their anxieties. Near hysterics, Claire clutched her sides. It plunged her into a pure moment where there were no fearful deans and unsure husbands and angry drivers and ghosted faces of accidental boys lost.

From their laughter, the clouds seemed to rise, lifting the normally low ceiling of sky that boxed in the terrain, opening it up with brilliant possibilities. There is that strange cavern of atmosphere that covers New England—even the Atlantic and her bays feel the limitations. Perhaps that accounts for the close-knit protectiveness of the culture, where newcomers are always strangers, and the shades are drawn at 5 P.M. New England can be a domed world, limited by the very borderless frontiers that gave it its existence. As with the southern French light that Claire knew at twenty, the region can merely define the flaws and bitterness.

The light at Angell and Thayer seemed to be taking forever. Their laughter had faded as quickly as it came. Richard's hands gripped the wheel at ten and two. Jaw clenched. Steam rose from a manhole cover. She had almost crawled into bed with him last night, had walked halfway up the stairs before turning back. She had only intended to hold him from behind. Feel the back of his lungs rise and press into her. But the intimacy scared her, especially on the night before she was due to leave. You can't lose something you don't have.

Claire spoke, breaking the quiet. "At least you'll have time to finish your illustrations again," she said. "No interruptions. No need to go to Cambridge."

He nodded.

"They really are stunning, Richard. And I'd swear that they could hang in an exhibit one day. You should think about showing again. They are that fascinating."

He still did not say anything. The light finally changed. They drove over the peak of College Hill.

"I am serious. When I return, I'll call on my contacts to get your drawings into a show. It could be called something like, 'The Art of Medicine.' It would be amazing."

"Okay," he said.

"It doesn't appeal to you?"

"I make illustrations, Claire. That's all I do."

"Oh, but that's not true. I felt something with that drawing in your room."

"Then I just made a bad illustration. It shouldn't leave you with any feeling. If you interpret anything I draw, then I am doing a lousy job."

"Or maybe not . . . But, really, let's think about doing something in a gallery with your work . . . When I get back."

He was quiet for a few minutes. Finally he spoke, "I appreciate what you're saying. I really do. I'm just not . . . I don't know if that's what I want to do. I am not sure . . ."

She wished he hadn't said that.

❦   ❦   ❦

BEGINNING AT AGE EIGHT, CLAIRE used to take the train by herself to visit her grandmother. Those were different times. It was a long ride for a little girl alone. In truth it was only about an hour and a half, but for a child who was not permitted to stay in the house alone, it was an excruciating journey. The Amtrak people assigned an attendant to the young Claire. They would check in on her regularly, and had made the promise to escort her off the train upon arrival and into the arms of her waiting grandmother. In some sense it was no different from having a babysitter; she was just outside the home. But once Claire was loaded on the train, given a deck of cards with the company logo on the back, and set up with soft drinks and a system for emergency contacts, she was a little girl left in a train that rushed her away from all the familiar, at breakneck speed.

It was an early taste of freedom. At eight years old, Claire had already understood the need to leave her hometown. Her grand-mother's town in the most southern tip of Ohio (indeed more Kentucky than Ohio) was by no means the promised land. Claire recognized it as small and dusty. She didn't know any kids, other than one who was the son of the daughter of one of Grandma's neighbors—a mean boy who was a year and a half younger and spent a lot of time talking about killing animals, with his one true goal to skin a dog. In a sense, it was all very boring. She spent most of the vacation days sprawled out on the living room carpet, shifting her elbows to avoid prolonged rug exposure, watching the giant television in the corner with faded colors that looked almost psychedelic. Still, she had been given the chance to live a different life, albeit temporarily. The illusion of the wombed home had been dissolved. With only eight years to draw from, Claire had discovered that the rules of the world were contemplated outside of 39 Emerald Street in Dayton, Ohio. Her mother and father were not the ones standing behind the curtain and spinning the earth on the tips of their fingers. She wasn't supposed to figure that out for another eight or nine years. But by that early age Claire was already dreaming of boarding trains that took her far away from Dayton. Deep into lands and lives that she didn't know. Anywhere but home.

Ŷ   Ŷ   Ŷ

As the 737 took off for Kennedy in New York (where she then would make her connection to de Gaulle), Claire looked out the window at her tiny state. It appeared even more delicate against the water's edge. Peaceful and still. Frozen in time. As though a god consciously had created this diorama at a distance, only to admire the beauty and the workmanship without having to be privy to the messy details. The world was idyllic from this high up. It moved with order and respect. It seemed almost impossible that waiting below was an interconnected web of pain and anger and rage all organized into a tightly knit system, drawing her into its bargain. Claire looked out at the clouds, and then down again to a shrinking Providence. She felt pity for the little Central American girl, no doubt compensated by a pittance to advertise complications that she should never know. But as the plane lifted higher, Claire took comfort in knowing that she was seeing the details of her world reduced to something she could scoop up with her hand.

PART TWO

Four Days

in

January

Day One

In May of 1890, having recently settled in Auvers-sur-Oise, Vincent van Gogh wrote a letter to his brother, Theo, in Paris in which he discussed among other things living with his ongoing melancholia. One hopeful moment, he had indicated, was in finally meeting Dr. Paul-Ferdinand Gachet, a local physician, art collector, and amateur painter, who had been recommended by Camille Pissarro. In the letter Vincent told his brother: "Dr. Gachet said to me that if the depression or anything else became too great for me to bear he could quite well do something to diminish its intensity, and that I must not think it awkward to be frank with him." *In that hopeful moment, following incarceration at the infirmary at Saint-Rémy, and desperate for some help, he wouldn't know it would be a matter of weeks before he would warn Theo that they should not count on Dr. Gachet because he is* "more ill than I am ... Now, when one blind man leads another

blind man, don't they both fall into the ditch?" *Barely a
month and a half later, Vincent would walk out into the wheat
fields that he had painted two and a half weeks earlier and aim
the revolver at his chest.*

His inability to control his disease had shattered him.

*But in May 1890 Vincent must have been elated. He was
overly hopeful about improving his mental health while writing
to his brother on that May afternoon, already planning a portrait of the man who would keep him sane. He was so optimistic that he might have even believed that the intended
portrait of Dr. Gachet would eventually command $82.5 mil-
lion in an auction almost exactly one hundred years after the
creation. And at that hour, Vincent would have argued that the
good doctor was worth every penny that Ryoei Saito will pay
one century later to preserve him in an undisclosed warehouse
in the joyous company of Renoir's* Au Moulin de la Galette.
*But during that second week of July, when Vincent stood in
the wheat fields watching the crows with a stain of black paint
on his brush, half aware of the psychological leash of Dr. Gachet, Vincent must have cursed the cure over the disease.*

Claire pushed her way through the crowds at de Gaulle.
Half in a daze she wandered twice around the horseshoe-
shaped terminal until finally finding the hall to lead her to
the RER. The airport seemed unusually quiet while she walked
through T-2, except for the regular business passengers who
shoved past her, keeping their stares trained down.

She passed three banks of phone booths. She had promised that
she would call Richard from Kennedy, but she hadn't had time.

And now displaced, exhausted, and feeling pressed for time, Claire decided to wait to call him until she reached her room in Auvers. She just would let him know that she had arrived safely. That she was feeling well. But, mostly, she would know that he was still there. Then, Claire could walk up the stairs to her room, pop a pill, chased by a hearty claret, and collapse on the bed and fall asleep with her socks on, and maybe wake up to a morning that, for once, felt like it carried the same possibilities as all the others once had.

She had managed very little sleep on the plane. Her temples throbbed. Her body buzzed. It had taken nearly forty-five minutes to get through customs. Somehow she had become caught up in a group of Turkish passengers, and only one officer was stamping passports. Everybody had been jockeying for position, and Claire had found herself feeling very claustrophobic, and overwhelmed. Finally she stepped out of the crowd, leaned against a back wall, and waited for the rush to thin out. When she finally made her way up to the desk to show her passport, the officer asked if she was here on business or vacation. She didn't know how to answer. Impatiently he stamped her book before she could reply.

Through the blue splays of airport boutiques, Claire peered in at the leggy young women working the floors, looking bored, like wearied fashion models caught in private moments between flashing bulbs. Her suitcase banged against her leg. For a moment she was tempted to run outside and grab a taxi straight into Paris. Order the driver to take her somewhere between the dueling neon of Les 3 Roses and Le Fet d'Cau in the red-light district. Maybe Le Cupidon, with its red and blue neon holding down the corner on place de Pigalle, bragging lap dances and table dances in perfectly lettered English. How easy it would seem to turn in her life for one at Le Cupidon, where instead of trying to live with her guilty conscious, she would be getting prepared for work, warming up backstage with stretches and hip bends, pulling her lace fringe just past her hips, ready to take residence in the district's risqué history.

She walked faster, feeling more manic with each stride. She had the complex of the fugitive, who becomes hyperaware of how he might stick out in public. Claire told herself over and over that she was a stranger here, no more interesting than the next person. But the paranoia from home still lingered. Especially in a crowded airport where so many worlds converged. Anybody could be watching her, anticipating the perfect misstep.

Getting out of here meant taking the RER B to Saint-Michel station in Paris, then transferring onto the RER C to Pontoise, just outside of Auvers. From there she would take a cab the short distance to her hotel in the village, where she planned to lie on her bed as still as possible, completely undetected.

With time to kill, Claire found an empty bench near the rear of the platform that left her with a view of the schedule board. Waves of commuters pulsed by. Passing through like any one of the single breaths out of the 17,000 taken each day. This platform was just a cut-through, a breezeway between the parts of their lives that mattered. But for Claire this was solitude. It was the pause when the fireworks sat in perfect formation before they started their collapsing descent.

When she and Richard had first separated, Claire often woke up from dreams in which she and Richard were laughing or running or, even more mundanely, cooking in the kitchen. She woke with a certain relief, the spark of love still flowing through her body. But only seconds later the cold reality had splashed her face, and she felt the knot tightening in her stomach, and the weight of guilt seeping through her. That hadn't happened yet with Ronnie Kennealy. The dream and the reality had not been separated.

As she fumbled for her bag to board the inbound train, Claire felt chilled by the reality of the concrete station. The solitude had been an illusion. A ruse. A temporary diversion from the world that had taken up arms against her, and to which she tried to surrender herself to its grief. But this was no battle. It was a beating.

On July 6, in the year 1890, Vincent took the train from Paris back to Auvers. He had been to visit Theo, Johanna, and his recently born nephew. He had stayed in Paris for only one day, a day reputed to be filled with tension. Easily overwhelmed by such anxieties, he would have walked briskly to the train station, taken his ticket before the conductor had time to return the change, and collapsed onto the wooden bench, already relieved at the solace that was waiting for him at the train's destination. Three weeks from that moment he will have painted Crows over the Wheatfield, *and later stood in the wheat field with the pistol aimed clumsily at his chest, speaking his final words to his brother once his body finally gave in two days after the bullet left the chamber. But in that one moment on the train, everything seemed perfect. He was in a moment that is the inverse of conflict. It is the dulling moment. Time stood in perfect harmony with the vision of how a life should be lived. And had he remained reclined on the train's wooden seat between Paris and Auvers indefinitely, he probably would have lived forever.*

Ω   Ω   Ω

SHE WATCHED THE COUNTRYSIDE STREAK by the window. Shrubbery and wheat blurred vibrantly with the passion of a watercolor. Then ripping past suburban neighborhoods that led into antiquated industrial parks, only to be dumped back again into a thicket that must have stood exactly as Vincent had witnessed. She had been to Auvers-sur-Oise several times over the years, but as the train sped closer, she found that she could no longer recall what the village looked like, other than the narrow roads that cut along the hills. It occurred to her that so much of this trip had seemed unfamiliar. As though since the accident she was leading a brain-damaged life that only allowed her to recognize the touchstones and markers along the way. She closed her eyes to try to recognize the town. She had stood in those wheat fields at the top of the hill before. Walked the path behind the church. But it seemed like another person's history. A ragged secondhand account that had been prejudiced by the perspective of its viewer. And the oddest part was that Claire could not remember if she had been there with Richard. Calculating the logistics had placed him there, but the details of her memory could not picture it.

The train was lightly populated. Most passengers ended up clustered on the upper level, facing forward along with Claire. She relaxed her shoulders. How could this all come to be? It was ludicrous that she would find herself alone, still too afraid to allow herself to forgive the mistakes in her marriage. But it was also absurd that she would become the focus of a Rhode Island family that was on a hurricane's path to publicly destroy her. Or even more absurd that she knew what it felt like to take a life.

Claire closed her eyes and thought back to first meeting Richard. They were younger than they thought they had been— late twenties but already feeling the initial weariness of adulthood. Both had had their hearts broken. Richard had been left by Marie Bechet, a Frenchwoman who had known a moment of notoriety in the Boston art scene for using acrylics and bedsheets in a contemporary homage to the art of batik. She had kissed him off suddenly, saying that she didn't want anyone in love with her. Meanwhile, not more than twenty-four hours after Miles Newton had professed his love to his beloved Claire, he had announced to her that he was leaving for a fellowship in northern France.

Within days of their losses, Richard and Claire had run into each other at a party in Somerville that neither had wanted to attend. They had known each other peripherally through mutual friends, but later each would swear that they had never talked until that night (although several of their friends disputed such accounts as romantic hyperbole). They had found themselves lonely and lingering over a cheese platter and a bowl of ice when Richard asked Claire how she had been. "Busy hating the French," she had replied.

He had grinned.

"Why are you smiling?" she asked, almost smiling herself.

"Because *you* can't hate the French. That is my arena."

In any other circumstance Claire would have felt the flush of humiliation fill her cheeks. She had known that Marie Bechet had ditched Richard. That news had made it through town on a wire. Claire had not been able to stop her words as she made the comment, but Richard's laugh had suggested that he was not wounded by the reference. In fact, it seemed it took him just as long to make the connection. Claire coughed. She told him about Miles Newton. "So it's probably not the French I should be hating, but the country itself." She bit into a cube of Swiss cheese and fumbled with the toothpick.

"How about I handle the French people," Richard replied, "and you take on the territory?" He was so charming in his loneliness, with a sadness that was inviting. She didn't fall in love with Richard at that moment, but she did sense a need to be with him. That was probably the first of her miscalculated expectations. In those long days she hadn't counted on her feeling of desperation ever going away.

Richard had been through a good stretch of showings in local galleries, getting attention for a series of sketches that detailed the body, a row of knuckles, an artery on the side of the neck or the temple. His most recent show at an upscale gallery on Newbury Street gathered some powerful attention, especially from the socialite Back Bay crowd. But Claire, whose own career was taking off with the publication of her second book on the way, felt overshadowed by Richard's current success. She saw the raw power that his work could have, while hers was deeply passive. The bigger reality of that initially had saddened her.

They had started taking small road trips into northern New England. Driving along twisted roads through New Hampshire. Occasionally venturing on marathon trips as far north as the Northeast Kingdom in Vermont, but always returning to Boston and into their own beds. She couldn't remember exactly how the trips had come to be planned, but Claire did recall that these were routes Richard had traveled many times alone. And he must have invited her for a drive the weekend following the party, because she couldn't remember a day since that night when she was not trying to map out every direction of their lives.

The conversations on those drives were full of knotted gut emotion, but without any sense of context. Claire would talk broadly about betrayal and emptiness. However, she rarely addressed the details. Never uttered Miles's name, and never referred to Marie other than in the generic "people like that." On one level it should have been pure and honest—as the stinging of raw emotions can be—but in a grander sense it was an evasion.

Richard would stare straight ahead at the road, two hands on the wheel of his Toyota, seemingly gone into other worlds. She didn't sense that he was interested in an emotional discussion, beyond responding to her questions. But then how many men are? Sometimes he would talk about work. He recently had been contacted about freelancing for Harvard Medical School, and, for the first time ever, *work*—in the grown-up sense—was starting to dominate his life. He alluded to the dilemma of crossing over from the avant-garde art scene into the commercial world, discussing the issue as though he were about to cross an ethical and moral boundary. Claire had suggested he could do both. "You have had some incredible successes already," she had said. "I don't see why some behind-the-scenes commercial ventures will harm those. You have already made a name for yourself in the galleries, and a place in the art community. Many artists and writers have straddled both lines for their entire lives in order to survive. No one will think the lesser of you."

He pursed his lips and nodded in kind agreement.

Richard had been a kind of child prodigy. His second-grade art teacher, Mrs. McCourdy, had declared her pupil had an instinctual understanding between spatial relationships and dimensions—seen through the usual fare of trucks and rainbows. She wrote in one report card that he had "a unique eloquence with his lines."

Mrs. McCourdy entered Richard's drawings into local contests, and then statewide, and then national. He had won medals and ribbons at each level, but all at a distance. He was never there to witness the judging, or to feel his stomach turning in anticipation as the names were announced. And as some fathers collect their sons' trophies and accomplishments, Ted Andrews worked on turning his son's avocation into a small industry that would at least ensure tuition to the future college of choice. He used his skills as a salesman to convince some newspapers and local TV stations to report on his son's accomplishments, all with the angle that Richard was some kind of strange elder being floating around in a child's body. On some level it was noble. Most fathers would have discouraged their sons' inclinations toward the arts, instead pushing for athletics and the regular rigors of pre-man training. But Ted Andrews had worked hard his entire life, and, at age forty-one, widowed with a seven-year-old boy, he hadn't been convinced that he would ever have the means to offer his son a better life. So early on he had seized what seemed to be the best guarantee.

Claire suspected that Richard's reticence came from that upbringing. In fact, Ted Andrews's plan had worked out, earning Richard an undergraduate spot at Dartmouth College, and a graduate fellowship to the Rhode Island School of Design. But Claire figured that along the way Richard had learned not to trust anybody. His father had somehow negotiated every social exchange as though it were a business transaction on his son's behalf, leaving Richard to dread more than the minimal social relationship with anybody. He would have been much happier left in his room to draw.

When she first met Richard at the party following his breakup with Marie Bechet, Claire could have predicted the whole history that she would later learn. In a sense, he was still that same little boy being fawned over for his talents, with relatively little concern for who he was, but rather for what he could produce—as though the product would somehow reveal the truth of Richard. It was no wonder that taking on commercial work had troubled him. In the car, on that first drive, Richard said he was lucky to have met an art historian. They understood the relationship between the art and artist, without the usual romantic reverence.

She never met Ted Andrews. He had died years before Claire and Richard married, but she somehow knew she would have detested him. Especially when trying to understand what lay beneath the confused eyes of her husband.

❧   ❧   ❧

CLAIRE EXITED THE TRAIN IN Pontoise with her lone suitcase.

She followed the other passengers up the stairs and along the pedestrian bridge that led to the front of the station. Her bag swung between her leg and the chain-link fence, whose once proud steel now looked dusty white. The Van Gogh tourists were made obvious by their daypacks. Few went to Auvers for the night. Mostly, they trekked to the upstairs of the Auberge Raveaux to see the room where Vincent died, looked at the various placards that noted the painting sites, ate lunch, and made a final pilgrimage up to the church, through the wheat fields, and out to the cemetery to be photographed by the graves of Vincent and Theo before heading back to Paris.

She had never been so aware of being alone. As with so many

other times in her life, once she had reached the goal, she had no idea what to do next. It occurred to her that she really didn't know what she hoped to find in Auvers. Never before had she ever subjugated anything so important to chance. Everything always had been outlined, mapped, and fully considered. She shook her head, swallowing, trying to hold down her breath, feeling the sweep of grief about to overtake her, knowing that halfway around the world it is six hours earlier, and teams of lawyers still are working late, trying to make a case against her. As Ron Bernard had told her, the truth of innocence and guilt doesn't matter. It is only how the case is made.

Pontoise to Auvers required an hour for the connecting train (for only a ten-minute ride). The truly ambitious navigated the local transportation system, looking for the 95 bus line. The restless types, such as Claire, would simply climb into the nearest waiting taxi and hand over the twelve euros, believing that sometimes decadence is necessary to counter the weight of decision.

The taxi drove along the banks of the Oise River, settled by homes constructed of old-world European elegance. It was interesting how quickly the globalization that has shrunken cities like Paris disappeared in the countryside. There still lived unique cultures that were meant to be shared but never assimilated.

Moments after entering the village, they were at the *mairie*. The driver pulled into the lot for the Hôtel de Ville, the site of one of Vincent's images of the village, but still an active hub of Auverian life. It looked strangely as though *it* were the representation to Vincent's realistic image. The cabbie looked back. *"Voilà, Madame . . . C'est bon?"*

Claire nodded, yes. *"C'est bon."*

The driver pointed across the street to the Auberge Raveaux, with its bottom-floor restaurant painted in rose, in contrast to the tan upper story that had once boarded the town's famous resident. "*Maison de Van Gogh*," he spoke, as though feeling the need to justify the location. And then he pointed down the road and to the hill, where he drew his finger up to the crossing tower of the church, "*L'Église de Notre-Dame*, and then wagged it to the right, where Claire knew the cemetery lie. "*Et voilà les tombeaux de Vincent et de Théo.*"

Claire paid the driver. She looked again toward the church. Her gaze climbed up the familiar tower that welcomed her back to Auvers, then dropped to survey the village. Aside from the day-trippers, Claire did feel a sense of solace here. Once the tourists left at dusk, the town would become quiet and still. And though she still felt as if the troubles she'd left behind could pop up around any corner, this town looked so innocent that you could spot the devil by the tops of his shoes and the frames of his glasses.

❦   ❦   ❦

SHE STOOD BEFORE THE AUVERS Guest House, her single piece of luggage weighing down the right side of her body, about to ring the buzzer on the outside gate. The home had at least a century of wear. The giant stone fence, with its arching iron gateway, stood as a relic to the elegant formality that once ruled the world's aesthetic. The air was crisp but did not sting or slap the way the New England winds did. It was as though she had become completely detached from the Claire Andrews of Rhode Island. She imagined that she had laid a velum sheet over a familiar picture, and was then sketching the shapes in wobbly lines, familiar enough with the intricacies to not have to detail them, but still curious enough to see their form.

She looked forward to the security of her room, hidden from all the threats. It was comforting to know that tonight she would sleep under a thin cotton sheet that gave figure to her body but still issued a protective layer.

Still, while the guesthouse appeared to be secure, like most safe houses it only provided a temporary shelter. It was reliant upon keeping secrets. But in time, secrets are shared, and the collusion can become impossible. In truth, there are no safe houses, only temporary hideouts, where the conversation is coded, and only the silence is trustworthy.

❧   ❧   ❧

ISABELLE, THE PROPRIETOR AND MATRON of the inn, made Claire feel as though she had returned home for a reunion. Claire had stayed there numerous times, but it was after her third visit, when she had mentioned Isabelle and the inn in a subsequent book, that the relationship had changed; Isabelle now believed that the perpetuity of linking their names in print bound them forever through history. "It is so nice to see you," Isabelle said, embracing Claire and kissing both cheeks. "Oh, and I do not want to forget, but I have a message for you." Isabelle handed Claire a smoke-colored slip of paper that was folded in half. She peeked at the message and saw that it was from Richard. He was probably worried. Claire would have to phone him in the morning, it was already too late with the time difference. She slipped the message into her pocket and smiled at Isabelle. "I'm glad to be here," she said. "Glad to see you."

Isabelle motioned to an overstuffed chair, with blue stripes that looked like shadows. "Sit," she said. "Sit for a moment." She lifted Claire's suitcase and ran it up to the base of the stairs. Then Isabelle returned, facing Claire in a matching chair. She was a handsome woman, not too much older than Claire, but enough to connote a generational difference. Her features were very pure—bold and pointed, and taken one by one out of context might have seemed grotesque, but all placed together were both strong and striking. Half of her face was hidden by her auburn hair, cut with angled bangs, leaving her left eye to peer out from behind the streaked blond highlights. "You had a good flight? Good travel?"

"It all went fine."

"And you are here for another book?"

"Among some other things."

Isabelle laughed. "You always work on Van Gogh. Is there more to say, really?"

"That's my problem right now."

"Now they all have interest in Gachet. Every guest that I hosted is here to find out about Gachet. It is some anniversary of Gachet?"

Claire thought about it, running dates through her head. "No. No milestones that I can think of."

Isabelle shrugged. "I don't know. But they look important, these people that have been coming. Maybe you know some of them? Chambers? Paul Chambers?"

"Actually I do. Anybody in my business knows of him. But he and I do go way back." They had known each other since graduate school in Boston. Both had been rising stars in the department, having built reputations in their fields prior to completing their doctoral work. Chambers had gone on to work as a restoration theorist, quickly founding a lucrative consulting business, where he and his staff advised buyers and sellers on the changing values that various degrees of restoration would bring to their investment. It had been all the news when he sold his business three years ago, exchanging it for freelance work as a dealer to broker sales of masterworks between sellers and anonymous buyers. His discretion had already been legendary, as was his ability to maneuver deals that protected any fiduciary details and concerns that arose in the process. "It must be something big," Claire said. "Paul Chamber is only involved when it is something big. A huge sale of some sort must be happening."

"He talked to his partners . . . whisper, whisper . . . hush, hush. Gachet. Gachet . . . whisper, whisper."

"It doesn't surprise me. He always has clients that don't want to be known . . . Although I can't imagine what is here in Auvers that he would be mixed up in. Nothing here has moved forever."

Isabelle shrugged. "I do not know. Only that it includes Gachet . . . But you are tired, no? You look . . . Well, you look tired."

"It's just exhaustion," she answered. Claire had resolved not to talk in Auvers about the accident. It was enough that it was in her dreams at night, and in her secrets during the day. The effects of the accident had taken up residence in her, but she did not want it to define her. She just wanted to try to remember what it felt like to be normal again.

Isabelle stood up. "We can talk more tomorrow."

They kissed again, and Claire headed up the stairs. She looked back once, and smiled to Isabelle, wondering if Isabelle saw her as she felt right now: her hair, although stylishly cut with a lightly colored henna, did feel broomlike and frantic. Her breasts felt hopelessly small, and her ass misshapen and winter-weight soft. She wondered if Isabelle saw the gravity in Claire that couldn't be hid.

At the top of the stairs she paused to look at Richard's note. The message was in fact a Mailgram. It had the deliberate typing that only comes over the wires, with the characters jumping around the lines.

> *Just want to make sure that you have arrived okay. All is fine here. Bernard seems antsy, though, because of a few things. Not to worry, as all is being addressed. Get your work done. Don't think about all the other stuff. I'll mind the fort.—Richard.*

The note was as cryptic as it was caring. Something was going on that Richard did not want to burden her with. From the way Bernard had been making it sound, this Kennealy family could be devious, with sacks full of manipulations. That Richard should be the one to handle any short-term crisis was both chivalrous and laughable. This was the same Richard who couldn't handle two projects at once. Who would go nearly hysterical when the supply store ran out of his pencils. She found his calmness to be alarming. The irony of that thought made her feel somehow safer.

Richard had not signed the message, *Love*. It didn't bother her. She wasn't even sure if there should be that expectation anymore. After all, hadn't they been trying to emotionally divorce themselves from the mutual dependence of love? So why should she expect him to retreat to it in a perfunctory manner? The very fact that he had written to her trumped the psychology of the situation—in all their years of marriage, Richard had never been one to send cards or flowers. But the accident had changed the dynamics. A different level of maturity had grown between them. Some people would take refuge in the growth. But to Claire, it made her nervous. What if the aftereffects of the accident were all that banded them? Would she always have to live with Ronnie Kennealy in order to live with Richard Andrews?

She refolded the letter along the original creases, and put it into her pocket. Then she climbed the rest of the stairs to her room, where she fell into the bed, as though she were finally home.

Day Two

She didn't wake until nearly 11 A.M. At night, the curtains had blocked out the world by creating an eerie cavelike quality about the room. They had given in all too easily to the morning, though. Creased, and hanging long to the floor, the cotton had taken on an incandescent quality, allowing the room to fill with an orange glow that brought the details into view. A small round table stood before the window, with high-backed chairs neatly tucked in on the sides. The light fixture hung suspended by plastic-coated chain links, evenly placed between two competing ceiling cracks, with three wicked fingers holding candle bulbs. Her single bag was placed near the door, with the zipper only half undone, apparently enough for her to have reached in blindly for her toothbrush. A digital clock sat on the end table. Its bright red digits had forced her to face it away during the night. But now, as she turned it around to see the time, it looked beautifully anachronistic against the antiquity of the room. The high ceiling and plank-floored room had remained unchanged over the past hundred years. It was strange to think that Van Gogh had passed by this house regularly to make his way up to the wheat fields, with his easel strapped to his back, and a pail of paints in his hand. And of course the one trip with a revolver tucked into his waist.

Claire might have slept longer had she not been dreaming about Ronnie Kennealy, his sudden appearance spooking her awake. She had scanned the room for a full minute, believing that he was there, remaining on edge, even once she knew it only had been a dream. It seemed he watched her every move, ready to pounce in judgment, or at least remind her that there were very few steps forward in this life without remembering the past. It was as though he shadow-trailed her along streets, airport security, and over borders. Once she left Providence, Claire had hoped he would stay behind to haunt New England on his own, leaving her out of it. But she knew that was impossible. They would dress for bed together every night for the rest of their lives, and wake up dreamy-eyed in the morning, side by side.

She sat up and stretched, trying to convince herself to get out of bed. She had tossed and turned all night, never quite getting the fold of the pillow right beneath her neck, feeling too disconnected to sleep, aware that jumping continents can only make you lonelier.

At least she had managed a few hours of sleep. Even as a child, sleep had been difficult for her when confronted with some form of anxiety. Usually it had to do with reliving some unpleasant moment from earlier in the day, or the queasy anticipation of a planned event for the following day. Her father, wary of overextending his medical benefits and deductibles, took to medicating his daughter with a double dose of cough syrup when she complained of insomnia. Nearly thirty years later Claire could still taste the medicinal mint, sometimes recalling the way the bubbles tickled her lips when her father's double dose foamed at the corners of her mouth. She had almost bought a bottle of cough syrup about a month ago when she had become so exhausted that she grew chilled. Instead she accepted that this was the way she now lived. Not even her father's best cure could relieve that.

Q   Q   Q

THE BREAKFAST ROOM HAD ALREADY been closed up, so Isabelle set up Claire in the kitchen, at a pleasant-size farm table that mirrored the sparseness of the room's decor. Claire had yet to uncover the basket of freshly baked croissants before her. A cotton towel trapped the warm aroma under its fold, as if to keep the sweetness preserved forever. She moved the butter dish back and forth, sometimes circling it around the jam jars. Isabelle checked in once or twice to refill the small porcelain coffee pitcher, but had since disappeared into the pantry.

The last of the coffee was lukewarm. The cream turned hazy.

She pulled the basket closer, fingering up a corner of the towel. The skin from the top of the croissant peeled off easily, thin and translucent, breaking apart in her hand. She wasn't hungry anyway. She was too restless to be hungry.

Claire felt anxious to get down to the village. It was the combination of familiarity and anonymity, like returning to the house you lived in when you were small. Comfort without expectation. She would roam through the wheat fields and the village streets, open to anything, but cautious of everything.

Q   Q   Q

SEVERAL LAYERS OF CLOUDS HUNG close to the village, with strata streaked in turbulent grays and whites. The air had the plaintive chill that comes just before a snow. Despite a darkening sky, the temperature seemed to warm suddenly. It was the moment before the beauty of the first snowflakes, few and tender. When the world feels so personal.

She could have existed on the streets a hundred years ago and still seen the world the same way. It was as though she had returned in this life several times over to walk the same footsteps and follow the same paths, each time unaware of the impending consequences. And she wondered, if she could be reborn in another era, would the series of events that constructed her life all hiccup at the same point, throwing her off course with such unbelievable fury that she would wish that she never lived her life at all? And at that thought, she felt the familiar constricting of her chest, where the nausea seems to rise into it, centered right under the lungs, as if that could be feasible, and it becomes impossible to breathe while her head swells and drowns, and she wills herself not to cry because she sees people looking at her, and she does not want to be looked at. It is in that moment that she gets thrown back into the accident. With every ounce of strength she forces herself to swallow, and let herself be distracted by something around her, understanding that this is only a wave that will pass as quickly as it has come.

Q   Q   Q

"THE MYTH OF MADNESS AND the artist," she had told her students on the afternoon of the accident, "is modern history's need to replicate the image of Beethoven." Claire proceeded to describe the torture of the composer's life. The mussed madman's hair. The bouts of insane stampings throughout the streets of Vienna. The brutalization of his nephew. His anger at the very concept of irony when he lost his hearing. Sawing off the legs of his piano to allow the vibrations to be closer to the floor. At the moment when it sounded too much like mythology, she played the last movement from Opus 135 of the late string quartets. There the rage and torment came through in a very real truth. But what made it genius was the beauty that hovered below the arrangement. The lone flower springing up in the fields of waste.

"That," Claire explained, "is why the mad genius artist is so tempting to those who write such histories. It is their hollow cry for beauty."

A student had raised his hand from the middle of the class. His face drew hard as he questioned with confidence. "But Van Gogh's craziness is well documented. He wasn't right." This was followed by a slight chuckle from the class. Even Claire laughed at his boorishness. "I mean, just the ear incident alone." The boy smiled ahead of the class.

Claire had folded her arms. She nodded, as though considering this statement for the first time—in fact, there was never a semester when someone didn't bring up "the ear." She looked at the boy, who she knew was from western Massachusetts, but was unable to remember his name. Her lips pursed, then relaxed. "Is there a question in there?" she asked. "Or at least a conclusion to draw?"

"I'm just saying that it's kind of more than myth, I think. Like I said, he was kind of nuts, and yet he made all this incredible art."

"Therefore . . ."

"His craziness and his talent went together. Into some sort of . . . Into a vision."

"Spoken like a true mythmaker." In truth, this was a difficult subject for her to tackle in a lower division class. The root of this discussion was much deeper than the issues it touched on. It was Columbus discovering America. George Washington chopping down cherry trees. Gardens of Eden. It was about the notion that myths are made to bring the illusion of truism to our lives. But, in fact, they can only make tangible the intangible in the same way that Cyrillic characters can represent the abstract concept of thought.

The boy would not let up. "But really, Professor Andrews," he countered. "You can't deny that killing himself doesn't speak volumes about him."

"Sure it says something about him." Claire was not even going to bother to retell the evening with Gauguin that shattered their illusion of idyll artistry. "But it only states a part of him. Yes, it is sexy. Yes, it has drama. And thus we give a single moment the power to define a life." She had found her voice rising. "Do we then let it define our perception of his art? Our perception of the inner life, of which we know absolutely nothing about?"

"But—"

"Wait, wait, wait, wait." Her face reddened as she raised her tone to an unaccustomed level. "You are suggesting that we allow one unexpected moment in a man's life to become the defining event of his history. Yes? . . . Now let's think about it: by letting a single mistake or accident live on to tell the tale of the life, we then dismiss the value of the life, and therefore miss the beauty of the life."

The class was silent, perhaps for the first time during the

semester having collectively given over their full attention. Although the boy from western Massachusetts appeared to want to talk, he sat humbly silent. Claire stood uncomfortable with the intensity of scrutiny focused on her. She felt as though she had betrayed the line between authority and vulnerability. In a clumsy command for strength, Claire snatched up her books and papers, a few notes floating down behind in a trail. "And now you understand the attraction of the hopelessly impassioned artist," she had managed to say. Then the professor marched a long procession through the aisle, out the back door, and into the parking lot, on the first night of standard time.

❧   ❧   ❧

As she came down into the village, Claire spotted a couple coming toward her, intent on catching her eye. They looked too young to be married. She guessed them to be recent graduates who were exploring Europe together for the first time. They talked in a conspiracy of hushed tones, pointing to the 8 à Huit market and its adjacent parking lot, and then up the hill toward the church. They looked uncomfortable, lost among the milling locals who clustered in front of the store, in concert with reprobates the world over.

The couple was well dressed, with the slightly tattered look of the heavily traveled. Both were wearing khaki pants and sneakers shaped as hiking boots. As they approached, the girl giggled and pushed her boyfriend away. He drifted toward Claire, almost walking side by side. "*Pardon.*" He spoke with an unconfident French accent. "*Parlez-vous anglais?*" The girl stood a pace behind him.

Claire nodded, yes. "I do." Her voice came out so soft, she wasn't even sure if she had spoken.

"Oh, that's great." The boy looked relieved. His girlfriend laughed. "We are totally mixed up right now."

"How is that?"

"We are trying to get to find the places where Van Gogh . . . Well, the truth is, we have absolutely no idea where we are." He looked at his watch.

Claire coughed. "It's all around you."

"It's crazy. We had no idea what we were supposed to . . . And once we got here . . . Well, the streets are so quiet with the weather, and . . ."

The girl piped in, "And you feel so helpless when you remember that you can't speak a single common word other than 'do you speak English.'"

Claire smiled at them, almost maternally. "I was just about to follow some of Van Gogh's trails. You are welcome to join me."

The two looked at each other, and shrugged, submitting to the trust that traveling brings. "Okay," the boy said. "Thanks a lot."

"But first, my coffee. Come along?"

Claire and the girl shared one side of the table, while the boy faced them. Claire learned that the boy was named Bobby, and the girl named Lauren. They were both from Marin County in California and had recently graduated from Berkeley. Now in the second of what would be four months away, they had decided to go on a "walkabout" before grad school to discover what they wanted of the world. They were tracking the whole journey in a journal that would somehow become a manifesto for the values to live by for the rest of their lives. Bobby had already been accepted to Yale law, with a year's deferment, and Lauren was applying to East Coast schools for sociology, already having been accepted at Cal

Poly under early admission, but that would not work if they were to continue their relationship. Stockton to New Haven was a long way. They were both "into art" but confessed little knowledge of Van Gogh beyond the "major works and the ear," but still were "totally fascinated with him."

Claire thought to ask them why they found him so intriguing, but she already knew the answer. It was the same truncated biography that compelled all young people toward him: the loner driven by passion, his submission to artistic expression, the teetering imbalance—he was the model for the young misanthrope. She too had been seduced by that. When she was their age, the prevailing narrative had far outweighed the aesthetic intricacies that would later absorb her. She had fallen in love with Vincent in the same way that her friends were falling for pop idols. Claire had put a poster of him on her bedroom wall—the one she would later know to refer to as *Self-Portrait*—and she would lay on her patterned quilt staring up at the painter in his slight profile, his mouth drawn shut, but not in a scowl, as though unnecessary words would only betray the importance of the moment. His reddish beard was trimmed and stylish, in almost perfect complement to his combed-back hair, which bloomed just perfectly above the hairline. Vincent's blue eyes looked down on her, casting an intense spell that connected the passion of two misunderstood people set a century apart. She had not fallen in love with a man, but rather with a painting. Later she would realize that she had fallen for an ideal, which really was no different from her girlfriends' various pop culture obsessions. Only she carried that ideal into a career.

The kids stood silently, waiting for her to lead the way. Claire looked to Bobby, without acknowledging Lauren. "I am sorry. Really sorry. But I need a few more minutes. I forgot that I want to call my . . . I want to call home before it gets too late. Then I will show you around. I am familiar with all of . . . With Van Gogh. Okay? I know I just told you . . . And then the coffee, but . . ."

Lauren laughed and told her to take her time. She lightly elbowed Bobby in excitement.

"Yeah," Bobby joined in, "that would be cool."

Claire turned, and began to walk down rue de Gl. de Gaulle to find a public phone. There was a quick patter of footsteps before Bobby caught up with her, just before the iron gate at the entrance of the Parc Van Gogh. He politely stopped her with an *excuse me* and a tap on the arm. Zadkine's spindly statue of the park's namesake peered over the stone wall, with his bronzed easel strapped on his back, and his straw hat rimming the top of his broad patina forehead.

Claire paused, startled by the touch. It was the touch of caring, an implied trust that overwrote frivolous intimacies and expected gestures.

"Sorry," he said. "It's just that we didn't make a place to meet . . . We didn't know."

"Right," she said. "Right."

Bobby stood still, looking down at his shoes, and then occasionally glancing at her eyes. He looked back once to Lauren when Claire didn't respond, shrugging his shoulders.

A group of tourists walked around them, armed with maps purchased from the tourism office, deciding whether to begin the tour with Van Gogh's death, work their way through in chronological order, or perhaps even begin in medias res in the wheat field. Nobody paused or stopped. They moved in diagonal paths, looking up from their maps, fumbling with their camera bags, and then disappearing up into the angles of the village.

Bobby seemed so alive. Barely grown, still with the sweetness of a boy, but carrying the growing confidence of a man. It occurred to her that she was witnessing a life in the making.

She reached out to touch Bobby's arm in a reciprocal gesture.

"I'll tell you what," she said, leaving her hand on his arm. It felt reassuringly real. "Ten or fifteen minutes. Ten or fifteen minutes are all I need. How about we meet here at the park? Inside the gates. There are benches. In front of the statue. Just ten or fifteen minutes. Is that all right?"

Bobby shrugged. "Sure."

"I could take you both to lunch at the *crêperie* across the street. And then show you around. Show you the fields where Vincent painted . . . The cemetery."

"That sounds really cool. But we need to leave around two. We're supposed to meet up with some folks later in Paris." He looked at his watch. They both saw it was nearly one. "But if you think there is enough to do around here, then I guess that we could hang for an extra hour." He chewed on his lip. Looked back down at his watch. "Yeah, that would be fine," he said, nodding. "So long as we're back in Paris by five, I guess." He didn't check with Lauren.

They reiterated that they would meet back at the park shortly. And although Claire felt invigorated by the notion of finding a purpose in Auvers, she also felt her body slacken at the realization of the finiteness of this day.

When Vincent first arrived in Auvers-sur-Oise, he wrote of the well-being in the air. He talked of the lushness, of the colors that filled the gardens and climbed the thatched cottages. And he declared to Theo, "You will see that to come to an understanding of a country, to see other countries, is all to the good." *One can only imagine Vincent walking around this village on his first day, far enough north to be freed from the bustle of Paris, but still within the city's cultural and intellectual grasp. He would walk the streets, still bundled from winter, despite the flowering of spring and the budding leaves. And on that first day, the only scar he would bear would be on his ear. His soul would feel temporarily cleansed, his past a lesson from which he had learned. He will have lost himself to the illusion of geography. Succumbed to the notion that place trumps the psyche. He will forgive his time in the South as one of a necessary healing, but will think of the North as his true calling. His feet would feel light when they first walked these streets. Hands dug deep into his pockets. Head held comfortably down. Never once feeling as a visitor. Instead willing himself to belong. Because to belong to the ideal is to live among the ideal. He would not have wanted to* learn *about this other country, he would want to be* part *of the country. That is where the good is. And on the first day his faith must have been extreme, even stronger than the belief in God. Because he knew that belonging was all he had. It was his only chance.*

Richard wasn't home. She left a rather long message saying that she got his note, and made sure to thank him for sending it. Then she told him about the weather, about the feeling of snow, and the sense of freshness in the air. And that being here did give her some sense of well-being, and as far as the book, she was feeling optimistic. She could feel Vincent in all her steps. He was coming alive to her, and although she may have no idea anymore what she saw when she looked at *Crows over the Wheatfield*, she was beginning to think that she might have a better sense if she saw it through his eyes. And then she told him that Paul Chambers had been there before her, and she wondered what that meant, since he was only ever anywhere when it involved a major sale, and the only thing left that she could even imagine was a deal involving *Portrait of Dr. Gachet*, but that was beyond unlikely, since Ryoei Saito had kept the painting veiled in some secret warehouse for how many years, with no known intent of ever bringing it back to market. She had still been considering the idea when the machine cut her off.

Claire paused when she saw Bobby and Lauren sitting on the park bench, lulled by the sound of children outside a school. They sat side by side, surveying the surrounding area, looking as wordless as a couple three times their age. She suspected they had not moved since she left them, instead politely waiting for their guide. The two of them looked so trusting. The kind of innocents you read about in the morning paper that have disappeared under the lure of a derelict's fallacious kindness. Claire wished that Richard was by her side, the Richard she had strolled with through the Public Gardens almost a decade ago; they might have been viewed no differently than how she saw Bobby and Lauren. She imagined the past version of herself and Richard grown into the contented version of what they might have been, instead of being surrounded by the complexities of what they had actually become.

Across the street a flower vendor peered over his nasturtiums in the reflecting glass, staring at Claire as if trying to remember where they had met. Probably putting it out of his mind before making the connection that the woman on the street had once come into his shop two years ago looking displeased and angry, arms crossed, while her husband, looking both desperate and chivalrous, had bought a bouquet of flowers.

Bobby spotted her first. "We were thinking of just walking around and seeing the sites," he called from the bench. "You know, not bother with lunch. We really are kind of short on time, to be realistic about it . . . Okay with you?"

Claire looked back to Vincent's statue, half expecting to catch the averted glance of peering eyes. There was only the usual pair of tourists, set and posed, waiting to confirm that the shutter had clicked. "Do you want to walk out to the cemetery first? See Vincent's and Theo's graves?" She wasn't that hungry anyway.

"That would be really awesome," Lauren said. She took Bobby's hand, a clasp that echoed dependence.

A group of the schoolkids entered the park, walking in neat, orderly lines. Soon it became a frenzy of children set loose, traversing broken lines around the park and the Van Gogh statue, weaving among the groups of tourists wading along the mannered paths, before their teacher restored order. Some of the boys continued to sprint, while the little girls sat delicately on the benches with their lunch bags, meticulously combing through them in an ordered discovery of what they should eat first. All the children seemed oblivious to the cold. Oblivious to the multitudes of harmful possibilities. Claire felt the dramatic irony of hope, looking into those pure eyes, knowing that heartbreak, disappointment, and affected and unaffected tragedy lie just beyond the door. And although she could watch their little hands cup the doorknob, using all their strength to twist and push, she would still secretly hold out with all her might that the door would never open.

"Well, shall we go?"

The couple moved alongside Claire before collectively falling back a step.

❦ ❦ ❦

Briskly, Claire led the way up the hill. She didn't walk as though on a tour, but rather as if they were in danger of missing a train. She suddenly felt the need to be out of sight of the center of Auvers. She continued thinking about what business Paul Chambers would have in Auvers regarding Dr. Gachet. She kept coming back to the portrait. It was all that was in his league. She didn't want to be paranoid, but if that was the case, every bit of research she was doing would be scrutinized. Because if the portrait was being sold again (and how incredible would that be!) it would dominate all the Van Gogh talk. Conferences. Journals. Books. It would be *the* story of the art world. And Paul Chambers would be controlling ever piece of it. If it was the *Portrait of Dr. Gachet*.

She positioned herself into the middle, letting the two kids shield her.

"It's a ways up here, isn't it?" Bobby said, stopping in front of the church. He breathed heavily. They paused to look at the sign that demarcated the spot where Vincent had painted the cathedral, highlighted by a miniature reproduction of the finished product.

"First we'll follow this path behind the building, and up into the wheat fields, and then over to the cemetery," Claire instructed. Veering off the road, they walked the church grounds, past a modern addition. A perfectly manicured hedgerow led to a trail that was cut as a canyon, with a pathway no more than four feet wide, but framed by hills that sloped in like manmade walls. The dead stalks, dried and yellowed, leaned over the tops of the path as though begging for reprieve.

"At least the grave was near the church," Lauren noted.

Claire didn't stop to clarify. She would have had to pause and catch her breath in order to explain that the Catholic Church had refused the burial on the grounds that Vincent had committed suicide. That he had been laid to rest without proper rites, at the time somewhat segregated from the rest of the interned, placed against the far fence. And that on some level he must have been content to lay in the peaceful solitude, but in true Vincent fashion, he was probably happily relieved when Theo's remains were exhumed in 1914 and set beside his. We can all use a little company sometimes.

"You don't need to rush on our account," Bobby said. The leaves crunched and broke under his feet. "We're not *that* short on time."

Claire kept moving up the incline toward the ridge that would look out over the river valley. The trail was sparsely populated, only made alive by the light breeze cruising the dried stalk and drafting up the pathway where errant patches of green lay ahead. She casually looked off to the fields that had captured Vincent's imagination, not even bothering to try to glance up to see one of the famed crows circling above. She walked with certainty. The dirt pack was cold and solid.

"Okay," she said. "It's just up here . . . Where he painted the crows in the field . . . And then right across is the cemetery." Claire turned her head to look back. She had the sensation that she had been followed from the church. But all Claire saw was her resident shadow, which was stretched longer and thinner by the winter light. She looked forward again, just in time to see an older couple coming down the hill toward them.

The husband was one of those jovial types, but without the requisite belly, puffed cheeks, and padded shoulders. He had a bone-thin face that rarely looked caught off guard, and his expression was so pleasant it was almost off-putting. He nodded as he approached them. Shook his head, and kept his smile. "Hang in there, kids." He sucked in a deep breath and wiped the shine off his brow. "The haul is worth it."

"Dan," his wife said, in a playfully scolding tone. She issued her reproach as perfectly rehearsed as a Broadway actor on the eve of her two hundredth consecutive performance. "It's not a haul, it's a—"

"Maybe for a kid like you—and for these three youngsters—it is something else, but for me it's a haul." He looked at Claire for a moment. He bit his lip, and then nodded his head, wiping at his brow again.

"Don't listen to him," the wife said. "You all enjoy yourselves." They walked off down the hill, breaking straw to form a trail behind them.

Lauren made a brief mention how oddly normal it was that the couple spoke English with the assumption that they would be understood. "I guess it's just the hubris of the American traveler," she concluded. Claire had immediately known that they would be speaking English. While she normally would have chalked it up to the undiagnosed confidence of the American abroad unconsciously colonizing each step that they take, Claire had sensed a familiarity about that man. She knew that she had never spoken with him before. There were no recognizable traits about the way he comported himself. Still there was intuitive familiarity there. And although he didn't look at Claire as though he expected to see her, this Dan did look at her as though he might have known her.

After a not very long but arduous climb, they found themselves atop the hill and in the middle of the wheat field. The narrow winding streets of the medieval village had quickly given way to an agricultural age, where the crops dominated the land instead of the retail fronts that their fruits enabled.

As with the church, a reproduction of *Crows over the Wheatfield* stood framed in the spot of its creation, the *plaque tableau* at the very axis of the three paths. The main path led to the church and its village. To turn right meant going into the cemetery. And to turn left was to proceed into the desolate unknown. Claire's stomach sickened while imagining Vincent frozen with those very thoughts, pistol in hand, in that almost peaceful pause before the collision.

"So this was where he painted his last painting, right?" Lauren stood contemplating the sign, stepping back to measure the accuracy between representation and model, as well as the difference in seasons.

"No," Claire answered, trying to avoid the classroom lecture. "Not the last painting, but perhaps the final statement."

The sky darkened temporarily with birds winging above,

while the wind blew through the lifeless stalks, cutting along the ankles. The three of them looked out over the town, where the church poked up through the skeletal branches of the winter trees. They inhaled deeply, taking in a strangely sweet air that smelled smoky with peat. And although firmly planted in the twenty-first century, with the sounds of jets rumbling above, this field still held the loneliness of a bygone era, in which any sense of civilization felt hopelessly alien. Even with the occasional tourist in the distance, the illusion was still maintained that they were the only ones there other than Vincent's ghost.

It was too much for Claire to stand in the painter's countryside. It was as though she was stuck in a quaking field that rocked her back and forth in a strange exegesis on the morality of indecision and the finality of chance. Lost in the strange in-between moment where everything is possible, but still a moment that is impossible to live in forever. A panic started to rise. She stood fully capable of being able to run, but there was nowhere to run to. "Let's go to the cemetery, now," she said, as much as directed.

They walked single file along the well-tread path that was bombarded by puddles and the fossilized tracks of paws from a season of dog walkers. The gigantic sky was as confining as it was embracing. It was quiet along the trail. Each footstep sounded louder as it broke the pack, but there was no resonance or echo—just a hard loud crackle that faded as soon as it arrived. Bobby and Lauren moved with an air of excitement as they got closer to the cemetery, carried forward by the same thrill of the rumor of a celebrity in a restaurant window. Walking quickly, without reverence. Fumbling for their cameras. Ready to document the evidence, as though it might disappear into the dark windowed limousine, and the true stories lost to hyperbole.

The end of the trail intersected a main road that quickly dead-ended into untilled farmlands. Before crossing the road to the graveyard, they passed a dilapidated wooden fence loosely strung by rotted and rusted barbed wire. Despite the winter cold, it was lined by small yellow roses that looked oddly displaced, as though part of some reclamation project.

Once at the large stone wall that guarded the cemetery, they pushed open an iron grate door, only stopping to look at the map that directed them to grave site number one. They walked under the *tombe de guerre*, a large arch that celebrated the commonwealth soldiers of Auvers, before fully entering the graveyard. The cemetery was still quite active, with many of the tombstones shiny and new. It was a strange mix of modern and antique, laying rest to generations of Auverian lineage. There were many monuments built high and proud to celebrate the lives once lived, surrounded by steel gates and capped lovingly in crucifixes, while others sat unremarkable with catalog headstones. But against the wall, off to the left and facing the farm fields, lay the brothers' graves, draped under a single quilt of ivy.

The graves had startled Claire the first time she had seen them. She had approached the site with the same enthusiasm, anticipating the symbolism of a young scholar finally meeting her subject. Still, she had not expected much that first visit. Her professional interests had been in the thematic connection between form and subject. She had long since stopped memorializing Vincent as a fallen idol. The young Claire had assumed the grave to be as most graves are—an attempt by the living to inflate the past into a permanent state of immortality. Where in the chiseled markings of the headstone, and the final tears that fertilize the soil, begin the first fictions.

"I don't know," Bobby whispered. "Do you think we should take a photo of ourselves standing by the grave? We should have something to show for this trip. Is that sacrilegious, though?"

"I think we can do what we want," Lauren answered. "It's just a memorial, right?"

But when Claire had first stepped before the grave all those years ago, she had felt a shiver run between her shoulders. She had been standing alone, faintly aware of voices ascending up the pathway to site number one. Professionally, she had been like the wedding photographer whose only purpose is to capture the critical moments and who never allowed herself to be invested with any emotion that might distract her from the stated objective. But the grave had raised Vincent from the shadows of the texts. She saw a man who had been laid to rest on a quiet hill. Been wept over. Where the lumps filled everyone's throat at the silence of that first clump of dirt falling, then hitting the casket top, while comforting arms held a sobbing brother. She had walked away quickly that day. Not even hearing a young woman struggle with English to ask if the tomb was near, while her sheepish husband stood a pace back, arms folded and smiling, dragging on his cigarette as though it were oxygen. Claire had bit down on her lip, trying to make the thoughts leave her mind. Her work would only have meaning if Vincent were a mystery. After all, it was her thoughts and interpretations that gave him life.

Bobby snapped a picture. He motioned for Lauren to move into the frame, but she stayed put. The wind gusted. Bugs impervious to the cold swirled among the ivy undisturbed. Lauren shivered a bit. She huddled against Bobby.

Simple granite headstones marked the two gravesites, perfectly framed by the sky. A few offerings were neatly placed on Vincent's side: plastic sunflowers, a cardboard painter's palette that held an apple, another sunflower, a slice of orange, a piece of candy, and some undecipherable words on a page of journal paper. All vastly understated in comparison to the monuments that neighbored them, like a lonely tourist in the valley of Manhattan.

"It was maddeningly hot that day," Claire said. The blank stares from the kids suggested that they already had lost the context of her comment. "When they buried him here. It was hot. A scorching sun. You would think it should have been cold. Dark clouds hovering, on the verge of rain. That's the kind of day it should have been."

"I'm sure that's how Van Gogh would have pictured it," Lauren said.

If she were in the classroom, Claire would have asked Lauren why she said that, pressed her for the logical and factual persuasions that led to that statement. But in this situation she accepted Lauren as a peer, only nodding in agreement. "The coffin was covered by sunflowers; his paintings were surrounding the casket. It sounds so beautifully lonely. Yes," she said, nodding to Lauren with a slight smile, "it is probably just as he would have pictured it."

Bobby had wandered off to take some more pictures, documenting every angle of the graves. Sometimes kneeling. Angling his body around. As though trying to make art of it.

"It's weird," Lauren said, "that just a little more than a hundred years ago people were standing in this very spot, probably desperately sad. And we stand just kind of curious." She looked around. "It makes you wonder if the space means nothing. Once the earth turns tens of thousands of times, all of this just gets wiped away. Like cleaning a blackboard. I used to think the tears and sorrow just went into the earth to become part of it."

Or like roads, Claire thought, where people travel daily, barely aware of the flower wreath that has wilted against a tree trunk in honor of victims like Ronnie Kennealy, soon to become part of the landscape of ordinary living. Perhaps heartbreak and words are no different from every breath that leaves our mouths, just disappearing with the exhalation. Claire told Lauren that maybe she was right. That maybe nothing really is immortal.

"Except art."

Claire nodded. "Except art."

Gachet had tried to speak at the funeral. His voice had choked up, and he could barely find words other than what a great artist Vincent was, and then stammering out a confused praise about how much he had admired the painter. Claire might have been standing on the exact spot where Gachet delivered his eulogy, facing where the half-circle of friends gathered around the side of the hole. The accounts of Gachet's statement had always struck her as odd, but it resonated even more now that she had become interested in the story between the two. It seemed strange that he could speak so endearingly of a man he had barely known. Her critics would no doubt tell her that that was a testament to the power of Van Gogh. That he had the ability to touch people, especially through his art. But he did not have the ability. Van Gogh did not have the childish charm that lies behind the gruff and delinquent skins of some troubled men. Nor was he the loner who chose the iconoclastic life in pursuit of his art and rejection of the world. He was a man who couldn't keep the company of others. Who drove away his friends. Who, in between his painting, dissolved into states of disrepair that warded people off not by shock but by fear. True, his brother had stood by him. But why Gachet? Why did this man, whom even Vincent didn't fully trust, stand before a gathering of intimates and utter words belonging to a blood relative? Other than his brother, it seemed as though the only people who could stand Vincent for any prolonged amount of time were those who wanted something from him. Standing before this grave, in the footprint of Gachet, Claire became even more convinced of the doctor's guilt. Even if it were not premeditated malice, the fact that he would admonish Vincent in the name of friendship and good health was equally culpable. Whether the motive was prestige and Gachet's own sense of worth, or just the pure intoxicant that some get from the realization of power over others, was yet to be determined. It made Claire sick imagining Paul Gachet standing at this very site, before artists such as Pissarro and Lauzet, declaring himself a part of the fraternity. The healer who had pointed the blind man to the edge of the cliff.

Bobby took a picture of Claire and Lauren. "We've got to get going," he said after looking at his watch. "We need to get going back to Paris if we're going to get together with Steve and those guys by five. Know what I mean? Especially if it starts snowing again. And who knows how many seats will be left on the train heading into the city on a Friday night."

Claire heard his words but didn't register their meaning.

"Come on, Lauren," Bobby said. "We're going to have to hustle as it is."

Lauren paused, and took one last look at the site. "This makes me wish I knew more," she said to Claire.

"About Van Gogh?"

"About everything. All of these incredible things that I have seen nearly every day of this trip. And they all have some meaning, but I don't even get the half of it. Four years of college. And it makes me sad about what I don't get."

"Come on, Lauren. We've really got to get going."

"All right."

"Don't want to spend the night in this place, do we?"

"Okay. Okay."

Lauren looked over to Claire, who imagined a two-way mirror of time. On one side Claire looked into the eyes of the girl she had once been, though never as naive about her possibilities but equally as romantic about the idea of knowledge. In contrast, she imagined Lauren looking at Claire, seeing the vision of what she might become. Would she be relieved to see that time does in fact shepherd wisdom? Or would it all seem a big disappointment?

"I guess we need to go," Lauren said.

Claire nodded. "I guess so."

Together they walked down the road, slowly winding back into the residential and active world. In his impatience, Bobby had gone ahead, probably believing himself to be setting an example. The two women strolled slowly. Passing rows of kale and twisting down the road bordered by rising stone fences with terra-cotta tops, just minutes before the looming church. "Please," Claire said, "remind me to give you my e-mail before you leave. You should get in touch with me once we are all back home."

"That sounds nice."

"I can help you fill in some of the blanks about Van Gogh."

"Are you a teacher?"

"Yes."

Bobby was several paces ahead. He stopped just before the

church and looked back. He might have yelled out if a delivery truck had not roared by at that instance, but instead clamped his hands to his hips and scolded Lauren through an irritated expression, rolling his eyes up and shaking his head. He turned to spit. Then reclaimed his pace down the hill.

Claire laughed. "At first I figured you to be the one who didn't care."

"You mean?"

"Yes."

"Oh."

"It's no insult. Oh God, I hope that I am not insulting you. We just stereotype each other. It's what we do. We can't help it. But it's no insult. It's just what we do."

Lauren said, "People are like that."

"But I mean especially women. We find those telltale traces of subtleties and immediately draw conclusions from something as simple as the pronunciation of a word to the shade of the eye shadow."

"Or the fact that they are even wearing eye shadow. Guys have it easy. No one picks them apart so, bit by bit."

Claire was glad that Lauren didn't feel insulted. Perhaps women are conditioned to that, and a certain immunity begins to build. While men battle with ill chosen words, women are more sophisticated to nuance. It is the look. The quip. The lightning assembly of puzzle pieces that intuits which one is malformed, or at least prone to weakness. And that thought brought back the image of the Delta 88 woman. Claire had been guilty of sizing her up. Rendering a pronouncement based on how she pictured the thickness and design of the mascara, and all the other usual characteristics that delineated social class. But the Delta 88 woman had handled it like a man, flipping her off while yelling *bitch*. Maybe that is what had thrown Claire. The rules of nuanced engagement were broken, and she didn't know it until it was too late. If she had understood that she was about to encounter male warfare, Claire would have just slowed down and looked straight ahead.

The *mairie* was in sight, with the traffic backing up along the central road. Bobby had blazed the trail so quickly that he could not be seen. Lauren looked as though she was getting anxious. She seemed strong enough to ward off Bobby's demands but probably did not feel like summoning the wherewithal to withstand the aftermath. She clearly walked the line between independence and subservience. And was teetering. Claire could picture the future Lauren either holding court on the world's stage or pulling lasagnas out of the oven in a mad dash before her blue-suited husband walked through the door, unknotting his yellow striped tie, tired and hungry and angry.

"Don't worry," Claire said. "You have plenty of time, I'm sure. Bobby said the next train doesn't leave for another fifteen minutes. And it is just blocks away. Fifteen minutes is a long time. There is plenty . . . Don't worry. Plenty of time."

"Bobby just gets so worked up about these kinds of things . . . The whole trip . . . He has to be at the train station an hour early, even when we have the tickets. We rarely get to enjoy wherever we are, because he is already busy getting us on to the next destination."

"I guess it is good that he brought the camera. He'll get to see everything sometime."

Lauren smiled. It seemed like she slowed her gait. Or maybe Claire was just wishing that she had. "Honestly," Claire said, "e-mail me. Make a list along the way of questions, especially works of art that you are curious about, and then send it along to me. What I don't know I will ask my colleagues."

"That's really nice of you."

They were just about to reach Bobby. He was fiddling with the camera case, trying to lock and seal it before the impending train ride. He was strangely out of breath and a bit sweaty. As they took those last steps toward him, Claire had the sensation of being afraid to let Lauren get away.

Like a longing parent, Claire stood alongside the train, just blocks from where she had met them a few hours earlier, watching the kids climb aboard the RER. Bobby hurried up the steps. She had made him nervous. And maybe rightly so, a strange woman who is double their age practically adopting them after less than three hours. In retrospect, perhaps she should not have offered to put them up for the night. She just didn't want them to have to rush back to Paris. Plus there is nothing more inspiring than the night sky as Vincent saw it. That was when Bobby retreated from politeness and nearly ordered Lauren to go. But Claire had known boys like him her whole life, the house cats who rub affectionately against you on their terms, and then scamper once the gesture is reciprocated.

She watched them find their seats upstairs at the back of the second car, passing the windows frame by frame. Bobby frowned with purpose. Lauren looked back through each dirtied pane, managing a lone secreted smile.

The train pulled out of the station, accompanied by a frightening scraping sound, metal screaming against metal. And Claire could have been anywhere, grinding her teeth together, willing her body to hold itself together, dropped into the same hole of emptiness that had been dug the night of the accident. Only now Richard was not coming tonight, and that feeling would bury her alive by the time morning came.

Q   Q   Q

A SNOWFALL DUSTED THE STREETS. Ordinary footprints easily upended the pristine pack, quickly diminishing any hope of a true winter covering. Claire stood on the porch of the Auvers Guest House too restless to go to her room, already feeling the loneliness set in. She breathed a smoke ring into the dusk, following its path upward into the same generic layer of clouds that one could expect from a New England winter, now curtaining Vincent's sky.

She pushed her hair behind her ears, and then dug her bare hands into her pockets for warmth. She rubbed her palms and fingers between the satin lining and the brown wool, then balled them into fists.

She should really have gone back inside, where the fireplace warmed the common rooms, catching up with Isabelle, finding out what was new with her husband, Philippe, and hearing about the various changes in the village.

Claire was too restless for conversation. She had come to Auvers to inform her project, and so far she had done little but be a tour guide for familiar sites. And the worst of it was that she still didn't know what she should do. All she knew was that she had her sights trained on Dr. Gachet. And, as with the others who seemed to be coming to Auvers these days, perhaps she needed to focus her attention on him.

A dark ornamental night might be the perfect setting to see Gachet's house again. Claire had viewed the house on her first trip to

Auvers. There was a photograph somewhere, but, as with most of the photos from that era, it had long since been boxed and sealed and shoved in a corner in the basement with a prayer that the mold wouldn't get it. At the time, Gachet's house had not meant much to her, especially with its newly built fence, which had obstructed the natural view. It was just another relic from the historical record given dimension. But now it had become the scene of the crime, where she imagined that somehow the doctor had betrayed the patient, driving him into an irrational state. A shadowed moment where worlds had collided to alter the course of modern culture.

Claire patted her pockets, making sure she had her keys. She walked across the driveway toward the gate. Her boots kicked up loose pebbles that were iced like marbles.

Sprinkles of snow lit up through the garden spotlight, emphasizing the crude iron of the closing gate. The mortar walls along the street rose endlessly. A fortress to protect this tiny lane. If she kept walking straight for another twenty minutes, Claire would cut across the hill on a slow incline to Gachet's house. She knew the night would damper its seduction. The gardens and grounds were so inviting. They had drawn in Vincent, increasingly more desperate for a sense of stability and acceptance. In Claire's estimate, Vincent had played the fly to Gachet's spider.

Most people's image of Paul Gachet comes from the portrait that hangs on the second floor of the Musée d'Orsay, the second variation that Vincent had painted for the doctor, presumably as a gift for his model, or perhaps in lieu of paying some untended debt. It is remarkably similar to the infamous original, capturing the doctor's expression in what Van Gogh referred to "as weary with the heartbroken expression of our time," *in keeping with the tradition of nineteenth-century physicians who diagnosed the mad through the visual arts. But while the original portrait almost screams out in passion, unnerving brushstrokes that enlivened the subject's almost melancholy expression—as though his self-treachery was being acted out on the canvas in concert with the various hues of blue as the sound track to the moment—this second painting seems duller. True, it probably had been painted in less than an hour, never meant to hang in a museum, but still it noticeably lacks the life of the original. It is a strange phenomenon, how one can use the same subject in the same place, even posed with the same expression and props, but how the difference of an hour or a day can render that person so much differently, in this case flat. Although it could be presumed that Vincent would have intended the second portrait to carry the same weight as the first, to have the same power and resonance, he must have also noticed the change, the flattening of the eyes, the redundancy of the paint. Perhaps that was why he didn't sign this version. In the second painting, Gachet looks harmless and bored. Maybe Vincent had seen something change in the doctor between the two portraits. And maybe Gachet noticed the recognition in his limner and patient. No one likes to have the mask stripped off. It can be too ugly underneath.*

Although Vincent's descriptions of the Gachet house are vivid, it is the Cézanne depiction that is best known. The slight steepled hill of rue Daubigny. Three tall trees guarding the grounds. And behind the third tree, the tallest, is a thatched roof shed set in profile, blocking off the corner of the doctor's residence. The three-story house is on the hill. Proud and lonely. Double red doors are directly in the center, with a slight space between them. They might be shutters; memory can rearrange it. Above the doorway is a pair of windows that look out like a set of sad eyes, distant and lacking in presence. Matching windows are on the third floor; they appear to be devious, looking ahead nonchalantly over the street while calculating a variety of possible perpetrations. All brightly lit up under a sky that is working too hard to hold back the light.

Cézanne's image is pure. It is the homage to the ideal. The sophisticatedly appointed neighborhood where no secrets lie behind the front doors. It is the one that art historians are desperate to preserve.

But was Gachet the tormentor, instead of the hero that history has made him out to be? Just a hackneyed painter who surrounded himself with artists the likes of Cézanne, Pissarro, and Seurat, becoming their so-called caregiver, while trying to align their talent to his mediocrity? And here comes Vincent. Gachet befriends him, says he'll help Vincent's melancholia by giving him drugs and therapy. Says, "just be honest with me," and the other deceits that all manipulators say. Takes him in as family, all the while trying to forge some false camaraderie between the two. When Vincent appeared suspicious of the doctor's intentions, Gachet must have gone through the roof. Knowing Van Gogh's vulnerabilities, imagine that one day out of the blue he started telling Vincent how messed up he was. How the demons would never go away. Imagine that under the pretense of medical counsel and drugs, he tells a vulnerable Vincent that there is no living end to this depression and compulsion, and then playing on Vincent's Jesus anxieties, tells the painter that this is all just leading to a painful crucifixion, fully understanding that Vincent is so engaged in his own paranoia that he would never recognize his gut suspicions as valid. Imagine that despite him being aware of Gachet's own sickness, Vincent remains fragile and always prone to trust others before himself, always idealistic about living in a more comfortable world. And, finally, imagine that Vincent stands in that blustery field with his paintbrush in hand, hearing Gachet's death is honor angel of mercy *of rap over and over in his head, while the birds pound their wings to push the storm away. He is just looking for a sign. Something to tell him that Gachet is wrong. Desperately hunting the terrain for something familiar. Trying to see those fields as he has known them before. But all he sees are the storm clouds overtaking the blue sky.*

It is amazing how one person can change a relationship so quickly, without fully understanding the consequences.

After three more blocks a chill set through her bones. She turned left and headed down to the village, deciding she wasn't ready to face Gachet. She hugged her arms to her chest, not sure if she shivered from the cold or from nerves. Who was she kidding? She wasn't ready for anything, except cresting through these days until she could thankfully look back and see them as her past.

The snow turned to sleet.

Claire dug her bare hands deep into her pockets. She walked with her head bowed, cupping her chin under the rim of her sweater. The village was quiet. A few people passed by. Tourists searched out dinner, absorbed by the ambience of the historic streets, while locals charged by with intent and purpose. Claire trained her eyes on her boots, watching the heel roll forward into the toe, making a rocking-horse track in the slush. She was thinking about Gachet. About how the most desperate moments demand the most unlikely promises. She could almost hear Gachet lecturing at Vincent, swearing that the treatments were working, to just give it a little more time, and have a little faith in something tangible for once in your life. And she knew Vincent just stared back mute. Nodding with a dumb expression on his face, one so void of passion that Gachet might have even questioned if he had the right man. If Vincent would have just said something to stand up for himself. Anything. Not just opened his palm to take the pill, relinquishing all his better instincts. Anything. Claire wished she could make her hand like a sculptor's, reach back into time, and mold Vincent's mouth so it could at least utter the word *bullshit*.

She did not realize that she was talking aloud until she nearly collided with a man in front of her as he walked out of Banette Boulanger with two baguettes tucked under his arm. *"Pardon,"* he said. *"Pardon."*

Still blocking him, Claire looked up, trying to catch the words that were still dangling on her lips.

The man hesitated. He was short, with a distinguished face, where every feature looked immaculately placed in awkward perfection. *"Eh bien, madame,"* he said with an air of disdain, and then stepped around her.

Claire waited for a moment. She looked back over her shoulder at him, a shadow of a long black overcoat with the collar turned up, two breaded wings sticking out. She muttered that it was just an accident, she was just lost in thought, and he didn't need to be an ass about it—although she knew her French failed her on the idiom.

The man did not look back. He barked back something she did not understand, as he brisked away.

She called out *imbécile*, but then stopped herself from saying anything else. She did not really understand why she was yelling. Mostly it was out of response to the man's reaction, and partly at the troubling sense of frustration about her work. Mostly it was exhaustion. She would go back to her room and try to get enough sleep to make it to sunrise. And then wait in her room through morning. In the past she used to trust that something would happen to guide her. She had had no reason not to trust her confidence. Now she would wait. Greatly unsettled.

§   §   §

BEETHOVEN HEARD THE NOTES IN his head. Lucky enough to have the discordant music of the world inaccessible, the composer was able to string the notes purely and honestly. The music was no longer in reaction to, or even in battle with, the competing sound track of the world around him. It was music in its purest sense. Where the only sounds were the subtly modulating keys and the blending of harmonies. His own vision of love and hate. His own aural ideal. If there was one romantic notion that Claire still carried about Vincent, it was her vision of him being the visual equivalent of Beethoven. Although his eyes could see, Vincent's view of the world was blinded. He did not see the noise and the catastrophes that played themselves out around him. Instead he sunk deeper into himself, for the most part hidden beneath the distractions in order to paint the truths, beyond the persuasions of those who tried to orchestrate the common perceptions. Claire liked to believe that he saw trees where others saw shadows. His tragic flaw being the intense fright that paralyzed him when he caught sight of the world around him. How different the colors were. The truths. You can almost hear his fingers clamping around Dr. Gachet's wrist for help. You can almost smell the envy on Gachet's breath.

❦   ❦   ❦

ISABELLE HAD BEEN PREPARING THE dining room by setting the table for tomorrow morning's breakfast. The heavy red drapes were pulled back, allowing the last bit of light to flow through, flooding a yellowish puddle across the middle of the table. On the opposite wall were two low cabinets whose tops were cluttered with antique serving utensils and bowls made of brass. A swinging door into the kitchen separated the cabinetry. Above each cabinet was a collage of framed paintings, all varying in size, and each brilliant in their colors, especially against the boldly painted orange wall. The collection made the statement that art in Auvers had not died with a pistol shot in the wheat fields a hundred years ago. This had always been a community of artists, and still was.

Claire had been fumbling with the lock at the base of the door, unable to turn the key, which was at ankle height. Isabelle took one step back, without breaking the rhythm of her tasks. With a simple flick, she unlatched the door for her guest, while at the same time instructing her twelve year-old daughter, Françoise, who had been assisting between the dining room and the kitchen, to remove the soupspoons, as they would not be necessary for tomorrow morning's menu. Isabelle smiled at Claire when she came through the door, but did not look at her. It was reflexive. Not necessarily disingenuous, but more like undirected love.

Isabelle stood hands on hips, watching her daughter remove the spoons. She wore a simple knee-length skirt textured in wool, with a matching olive jacket, whose buttons crossed in a series along the front in the subtle understatement of a master designer's hand. Isabelle was stately and chic, with the quiet French grace that certain American women clamor for in their fashion magazines. "It was a nice walk for you?" she asked without looking up. Her voice was soft and hoarse, yet still commanding.

Claire paused for a moment. She had imagined herself looking as threadbare and worn as she felt inside. She wondered if the word of her outburst had already made its way through the small town, almost as a warning to avoid the crazy American woman parading the streets. But Isabelle's tone spoke as though all were normal. "You know the sites very good by now, yes?"

Claire nodded, relieved by the sense of normalcy that had greeted her. "It is good to see them from different perspectives, I suppose."

"Let me understand this with accuracy, if I will. You have went to the cemetery, yes? But Van Gogh's room is closed down for winter, so you have missed that. But you have been there in the past?"

"On my first visit. Years ago. You know that." She smiled. "You remember, don't you?"

Isabelle still had not looked at Claire. She had been moving along the perimeter of the table, straightening plates, evening out the flatware, and waiting for her daughter to return with the coffee cups and saucers. "It is dark, that room where Van Gogh lived.

Makes me feel very tight inside when I have visited inside of it. I find it hard to have breaths in there. But I guess that is how he lived. That is why you travel here to visit the room. To stand in the shoes."

"Yes," Claire said. "To stand in the shoes."

Isabelle didn't react. She had become distracted, counting the place settings with her right index finger, once around the table, and then back. "*Merde*," she said. Then she barked back to her daughter in the kitchen, "*Françoise, nous manquons un couvert. Dépêche-toi! Dépêche-toi! Nous sommes censées être dans la voiture dans dix minutes pour rejoindre Papa à la gare et puis sortir dîner. Dépêche-toi, s'il te plaît!*"

Claire asked, "Is everything okay?"

"I am sorry," Isabelle replied. "We are one table setting too little. There are only five when I need six. Françoise and I are to receive my husband at the train station in twenty minutes. This is not good managing of time."

"Can I help?"

This simple question seemed to alter Isabelle's demeanor. The smile came back to her face. The air of hospitality returned, as though she had been embarrassed by the glimpse into the private family rooms. "Thank you, no. You are my guest. But Françoise, Philippe, and I do not return until late tonight, okay? We take Philippe out for his birthday. It is surprise meeting." She laughed. "And he does not like the surprise."

"Where is he coming in from?"

"He arrives from Paris." Isabelle waved her hand as though the information were of little interest. "With all people in Auvers, he works there . . . Not hardly a person here who is not working in

Paris . . . But before I forget, I hope that tonight you will be able to meet two of my guests, without my introduction. I have told them of your name, and the husband knows of you. He too is a scholar of art. He said he is charmed to be in the same house where you stay."

"Do you remember his name?" She hoped that Isabelle was not going to say Paul Chambers. "Now you have me curious. I wonder if I know him."

Françoise came scurrying out of the kitchen with the plates and silver balanced between both her hands, trying to work quickly and efficiently. The expression on her face suggested that she was willing herself not to drop the porcelain to the floor. It was easy to picture Isabelle as a young girl by looking at her daughter. Françoise had the same chin and nose but with chaste skin, as yet unblemished by worry and experience. The girl must have only taken after her father in terms of height. Already she was taller than her mother, walking with an uncontrollable bounce to her step that caused her ponytail to swing back and forth in tribute to its namesake, as though instinctively swatting at flies.

Isabelle stopped and looked upward to search for the other guests' names. "He is called Gould. Daniel. His wife is Kathy." She smiled at that for no particular reason.

Claire thought for a moment. *Daniel Gould. Daniel Gould.* Not a familiar name. "Are you sure he is a Van Gogh scholar?" It would surprise her if he were, especially if he had done anything substantial, as by now she had come to know nearly everyone in the field, including the up-and-comers, who all wrote to her for advice.

"I do not exactly know. Gould talked to me of Van Gogh's . . .

I do not know, really . . . Maybe one of those Gachet people . . . *Françoise, dépêche-toi! Dépêche-toi* . . . I am sorry." She looked up at the clock. "He works for a museum? I cannot recollect right now. But you will make the introduction tonight, okay? There is some something they are engaged to, but they plan a return at around seven o'clock. And they want to meet you. Especially Daniel Gould. Perhaps you will give them some of your knowledge." Isabelle clearly relished her role as hostess.

Claire smiled, as though indicating that she would make the introduction. In truth, she knew that she would vanish into her room, perhaps slip out to the 8 à Huit to buy a baguette, some cheese, and a bottle of red wine to bring back for an indoor picnic in solitude. The day had exhausted her, and although her nightly panic about being alone began to set in, she felt fully depleted of personality. She might check in with Richard. Otherwise, she would lie in the dark and try to convince herself to fall asleep.

Françoise laid down the final setting, and then punctuated all six with the cup and saucer at the top right. She smiled at her mother, looking for the compliment that she undoubtedly was accustomed to, but tonight, her mother being under the sway of a quickly moving clock, all Françoise received was a whisk of the hand, followed by the instructions to get changed and meet in the car. *Dépêche-toi! Dépêche-toi! Ton père attend.*

"I am sorry that I am not hosting very well tonight." Isabelle patted the sides of her hair and looked over the room once more. She clearly did not plan to think of work until morning. "It is just the way some things sometimes are falling."

Claire told her she understood, and not to worry.

Isabelle reached for a set of keys hanging off a hook beside the door. "And you have everything you need for the night?"

"I am fine, thank you. I might need to use the telephone is all."

"You are welcome to use the one in our living room if you require privacy. We do not arrive home until much after eleven."

Françoise came angling down the stairs, slightly short of breath, with an insect's stride. She wore the same brown wool pants, but had changed into a beige blouse that flowed loosely in stylish contemplation for a girl her age, clearly meeting her mother's expectations. Without discussion, Françoise opened the front door, and then held it for her mother.

"Have fun," Claire said. "And wish Philippe a happy birthday for me."

"You can tell him yourself in the morning." Isabelle smiled, and then she stopped as she was almost through the door. "Please don't forget the Goulds. They are so interested to talking with you."

The house was silent once the door closed. Usually there was some family member present to conjure up life. A television playing, a ringing telephone, or the march with cleaning brush batons to the emptied rooms and toilets. But all was quiet enough to hear the bare branches, brittle with age, scratching against the upstairs exterior. There was only the smell of a recently extinguished lavender-scented candle. Claire had the sensation that nothing was familiar anymore. She was not yet able to ground herself into this one world where she is the expert, something that should have given her a feeling of balance during these doddering days, while the rest of the business of living had become even more unbearable. Where minute by minute, as though on a continuous reel, that October night on a country New England road plays in a low hum across the back of her skull. The restlessness hurts. She feels paralyzed. She wishes she could stay in Isabelle's guesthouse for the next several months, and be tended to by the dutiful Françoise until her strength of will has returned. And yet she will have to move on soon.

Nothing is safe.

Especially as these in-between days seem to feel more and more permanent, and it becomes impossible to believe that they will ever pass.

Nothing is safe.

In May of 1889, not long before deciding to migrate to Auvers, and following a series of breakdowns, Vincent wrote a letter to Theo from the sanitarium in Saint-Rémy where in part he advised his brother, "I beg you not to fret, or be worried about me; the ideas that you get into your head of this necessary and salutary quarantine would have little justification when we need slow and patient recovery. If we can grasp that, we shall save our strength for winter." *How relieved he sounded to be taken care of. As though all those misbegotten hopes of the past had never occurred, again Vincent spoke as if he had finally found his cure. And how delighted he must have been to give comfort to his brother, who had supported him through the best and worst. Nearly a year later, in a letter from Auvers, following another bout of hope, he credited Theo for his* "part in the actual production of some of the canvases." *Vincent*

must have felt the inexplicable relationship between crutch and
injured limb, where one is dependant on giving hope, and the
other on giving meaning. But separately they are worthless.

Claire sat on the edge of Isabelle and Philippe's couch, cautious
not to make herself too comfortable. She had never been in their
private quarters before, and despite the welcome invitation she felt
something of an intruder. It really did not look too different from
the rest of the house. There was nothing more personal in here
than in the other rooms, save for a family picture at the beach set
upon the bookshelf, and a series of old cracked and sepia-toned
photos hanging throughout the room, which Claire took to be the
family history.

She dialed the phone slowly, trying not to invert the numbers
of the country code before finding the more familiar 401 of Rhode
Island. She did pause momentarily at her own phone number—but
why shouldn't she? She had been long out of the habit of calling
her home.

The phone rang three times. It must be close to 1 A.M. in Providence. Richard was still likely to be working upstairs, hunched over
his drafting table in the makeshift office.

The machine picked up, clipping off the fourth ring, his eyes
heavy, with the hope of just completing a few more details, before
he then would go off to bed. She knew the process would continue
well into the early hours of morning.

It was Claire's own voice reciting that she had reached the
home of Claire Andrews. She had recorded the message the morning of the accident, seeing the time change as an excuse to update a
greeting that had been eight months old by then. It was the voice of

another woman. One who had recently decided to test being single, was continuing to soar in her career, and who concluded that the worst of her days were behind her. The voice was full and bold. Spoken with pulled-back shoulders and a bellowed chest, enunciating with confidence. Claire should have been reassured to hear this stronger version of herself. Instead she darted her stare around the room, waiting for it to finish, with the same detached impatience of listening to instructions from an automatic voice messaging system while longing for human contact.

"Richard," she spoke following the beep. "I just want to check in. There is so much to——"

"Claire?"

She had no plan of what she was going to say, other than to know that Richard was still there.

"Where are you, Claire?"

"I am in Auvers now. All is fine," she said. "Fine. In Auvers." She felt a sudden caution, unsure about how she was supposed to talk with Richard. They were still like neighboring territories, cautiously waiting for the borders to be drawn.

"Well, I am glad you called," he said. "Things have turned crazy here. And it's more than I would have expected. Even Bernard is acting stunned."

The tone of the conversation already recalled those awful days when their relationship had turned to all business, a series of detailed strategies and flowcharts to avoid seeing what happens when two expectations collide.

"I am sorry this has fallen on you," Claire said. "How is Cocoa?"

Richard replied, "How is Cocoa?" After a long breath, he proceeded to detail the explosion taking place back home. He paused, scraping for a positive way to describe that yesterday alone three reporters from the local Eyewitness News Teams had knocked on the door with unsubstantiated claims that there were two witnesses going on record to say that Claire had been driving so recklessly that she did not even have a split second to avoid hitting the child. Bernard was managing that, and as of now saw it as a bullshit claim, but nevertheless one that was out there in full view, and now generating overwhelming media interest. The floodgates had opened. In light of the TV news report, an inaccurate but still compelling narrative of their marriage was reported in today's *Herald*. The word *fugitive* had not been used, but the implication was the subtext of the article. The university had started calling; not her dean, but instead a hired publicity gun charged with protecting the reputation of the school, and whose primary concern— by his own admission—was to preserve the good name of the institution, not one of its faculty members. And a teaser for the five o'clock news announced that tonight's Night Beat *"will find out why an unnamed member of the Kennealy family is out to tell the whole of Rhode Island that 'hiding out in the ivory tower' won't stop justice."*

And that didn't even begin to cover the legal machinations. Richard spoke with the expertise of the desperate amateur, suddenly immersed in the vocabulary and procedures of foreign systems. He explained how this case, supposed to be determined on the rules of evidence and presented to the jury without prejudice, has a legal strategy that figures it will only take a sprinkling of nonprejudicial evidence—a witness statement, a kink in the investigation—to allow the introduction of sympathy and emotion into the proceedings. Logic suggested that the prosecution was basing its case on what is typically called "*the failure to keep a proper lookout*," where a driver is responsible for being fully aware of all the conditions around him, as with road rage cases and accidents involving cell phone users. The state of Connecticut recently prosecuted a dart-out case very similar to Claire's on this same precedent, and that, according to Bernard, they need to take away all potential conjecture. Stop the prosecution's march to the sympathy vote.

"Bernard needs you home as soon as possible," Richard concluded. "He said that he completely underestimated the force that this would come with. He is especially concerned about how this craziness might be poisoning public perception, and even the jury pool, if it comes to that."

Claire sat quietly, looking up at the antiquated face of a stern Frenchwoman hung above the television. She took it to be a portrait of Philippe's mother, bearing a slight resemblance to Françoise but none to Isabelle. "I don't understand, Richard. Do you?" This should be somebody else's story that Richard told.

"Claire?"

"I have to see it every night as I am about to fall asleep. To lose my breath in panic when I see a child anywhere near a street. To look into the eyes of every one of my students and imagine them as children, but find it impossible to see them as fully matured adults. I have paid every minute since that night. And I will continue to for the rest of my . . . Jury pools? It's already poisoned. This whole nightmare is poison."

"I just don't want to see things get any worse for you."

She sensed an urgency in his voice that was beyond his normal capacity for stressful situations. Richard was not structured for this level of tension. He was somebody who needed to keep things organized, unwilling to be surprised by the unexpected, needing to preserve his sense of order.

Among Claire's later regrets will be that she didn't let Richard know how much she appreciated what he was putting himself through on her account. She actually had felt a surge of passion shoot through her, charmed by this sacrifice of which his only gain was seeing her betterment. That was the core of what she had loved about him. It was just the details that did them in. His anxieties, and the stupid ways he expressed them. If only they could have found a way to exist beyond the surface and into that core, Claire would have continued to love him the way she loved him now. But even Socrates knew that one eventually had to return to the cave to live among the changing forms. One couldn't survive on the purity of ideals alone.

"Son of a bitch," Richard said, lowering his voice. "There are more reporters right outside the window now." He paused. "They are cupping their hands and peering in for Christ's sake. It's the middle of the goddamn night!"

Claire heard footsteps in the guesthouse driveway. The door unlocked, and two voices spoke in English, one deep, the other light and melodic. She looked over at the clock. It was barely six. According to Isabelle, the Goulds were not supposed to be back until later. Yet here they entered, lingering around the foyer. Probably lying in wait to see her.

She scrunched her shoulders. Her legs balled up. She leaned in closer to the phone. "Richard," she whispered, "I have to go."

"When should I tell Bernard that you are coming home?"

"I will let you know. I'll call once I . . . I really need to . . ."

"Claire . . ."

"Richard?"

"Yes?"

Her whisper was barely audible. "You didn't tell me how Cocoa is."

"Holy shit. Now they are feeling around the goddamn mail slot . . ."

She hung up the phone when the voices stopped suddenly. She could feel their attention drawn toward her direction.

She sat in Isabelle and Philippe's parlor for another half-hour. Her knees curled tightly, unwilling to move, even though her calves started to spasm and her arches began to strain. She remained still until she heard them proceed up the stairs, slamming the bedroom door for the night.

Claire crept out slowly. Once in the foyer she peered into the dining room. Then into the common room. And then she looked upstairs, listening for any kind of movement. Frozen in place, she waited for the best moment to escape down to the market for dinner.

She reached for her keys. They fumbled in her hands, dropping to the floor. The metal falling against the tile echoed as though a vase had shattered.

Footsteps quickly treaded along the second floor, and then made their way down the stairs. The light switched on, and standing on the landing step before her was the man from the trail. "Oh sheesh," he said. "I thought I heard a terrible noise."

Claire stood flustered. She couldn't bring herself to look at him. "It's just my keys. These giant rooms."

He paused. A huge grin came over his face. "Claire Andrews," he said. He pointed at her, wagging his index finger. "Son of a gun, I thought that was you today. On the trail. With those kids."

She nodded.

"My wife and I walked right by you just as I was about to pass out from exhaustion. But I thought that was you. I told my wife I knew it was you. I even said to her, '*Kathy, I think that is Claire Andrews.*' Of course it isn't so surprising to think that I would see you in one of the Van Gogh villages. Still, imagine the coincidence. When I asked Isabelle, and she confirmed . . . I should have assumed you would spend a lot of time here."

"Enough, I guess." She bent down to pick up her keys. Trying to figure out how she could make a clean escape, in spite of the awkward lock at the bottom of the door.

"Dan Gould," he said, introducing himself. "We haven't officially met before, but I am so darned excited to meet you. I have read all your books, and have heard you speak at several conferences. You even inscribed your first two books for me at Clark."

"Have we met before?" She paused, and reconsidered. "Oh, I'm sorry, you just said we had . . . Sort of . . . Isabelle mentioned that there was a Van Gogh historian staying here." Claire could not see a way out of this.

"Well, I would hardly say that I am a Van Gogh historian, or any brand of art historian, for that matter. I am just a forensic scientist for BCE labs."

"Is it BCE that discovered the forged Cézannes? The ones that Gachet supposedly painted. Something about saffron in the yellow instead of mustard seed."

"That was us. And yes, it was the pigments that gave those away. I was on the team that wrangled that one out."

"So what brings you here?" She immediately thought about Paul Chambers's snooping around about Dr. Gachet.

"Kathy and I are just here on a little R & R. A little getaway. I am something of an amateur Van Gogh enthusiast, that's why I know the books and the conferences as such, and after I saw you on the path . . . And by the way I can't express what you must already know, how amazing it is to see the wheat fields in all their living glory. You read about it, study it, but there is nothing like standing within the history . . . Once Isabelle said . . . Once she told me that you were . . . I was just hoping I could be able to talk with you. Just have a chance to meet you and tell you how much I have learned from your work."

Claire smiled politely.

He lowered his voice. "The rest of the story is that I was on a job in Paris for an art dealer, whose name I am not allowed to say." His voice lowered even deeper. "On the *Portrait of Dr. Gachet.*"

Claire's breath caught in her chest. She couldn't swallow. "The one in the Orsay? The second one . . . ?"

"Both." He stared at her. His eyes, wearied and confident, now looked sad.

"*And* the original? You were testing the . . . ?" She swallowed, making the connection to Paul Chambers. "Saito's purchase?"

"If you can call it original," he muttered.

Claire stepped back. The anxiety she had been feeling earlier was strengthened by a burst of adrenaline. For one second, she felt a sweep of power, shoving the dramas back home to a distant and removed, albeit temporary, space.

"This is all in confidence." He glared at her for confirmation. "You can't breathe a word of this conversation."

"But *what* are you saying? About the painting."

"You know, Miss Andrews . . ."

"You can call me Claire."

"I guess what I am saying is that I can't say. Only that what I have experienced in the past week is enough to make you want to quit the business altogether."

"What did you find?"

"It's amazing how the outcome of a couple of days can alter your entire perspective. I guess that is why Kathy and I came up here. Feel a little less jaded being away from the professional world of what I do. To remember what the art is all about. Caught up in the science and the business, and the . . ." Gould looked away in disgust. He looked as though he were pushing the next string of words back down his throat.

"But you are not telling me what you found. Or why you were even testing the *Gachet*."

"I have signed so many gosh-darned confidentiality forms that I am not sure that I can even talk about what I had for dinner." He shook his head. Swallowed. Kicked his feet against the floor. Then he lowered his voice to a whisper. "You ever hear about drug companies that hire doctors to test their new products? Well I'm sure you know that not every doctor is going to give a positive report, in fact some will tell that the drug had negative effects or was just plain hooey. And you know what the pharmaceutical company does with that information? Puts it in the shredder. And you know what the doctor can do about that? Absolutely zilch. Why? Because he has agreed up front that his results are the property of the company."

"And who exactly are you working for? You work for BCE, right? BCE."

"I told you, BCE. You know I can't name the client."

"Jesus, if he knows you are talking with me . . ."

"I didn't even know you were on the same continent until I spotted you on the trail, and I just looked at Kathy after we passed . . . And then Isabelle confirmed it when I asked her if it was . . . And . . . How would he know? The client couldn't know."

"Right, how would he?" Claire was cautiously suspicious. Clearly Dan Gould had discovered some flaw in the *Gachet*. The distress was in his posture, the way he bit down on his bottom lip and chewed on it while trying to look proud. She could see the weight of responsibility that he felt, the torment of the guilty who are complicit not by the actions they take, but by the knowledge they have. Still the coincidence seemed too fortuitous. One more degree of paranoia would lead her to believe that she was being tested by Paul Chambers. But wasn't history gleaned from moments like this? Rembrandt's copperplate of *Abraham Entertaining the Angels*, stuck to the back of a painting by Pieter Gysels for three hundred years. Whitman's lost interview, which advised aspiring poets not to be poets, found in a university newspaper's archives. Attics and garage sales and cellar archives were filled with stories like this; they were the true keepers of history, waiting to be stumbled upon by the one person who cared. Sometimes you can't question the collisions of the world.

Claire asked him if he was free for lunch tomorrow. Would he like to join her? "Just to tell me about the work you do. How the real portrait looks these days. That is, what you can."

Gould smacked his lips. He looked up toward the staircase. "I don't know; Kathy has been feeling a little bit exhausted by all this, and, well . . . I don't know . . . I mean, I suppose it would be . . . Well, yes. Let me just say yes." He was halfway up the stairs when he turned and lifted his index finger for a wave. Then he crept the rest of the way up the staircase.

Claire paced the entryway. She would not ask Dan Gould for the details of his findings—she respected his professionalism too much for that inconsideration, but she hoped that he would give more context to the project, the general notion of what he had stumbled upon. It couldn't be good. That's why Paul Chambers had been here. Something had been discovered that had changed everything, and Chambers wanted it to go away, to pretend that his own disaster had never taken place. For the first time in the past months Claire felt a tinge of life come back to her. She could feel that lost sensation of control returning. Where her own hands formed the actions and the consequences.

Day Three

Sitting at the back of Crêperie l'Auversoise, Claire cut into her crepe with the edge of her fork. She pushed the piece around the edge of the plate, letting it soak up the mushroom sauce. A bouquet of savory and butter wafted up from the plate. She had never smelled anything so fragrant in her life. Yet she was not able to bring herself to take a bite. Bringing the fork near her mouth caused her stomach to clamp at the center, while a sickening bile worked its way up her throat. One day she would be able to eat regularly again.

Dan Gould didn't seem to notice. He had finished his ham crepe in two quick swipes and as quickly inhaled a lemon crepe for dessert. His table duty had then become relegated to keeping the water glasses full, pouring from the shapely bottle at the center of the table. He asked Claire a lot of questions about Van Gogh, trying to ferret out differing versions of various mythologies, especially interested in her various thoughts on *Crows over the Wheatfield*, having attended the lecture at Clark. After she explained a bit of her current intrigue about the work, Gould then asked her why she was in Auvers, what more research could she possibly get from this town—it was hardly the hub of anything substantial, other than as a moving memorial.

That was it, she told him. She was coming here to research Vincent as she never had before. "Just as you are saying, I have always seen this town as a memorial, or a place to weed out symbols to support my interpretation. But I am beginning to think my goal is to understand Vincent's last days, and I can only understand them if I allow myself to see this village just as he saw it—not as a researcher would. There are no more primary sources for me to research. No data that I haven't exhausted yet. But the one thing I have failed to do is look through Vincent's eyes. Especially how he might have seen Gachet in those final days. That's what I have left. Because, really, there are no more stones to upturn."

While she spoke, Gould had been trying to fill his water glass. He missed the lip completely, but pulled back the bottle in time to avoid a substantial spill. He laughed nervously, darting his eyes in place of an apology as he soaked up the few droplets with his napkin. "There might be one stone," he said. "One stone left."

She dropped her fork. It tinged against the plate. "What did you say?"

"One stone," he said. "One stone to upturn."

"What do you mean?"

He looked down and scratched the back of his head, inhaling heavily through his nose. His lips pursed while his stare was drawn toward his lap, as though he was about to commit an act that he understood could undo him. "The Gachet portrait," he said. "It's a fake . . . A fake, it is. That's the stone."

It was obvious how much it tore him up to say that, as he blurted it out with some type of wounding intent. Instinctively, Claire reached over and touched his arm in collegial comfort. This clearly was the observation of an amateur. "It's okay," she said, shaking her head. "You're only betraying what people have suspected for years anyway. It has always been seriously considered that the second *Gachet* could be a fraud. Don't beat yourself up over this."

Gould didn't reply. He didn't even look up.

She continued, "So you have confirmed it. It's okay. It may be a shock to you, but only a bit of a surprise to someone like me, as I have heard the rumors for years at various conferences, backed up by some pretty convincing anecdotal evidence."

"But that one is not the fake, the second one." Gould was whispering, not from a conspiratorial tone, but from the physical incapability of talking. "That one is Van Gogh's."

"Then what are you talking about? . . . Oh, Jesus Christ . . . But that's impossible . . . You mean to tell . . . Are you serious?" And she wanted to start laughing, not at the joy of the act or the deception, but at the joy of discovery, at the sense that there are still things in this world to be found, to be understood. But that feeling quickly passed, and she found herself huddled over the table, leaning toward him, speaking in the same hushed tones. "Are you sure?" she said. "Are you absolutely sure that the *Portrait of Dr. Gachet* is a fake? The one that sold for eighty-two and a half million dollars? That I assume Paul Chambers is negotiating for a new seller at this very moment?" She broke into a smile.

Gould didn't even bristle when she mentioned Chambers by name. It was as though he didn't hear her. "You can't breathe a word of this to anybody. Nobody. Not a soul."

"I won't ever mention your name."

"I decided today that I will put my findings in my will. That's when they'll come out. So you can't . . ."

"I won't . . ."

"Promise me."

"I swear."

There was a lull between them. Gould looked at his shoes, grinding his toe into the floor. Claire, hunched over the wooden table lit by dancing candlelight, staring at him.

The waitress set the check between them. She was a young girl of about seventeen whose parents no doubt ran the place. When not in service, the girl sat at a table nearest the kitchen, dragging on a cigarette and bantering with the locals seated across from her. She played the part of an American teenager, dressed in a short tartan skirt, a white button-up blouse with the top flared open, and clunky black work boots. Her red hair was mussed to perfection, and she worked hard to conjure a snarl over a face that was equally as innocent looking as Françoise's.

Gould looked up out of the corner of his eye. "I shouldn't have told you. I shouldn't have said anything. You won't say anything, right. You said you wouldn't. We agreed on that, right?"

"I told you." Claire nodded.

"Because he just thanked me for my work, and said that was all, and reminded me of the nondisclosure clauses. He was going to have to work with a different lab, he said. A different lab that he knew would understand the history better. Better, he said. You said you wouldn't say anything, right?"

Claire smiled. "Again, yes. Trust me . . . But how did you know? That's what interests me. What gave it away?"

Gould shifted. He straightened his posture. "Well, the gel electrophoresis gave the first indication that the color composition was inconsistent with what we knew to be Van Gogh's." His voice livened. As with Claire, he clearly felt most comfortable in the world of his work, rattling off a litany of scientific terms that defined his process en route to the discovery. "It was only preliminary," he concluded, "but it, of course, was not the expected or intended result."

"I should think not."

"The hope was that I could definitively show the second painting to be the forgery, in order to further increase the gosh-darned value of the so-called original. I was only testing the original as a control. That was when it all started going haywire."

"Is that when they stopped you?"

"Heck no. The client couldn't believe it. I told him, 'I don't know, I'm just a scientist and I'm only looking at the results,' but he insisted that I get a more detailed reading. Called up my bosses, and they called me. He wanted the whole works. So I was able to run a gas chromatography. That test will pinpoint all the dyes and pigments that went into the original paint—it does not lie." He went on to explain the details of the scientific inquiry in a technical language that Claire was vaguely familiar with from past readings on the subject. "And you know what it came down to?" Gould said. "The saffron in the yellow again."

"So you're saying that Gachet painted the portrait, as well. Just like the supposed Cézanne."

"I am not saying anything. Only that there is a common trait between the two. That's for others to draw the conclusions. But that fellow acted like he didn't believe my results. Going to get someone who understands the work better, he said. He's going to broker that painting like it's real. And someone is gonna pay for it like it's real." Gould sighed. He puffed his cheeks out, for a moment erasing the lines in his face, ones that were no doubt going to deepen in the coming months and years. "I can't afford to lose my job over this. I've got kids in college, Kathy teeters between sick and well . . . This is one time where I have to swallow my conscience. Just go along on my way. You know what that means to a scientist? Do you know?"

Claire didn't know how to respond. She pushed her plate away while considering. "Maybe knowing you have discovered something important is enough. And what you've found *is* incredible. Who knows, maybe one day people won't think it's as good if they find out it's worthless. Or they'll suddenly find the brilliance in the second *Gachet*."

Gould nodded.

"But the very fact that he was forging his own patient's work says something about the man. He wasn't interested in cures. He was only trying to build his collection, from every angle. No wonder Van Gogh lost hope. All the trust was betrayed."

Gould examined the check, then reached into his pocket and laid down thirty euros. He pushed the bills to the edge of the table, just under the flickering candle. "I told you I don't know about that stuff, only the data. But I have to say, hearing all that makes it a little bit worse. Because I have to live alone with the secret of the truth. Nobody will ever know any of those things you're talking about. At least not in my lifetime."

The waitress returned, pushing her right hip out. In one hand she held a cigarette, the filter a bright red from her lipstick.

"Thank you," Claire said to Dan Gould. The girl, thinking Claire had been talking to her, made an exaggerated curtsy and looked over for a laugh from her friends. She snatched up the bills from beneath the candle.

"So what do we do?" Claire asked him.

"Try to go back to being normal. Do our best to live like it never happened."

Q   Q   Q

ALTHOUGH IT WAS STILL FAIRLY early, it already felt like dinner-time once they got back to the guesthouse. It had been a slow, quiet walk. Winding up the hills, climbing narrow staircases between stone houses, the sound of their footsteps patting behind them. Gould walked stooped over, breathing heavier with each step. On occasion he winced in pain, nothing apparent or specific, probably symptoms of general weariness.

She didn't talk with him all the way back. His regret at telling her was obvious. He could barely make eye contact when she did catch his glance, like two midnight lovers facing each other in the morning's light. In the end, though, she knew that he would feel himself lucky to be unburdened of having sole propriety of the se-cret. At least Dan Gould could live his life knowing that someone else, for whom the information impacted the same, also knew the truth.

At some point Claire knew that she would have to ask his permission to use the information for her research. She would cite it as evidence from an anonymous source, somehow invoking the same shield law that journalists use. Bill Harrison would know how to handle that. Gould would not have to worry, as she would deny up and down any trail that led back to him. Nor would he need to be concerned about Paul Chambers, who would have to build a fortress around himself in order to distance himself, and protect his supposed integrity and reputation. One thing Gould was right about, this was important, and it did need to be told. They had the researcher's responsibility. And once the secret became everybody's, it would not seem so ominous anymore. It would just become part of the world that everybody knew.

But she would broach that subject later. The dust needed to settle. What seemed shocking for the moment needed the time to become normal. It is only when the deformed leg becomes a routine part of life that one can start to figure out how to walk on it.

When they reached Isabelle's, Claire stood on her tiptoes and kissed Dan Gould on the cheek. "I just have one question," she said. "One question. Why did you tell me?"

Gould looked at her, shaking his head. "Sometimes you have to say something out loud, just to hear how powerful it is. And you have to say it to someone that you trust, and who understands why you're saying it . . . That's the best I can say."

He looked browbeaten. She expected she would hear him toss all night across the hall. He turned to go upstairs. He might have cried.

She went into her room and drew the curtains. The art world was about to get the conclusion to one of the great enigmas and mysteries of modern art, complete with romanticized eccentricities and the lessons of greed. But Ryoei Saito's purchase and its aftermath had been too much of the story of the piece—so much so, it probably had devalued the painting. Tainted it. From the buyer's perspective, its historical significance would need to be inflated. Chambers, himself, would be behind the scenes, reinventing the life and importance of Dr. Gachet, making advanced deals with museums around the world to allow showings of *Portrait of Dr. Gachet*. The grand return of one of the world's lost treasures. And quid pro quo, they will all agree to promote this idyllic legacy of Gachet as the man who tried to save the flailing genius. If Chambers knew she were here, he would be monitoring everything she did, making sure that nothing she was working on reflected negatively on Gachet. He would make sure that it all stayed clean for the buyer. He would know everything necessary. And he probably would know about the accident too.

❦   ❦   ❦

CLAIRE WENT DOWN TO ISABELLE'S parlor to call Richard. She misdialed the country code twice. Richard did not pick up with the machine. She left a message telling him about Gould's discovery, saying twice that he had to swear a thousand times over that he would not tell a soul, that Gould was genuinely freaked out about the possible ramifications. She couldn't find another word besides *incredible* to describe the information. She must have said it five times in the short message, before rambling on that she wished Richard had been there, and then stopped herself, still jarred by the confusion of their relationship. It had felt good to tell him. She liked remembering the feeling of sharing her excitements with

Richard. But what was acceptable and unacceptable seemed so murky these days. And as with most gray areas, that only saddened her. She managed a good-bye that surely sounded as confusing as the initial excitement. She folded her arms over her stomach, trying to keep the impending knot from coming.

She ran upstairs to get Bill and Maggie's number, walking gently past the Goulds' room. She could imagine the quiet behind that door. The way in which Gould probably had turned away from his wife when she sought to comfort him. How he must be dazed, his eyes fixed on the wall. She knew the posture well.

Maggie answered on the first ring. The television was playing in the background, blaring a lush sound track. "Turn off the TV, Maggie, and get Bill on the other line."

"Claire? Where are you? Are you back already? Oh my, is everything okay?"

"Maggie, please put Bill on the phone as well." She whispered in insistence.

Claire was convinced that she was not about to betray Gould's confidence, she was only going to tell Bill that the book had clicked into place. She not only would assure confidentiality from Maggie and Bill, but as a precaution, she would bend the story a bit to make it sound as though all of this was still only a remote possibility, not the certainty that she knew it to be. She would refer to the *Gachet* not by name, but only as "an important painting, one of great interest to the art world, and one that would be a tremendous indicator of Van Gogh's final days." Her source would be "someone who knows somebody." And, for Maggie's sake, she'd let it slip that it probably involved Paul Chambers. If she wasn't so damn excited!

When they both spoke into the phone, Claire proceeded to tell her version of the story, already weaving the scientific fact with the social and psychological conjecture.

"That's a good story," Bill said. She could picture him shaking his head.

"It's all hypothetical, right now," Claire said.

Maggie immediately started in. "If this is Paul Chambers's bullshit . . . How someone who once defined integrity in the field, can come to define its antithesis." She hoped that the entire art world would read Claire's book, and extrapolate Paul Chambers from the alias he would have to appear under. "We work our whole lives to find even fractures of these answers, and he goes and . . ."

Claire smiled to herself. "I appreciate you keeping the torch of anger for me."

Bill said, "I do think this has to be the book. This is the exciting part of the story. Where the real drama takes place."

"You have to get that information out, documented or not," Maggie said. "It is too important not to consider. Son-of-a-bitch-Paul-Chambers."

"I don't know if the person I know is willing to confirm the information."

"Certainly they understand the responsibility," Maggie said. "If they have any connection to the kind of work we do, then there can be no question, despite the personal risk and sacrifice."

Bill said in the long run it didn't matter. The facts and details could be disguised enough to mask the person's identity. "You have to go ahead on this," he said. "You have to."

"I figured you would both be as excited as I am," Claire said. Only now she felt a little awkward. She had not given anything away about the details of Gould's research, nor in fact even given an indication of what level of inquiry he was involved in; however, she felt the power of his secret, its private grief, which she was denying due process. Even speaking speculatively had already turned this into something larger than all of them.

Bill advised Claire to try to talk with her contact. He would also be happy to speak with her source to review all the legal implications. Claire would have told him that it wasn't about legalities at this point; but to try to explain that to Bill right now would be like him trying to tell her that this wasn't about excitement.

"I'll figure it out," Claire said.

"Claire," Maggie said. "Congratulations. This kind of thing only comes once in a lifetime."

Back in her room, Claire closed her eyes, trying to give way to sleep. She was torn between her loyalty to Vincent and her loyalty to Dan Gould. As her thoughts become heavy, she realized that in the excitement she had, for the first time, not thought about Ronnie Kennealy during the course of an evening. That the quest for the intangible had trumped her real emotional state. She wished she could see that as a good thing. That sat in her stomach as she finally fell asleep. Taking its place among other regrets, great and small.

※   ※   ※

CLAIRE WOKE UP ON THE edge of screaming. She caught her breath to keep the panic at bay. In the darkened second-floor room she could make out the edges of the drawn curtain. She knew exactly where she was but had lost all sense of the dimensions of the room. It seemed smaller than she had remembered it being. And although it felt as if it were the break of dawn, the clock on the nightstand showed that it was only 1:12 A.M.

Her dreams had been all over the place. It took only one day in Auvers for a collage of eras to pastiche themselves across her mind.

Claire awoke with a single image, one as real as anything she had seen in this waking life of hers. Beside the ivy-laden graves of Vincent and Theo lay the headstone of Ronnie Kennealy, with the granite equally weathered, and the ground as aged and hardened, breaking and cracking under the four-way tug-of-war of the seasons. All three graves shared the same pasture of ivy.

It felt impossible to breathe.

And it felt too real to have been filmed in her head.

She kicked off the covers, as though their weight was somehow culpable. She sat up, hugging her legs, feeling her knees press into her collarbone. By all rights Claire should have been exhausted, too wearied to do anything but close her eyes and fall back into sleep. But it felt impossible to sit still. The image continued to flash before her like a slide show against the dark.

The room felt more and more cramped. She felt the need to be moving.

Gachet's copies of Vincent's work overwhelmed her. The possibilities swirling inside her head of justice and redemption and acceptance. Maybe Gachet had not killed his patient, but his own agenda had certainly prevented him from averting it, at the very least willingly ignoring the professional signs and encouraging the confused state. And to think, the doctor had stood above the grave, dropping tears into the freshly tilled earth.

Claire's eyes darted around the room. It seemed too unfair how the truths of one's life can be held in secrecy by a select few. How could Vincent's remains be within fifteen minutes of this room, laid to rest in full ignorance?

She intended to go to the cemetery. It seemed only right.

She stepped nimbly toward the stairs. Staying in her pajamas she slipped yesterday's socks on, and over them laced up a pair of sneakers. She protected herself from the potential cold with a thick wool sweater imported from Ireland, and then draped her black overcoat along her shoulders, reaching into the pockets to ensure that her keys were still stuffed where she had left them.

The first-floor lights lit a nebulous pathway along the hallway, the orange glow giving the otherwise shiny floors a sepia finish. She passed the Goulds' room. Kathy Gould's sweet breaths whistled in the bliss of slumber, while rustling sheets suggested her husband's restlessness.

Claire gripped the banister. Confining her steps to the red runner to avoid creaking noises. Careful not to knock the brass carpet stays out of place.

As she neared the front door, Claire heard the TV from the living room off to the right. The light from the set flashed through the doorway like blue lightning strikes, second by second.

She took one long stride past the living room entrance, glancing in briefly to see Isabelle fast asleep on the couch with her legs dutifully crossed, reading glasses slipped down her nose, and a fluttered magazine spread across her chest. She looked peaceful and unsuspecting. But why should she think otherwise? It would seem highly unlikely that anybody would venture into the village this late. Even nefarious misanthropes keep regular hours.

It would be an awkward confrontation, Claire fully dressed about to lunge into a village that was tucked in and snoring soundly until morning. There would be no way to explain why she needed to walk up to the grave site in the middle of the night.

Claire paused before the doorway, wishing that she were the horror movie villain that could shift into a bat and drum its wings invisibly against the dark sky.

She bent over and inserted the key at the bottom of the door, just above her right foot. A simple twist, followed by a push, accessed the outside in near silence. Claire sighed as she gently closed the door. Relieved that she had gotten out ahead of the telephone that had just started ringing in the office.

Walking over the driveway rocks took great care. Each step sounded three times louder than its actual volume, evoking the sound of a prowler or a wild animal in search of trash. She closed the iron driveway gate with great care and finally found herself freed, on the road.

Shutters were closed on all the houses. The only light came from a distant sliver of moon, tossing off black and white shadows in barely visible shades. She walked along the inside of the parked cars, squeezing her body between the side-view mirrors and the stone retaining wall, taking each step gingerly. The wind shot up the street as though on a breezeway, quickly gaining momentum as it negotiated every twist and turn.

Claire looked once to the church, the generous lighting showed the stone's brilliant perfection. She then turned right, proceeding up the hill to the cemetery.

Still keeping close to the side of the road. Marking her path by the retaining wall.

Still conscious of being conspicuous.

Vincent's wheat fields on her left were invisible and unemotional in this hour.

She thought she heard voices. They chattered indistinguishably, more in sounds than words, as though engaged in a primitive discovery of language. Claire stopped. The voices stopped. She moved. They started. She stopped, and then took another step and heard the voices again. It took two more moments of childlike experimentation to realize that the voices had not been chatter and conversation, but instead were the combination of strange echoes of twigs breaking under her soles and phantasmal paranoia.

The wall disappeared and gave way to fields, where dying heads of kale lay orderly and humanlike in the dark. It was as though they might start singing in chorus, rocking back and forth in unison, sharing secrets when her back was turned, and perfectly still when she whipped around to catch them.

Claire pushed open the gate near the rear of the cemetery. The moon lit up the headstones like rows of aged teeth. There were few sounds of note, yet the grounds were not quiet. Perhaps it was the occasional car that motored in the distance, or the airplanes jetting out of sight beyond the clouds, or maybe the buzz of trembling spirits.

She walked along effortlessly, momentarily considering that she was the lone ghost haunting the graveyard, which made some sense, when considering the reversing of the worlds. That suited her fine. It was not the fear of running into the waking dead so much as the wandering living. She would be petrified much more if she were to turn the corner and confront another midnight loper. At least as ghosts, there was a sense of belonging. Still she moved carefully down the rows, focused on staying on the path, and not treading over anyone's designated resting space.

While Claire was relieved to be the only person in the cemetery, it did strike her as fascinating. Out of the billions of people in the world, she was the only one in this moment about to approach Vincent van Gogh's grave. Surely that thought must have crossed somebody else's mind in tandem. It seemed as though it were a sociological impossibility to move through such a well-traveled cultural phenomena alone. But here she was, standing before the headstones of the Van Gogh brothers as though she were the only person on earth who cared.

Claire knelt down at the foot of Vincent's grave. The ivy shivered in the breeze. She hugged her arms to her chest for warmth, watching the steam of her own breath form under the moonlight.

This was the moment of vindication. The moment in which she could lean forward with a whisper to say, *I know what happened. Even more so than you. I have learned of the proof. And trust me, you are not what they say you are,* and then lean over toward Theo's plot and nod, *And I suspect you knew this too. There is nothing that you could have done.*

She wanted to preserve this moment. Melt it deep into her pores until it became part of the very lifeblood. And yes, it was inexplicable to the likes of Paul Chambers that one could sit here at the foot of a man's grave, surrounded by the souls of so many other generations, and for the first time see your protagonist beyond a theory or a product or a shapeable narrative, instead seeing him as a person who deserves to know the truth of his own life.

If she had to, Claire was willing to sit at the foot of the graves all night. Sharing the sense of liberation that a truth uncovered always brings, even if it is cobwebbed and dusty.

Tomorrow morning she would rise, willing to accept that she must return to New England at Ron Bernard's behest. There was no point in waiting any longer to go deal with the legal issues there, and in her head she still thinks *there* and not *home*, because she no longer sees Providence as anything other than a place where her dog and her things are housed. She knows she will have to pay the penalty fee on her return ticket in order to take the first available flight out of De Gaulle. And she can picture Isabelle kindly driving her to the *gare* in Méry-sur-Oise while Philippe is already off to work, and Claire has still not had the chance to wish him a happy birthday. Isabelle will ask if Claire got the chance to meet Dan Gould, and Claire will not lie, but she will skirt the issue. She and Isabelle will hug at the train station, and as her lips graze each of Isabelle's cheeks, Claire will savor the warmth. Soon she will be shaking and sweating, realizing that the life that she had said goodbye to on that snowy Providence morning is indeed still there, only now larger and more beastlike. She knows it will feel strange to greet Richard. On the one hand it should seem as though they should fall into an embrace, realizing their need for each other and the ridiculousness of their separation, much in the same way that a large-scale catastrophe makes the smaller details seem so petty. And yet despite how close they have become, it seems as impossible to imagine a life with him again as it is to have imagined a life ever lived with him at all. Her only certainty is that tomorrow will not be the future, rather an extension of the present.

But for the balance of the evening, she remained before Vincent's grave, growing more and more determined to find a way to let Dan Gould allow her to tell her story, in order to vindicate the painter. She would talk with him in the morning. Convince him that it was not only safe to allow her to reveal his findings, but mostly that it was the right thing to do. They had to show that Van Gogh, a man whose life had been guided by accidents of grand proportions, had taken a final stumble that caused the final days of his life to be manipulated and stolen by the greed of another man. Regardless of Paul Chambers's avaricious intentions, they owed Vincent that much.

For a single moment, she turned her head to the left and looked off into the night where stood the wheat fields, a five-minute path to the very crossroads that Vincent painted, where he seemingly couldn't face the choice.

Claire imagined herself at the same point. Only for now she was choosing a direction.

Day Four

The next morning went as she had imagined. Isabelle graciously had offered to escort her to the train station after Philippe left for work and while Françoise cleaned. Claire had brought her bag down to the landing by the stairs, where a dutiful Françoise had been instructed to place it in the car while Claire went back upstairs for a last-minute survey of the room.

As she came down the stairs Dan Gould brisked past her on his way up to his room. He did not make eye contact, drawing his stare away in an oddly dramatic fashion that only further served to bring him attention. He pulled his arms in tight, as if to avoid any accidental touch, or even acknowledge that they shared the same space. "Can we talk?" she asked. "Please. I am on my way out, and I'd . . ."

He stopped at the last step. "I don't know," he said. "I don't know."

"Please."

"I have already said too much. I know I have. Much too much."

Isabelle called from the dining room. "Claire? It is time we must have to go. I do not want for you to be late for your train. And please do not let me forget a message I have for you. Always a message for you."

"One moment," Claire answered back. "I'll be right there." Turning back up to Dan Gould, she said, "Please, Dan. Give me a minute before I go. Just a minute, please."

"I know what you are going to ask." He shook his head back and forth, wiping the back of his hand against his mouth. "I know what you are going to ask. I knew it as soon as I told you at the restaurant yesterday. Knew it as soon as I was done talking."

"We have no choice."

He looked up toward his room, and then back to Claire. He barked out in a whisper, "I can't. I told you I can't afford the consequences."

"Please hear me out."

Isabelle called up again. "We are losing our time."

"I knew I shouldn't have told you. I went to bed . . . And I just knew I should have paid better attention to what I was . . ."

"Well, let's turn it into something positive. Make it a good thing. Let's." She had never felt herself be so aggressive about not letting something drop.

"You don't understand."

"At least give me your phone number so we can discuss this further. There are ways to get information out that are not as devastating as you think. I know these things. Believe me. At least your number. At least we should talk this out when we are both back home. Away from the drama of the moment."

It wasn't clear if Gould acquiesced from understanding or to end the conversation, but he took a step down the stairs. "I don't have a pen," he said. "I don't have one. I never carry them on me."

Claire took one from her purse. She handed it to him with her old Air France ticket folder, which was still in her coat pocket. "When will you be back?"

"Day after tomorrow." He didn't look up, trying to steady the paper enough to write down his information. "Here, okay? It's my home number. Not my work number. My home number. I can't have any of this conversation nearing my work. You understand? Promise? . . . I don't know that I want to talk with you anymore. I don't want to be involved." He handed her the folder and pen, watching her push it all into her coat pocket before turning around without saying good-bye.

At least he actually had done that much.

❦   ❦   ❦

THEY ARRIVED AS THE TRAIN was pulling up to the platform. Isabelle grabbed her guest's bag and ran off to hold the train, while Claire stopped to hurriedly purchase her ticket. Isabelle was braced in the doorway of the commuter car, keeping the doors from closing under the rueful eye of a conductor too complacent to do anything but stare disdainfully.

They hugged quickly in the doorway, and as Claire turned to head up the steps, Isabelle called out to her, "Claire, *arrêtez*. Stop. There is the note, here. The message."

Claire thanked her, and tucked the message into her palm. Again they hugged. The train pulled out of the Méry-sur-Oise station in a slow grind, before soon hitting full speed. She waved to Isabelle out the window. She had the sensation that it would be a long time before she saw her again. It was Lauren's blue eyes all over, staring at her through the fogging window, as Claire had stood on the platform and watched the train pull away. The intense sadness in Lauren's watery eyes had tried to be hopeful. But they both had looked away at the last minute, knowing they likely would never see each other again.

Once settled in her seat Claire unfolded the Mailgram. Of course it was from Richard, simply congratulating her on the information she'd gotten from Dan Gould. He also had told Bernard that she would be home soon, and he looked forward to seeing her, but wished he knew when she was arriving.

> *But regarding your discovery, go slowly. I know how you tend to run with things. But be careful with this guy. It sounds like he could retreat just as easily. Just felt like I should say that.—R.*

She smiled at his concern, and then put the note into her pocket, where it sat against his last message, which she still had been carrying. Pushing her bag away from her feet, thoroughly exhausted while still overly enthused, she reached into her pocket to look at Dan Gould's contact information.

She looked at both sides of the Air France folder. Son of a bitch. There were no numbers. Just a single sentence near the bottom of the back asking that he be left alone, followed by the word *Sorry*!, capped by an exclamation point.

In less than a second she knew that she had lost Gould. She had played witness to her own stupidity in trusting that he understood the obligation of sharing his work. She should have known that something was amiss the moment she had seen him scurry up the stairs without a good-bye.

Claire didn't feel as though she had the time to be devastated. She scrambled though her pocket for her pen, trying to reconstruct all of Dan Gould's information from an exhausted memory. *Gas chromatography. Thermal conductivity. Mass flow dependant detectors. Organic compounds that compose the colors. The consistency of saffron in the yellows, same as the forged Cézannes* (he couldn't be more specific?). *Building regional colors. Gel electrophoresis. Macromolecules, proteins, physical properties. Microscopic paint chip analysis. Spectroscopy. X-radiography. Electromagnetic spectrum. K_2CrO_4. Or was it K_3CrO_6? Yellow precipitate. Layered paints. Premixed paints.* She didn't even know what she was writing, only cataloging all the vaguely familiar terms that Gould had used in his technical explanations. It was like stringing together consonants with no vowels. If she could keep some of Gould's process in her head, then she could certainly find a chemist at the university who could put it all in the proper context. From there, she could tie in the historical aspects that would support and complement the data. It certainly would be enough to support a theory. At least enough to get the ball rolling. Her stomach turned hard, and her breath lodged into her chest. All she could do was close her eyes, and hope that sleep would retrieve what she had once known.

PART THREE

Six Days

in

Four Weeks

Mikey hasn't worked here for a month. It started with him joining a band, then trying to write poetry; now he is gone somewhere living off his parents' dough trying to write a book. All for a girl, of course. Off to impress her by being the artiste. Turned out that the girl he wanted wasn't as impressed by his reciting of smart things; she wanted him to be someone who did the stuff that people say smart things about. So he's off. Crazy part is that girl will be gone before he figures out what he is doing. You and I are both old enough to know what I'm talking about. It all seems so concentrated when you're young."

Claire stood in the lobby of the Ocean Front Motel. She was inquiring at the desk about a student of hers who had worked there while he finished graduate school. The last leg of the flight from Philadelphia into Providence had been especially exhausting. Following a three-hour layover, there had been a mechanical delay of some sort, the kind that is never fully shared. Then, according to the pilot, they had lost their place in line for takeoff and ended up sitting on the tarmac for an extra hour with a noxious odor that blew pungently through the cabin. It seemed as if it took nearly as long to get from Philly to Providence as it did to get from France to the United States.

She had landed in Providence tired and exhausted. The realization of not having Dan Gould's support or permission drove out all her enthusiasm. She knew that she could track him down, but at least for now, his position on the matter was obvious. And yes, he likely would come around to see his responsibility, but that could take years; enough time would need to pass until he felt as though he had nothing to lose by jeopardizing his career. Maybe Bill Harrison was right—she just needed to write the story because it was too important not to write it. Gould would be protected, legally and publicly. He would only be a casualty in his own imagination.

On the return flight she had sunk into a deep sadness. For a brief moment, Claire had almost believed that she could reenter her life with a newfound distance, able to have gained some perspective on the accident. But the moment that the plane departed from the Philadelphia airport, Claire again was overtaken by the dread that she was flying to a home that no longer welcomed her. By the time she had landed, Claire was too distraught to phone Richard. She needed one last pause before reentering the drama of her life.

Claire chose the Ocean Front Motel because Mike Wilson worked there. She had been his thesis advisor in the graduate program. Extremely loyal to her, he had researched tirelessly on her behalf on numerous projects, and last year, Mike had even made a daily trek into Providence to walk Cocoa and sit with her while his professor was at a four-day conference. He would be respectful of her need to ease back into the fray. If her name was as criminal as Richard had led her to believe, then she just needed a private respite in order to gather the strength to hold herself together, all for the next phase. Mike would have offered a sense of something familiar, yet still allowed the anonymity, giving just enough time to settle back in. But Mike was gone.

She didn't respond to the desk clerk, merely took out her credit card.

"How long do you plan on staying?"

She shook her head. "Not sure."

"Got a ballpark?"

"Excuse me?"

"A rough estimate. An idea. We work on reservations here, you know. I just need to know so I don't get you into a room that you'll get booted from in another night or two. I just need to know. It's the reservations. We work on them here."

Claire felt a little flustered. Still she managed a smile. "I am sorry. I'm just a bit tired. It was a long flight. Maybe two days for the room will do. Maybe a bit more. I guess it could be just one. Can we just start with one?"

"Fine with me. But I can't promise an open room the next night. Can't promise you what you don't reserve."

She said she understood, even though it was hard to understand his concern. It was hard to imagine that there were any other guests at the motel.

The clerk put on his glasses and shifted the lanyard back behind his neck. He still squinted behind the lenses, balling up his thin face, the desk lamp highlighting his corroded, pasty skin. He gave her a registration card to fill out, looking out the window as she filled it out, and told her she just needed to write down her name, and then he'd take a credit card number. "First time in Providence?" he asked.

"No," she said quietly.

"Shoot, that's right. You know Mikey. How do you know him again?"

She paused. "I helped him with a project once for school."

"Well, I hope he doesn't give up on college for a girl, you know what I'm saying. He's a bright kid who doesn't quite know it." He placed his index finger against his temple. "Mikey's got them stuffed up here. Brains and more of them. As long as it doesn't go to mush is what I am saying. That's all I'm saying."

"It will pass, I'm sure. Kids like him go through these kinds of phases."

"Speaking of the boy, I suppose you've heard about that teacher of his out at the college."

Claire didn't move.

"Hit a kid, and then fled from the country. Gone. Or something like that. Been all over the news this past week. But it wasn't just any kid she hit. Shouldn't mess with Fletcher Kennealy's family. Not in this town anyway. Accident happened a goddamn month ago, and this is the first we're hearing about it. That's classic Kennealy for you. If the old man still has the *cajones*, then somebody better look the *F* out. Fletcher Kennealy might have been forgotten about in this area these days, but I guarantee you that he still means something to the old-timers. And man does he know them all."

"I've been away for a while." She handed him her credit card and watched him swipe it through the machine. Either he didn't look carefully at her information, or he just wasn't making the connection to her name. Mostly, it seemed, he was more interested in chatting than working. She tried not to appear too conspicuous, but felt her palms break a sweat in anticipation of probably being recognized, and then seen as the villain that she was. Or was she? If only Mike would come to his senses in the next five minutes and return to the front desk from wherever he was. "I am not up on all the news," she said. "Not up on it all."

"Well, it's definitely the story around here these days. You know how they do that, those local news people. Beat one thing to death. And they are all looking for the angle. Something new to say. Of course they don't have much, since she's not even in town."

The clerk offered to assist Claire to her room. She turned her back quickly and grabbed her bag, latching her index finger around the key. "It's all right," she said. "Thank you though."

"Checkout time is eleven, whichever day you decide to leave. And just so you know, I clean the rooms promptly by eleven-thirty. I don't like things lingering."

"Got it."

"So if you need anything you just call on me. Press the zero is how you'll reach me. If somebody else answers, just ask them for Tommy. Zero for Tommy."

She thanked him again and walked out of the lobby, pushing the glass door open with her foot. The ache in her knee still lingered.

The motel was a relic from the days of road-wearied tourists in search of motor inns. In its heyday it likely had been a stop for travelers heading up to the Cape, long before I-95 had eased the journey into a simple day trip from Providence. The building stretched long and unnoticeably on each side of the office, winging out with ten rooms per section, and then stopping at a vending machine that practically butted up to the room behind it, blocking off part of the window. A set of stairs took you up to a second floor that replicated the ground level. Although it was named the Ocean Front Motel, in fact it really looked out over a stretch of I-95, just before the highway offered the option to break toward Cape Cod or to continue northward to Boston. Across the highway sat the Providence River harbor, a disregarded memory of more prosperous industry, now looking lonely, awkwardly still and forgotten. Claire stood on the balcony, staring out over those waters that would pass through the hurricane barrier, eventually filling a series of upscale bays, and then becoming lost into the Atlantic. She gripped the railing. It occurred to her that this motel was built with the same 1960s mass design as the Lorraine Motel in Memphis, where Martin Luther King Jr. also stood on the second level, unaware that a bullet was bursting across the sky.

The room was as expected. A thin carpet, worn by the door, lay in a muted color that could not be named. The bedspread was patterned in random colorful shapes, thick and stiff when she tried to move it. Opposite the bed stood a small blond desk, and above it a television was bolted to the wall. A framed seascape hung over the bed, thick in faded oils, with identically precise seagulls cresting the waves. It was for this very reason that she used to travel with small reproductions of masterworks, to temporarily cover the hotel pieces during her stays. It had started when she was a child. Her father, who loathed being in nature, considered a string of budget motels to be the family camping trip. He was the one who taped *National Geographic* pages over the framed pictures, as though simulating outdoorsmanship. Any night in the Motel 6 could be a different part of the world. It was one of her few memories of laughing with her father, as they carefully chose each night's theme.

She might have taken the seascape down and placed it in the closet, were it not permanently fastened.

Claire sat up on the bed, holding her legs against her chest. Just being in the vicinity of her so-called home made it impossible to breathe. She had to instruct herself to inhale, hold in the breath, and then exhale, until, like a stubborn motor, it finally caught on its own. This was her minimum security holding cell. The place to sit and wait out the future, safely sequestered from the rest of the world.

She then reached into her pocket to read her reconstructed notes of Gould's discovery. There was a slight pang of hope knowing that at least she had had the fortune to witness the raw truth in Auvers. The flattening of time on the airplane, coupled with the bureaucratic maelstrom of the flight delay, had made last night at the cemetery seem as though it were another era of her life. Still the deviousness was present. She read the notes twice, trying to integrate them into a unified theory, and then reached for her pen, drawing lines between various terms, hoping to map them together, as though this exercise would reignite the memories that already seemed to be fading. She stopped when she realized that she was only organizing and reordering the facts with the same mechanical distance as the typewriter arranges letters into words.

A semitruck lumbered down I-95, banging its load, followed by a ghostly rattle of chains that threw out sparks along the macadam. It seemed almost impossible to imagine that the borders of her town stood in that darkness. Her professional marks were made within those frontiers. Her collapse into love and its commitments, and her collapse right out of it. And out across the harbor, Route 111 surely looked exactly as it had that very night of the accident. A trail of cars inching along in pulsating brake lights. By now that section of road betrayed no trace of what had occurred, becoming just another part of the lore of spilled blood in the region. How many people must pass that spot hourly without ever contemplating the tragedy that happened there? Do they get some kind of sense? Is there a tingling? A cold sensation? It is almost impossible that there could be such a cataclysmic event that would unearth the very foundation of a world, yet leave no resonance.

Claire slipped off her pants and unbuttoned her blouse, leaving just her T-shirt on. Both discarded items formed a familiar pile beside the bed. She pulled back the heavy comforter and tucked her body under its weight, secured by the tight sheets. For a few minutes she stared up at the blank television screen. The concave glass, heavy green and almost black, brought a slight luminescence to the darkened room.

Claire closed her eyes and let herself fall into a light sleep, tucked in comfortably by the truths still lingering in her head.

۞   ۞   ۞

SHE DREAMT THAT THERE WAS a wake for her. All the students she had ever taught were milling through her living room, animating about as though there was no influence of time and era. But ascending from the top of the stairs came Ronnie Kennealy. He stared out with the exact same expression as he had through the windshield. He stopped on the third step and looked out over the room. She looked away for just a split second, distracted by someone's laughter and an acoustic guitar player, but in that second Ronnie Kennealy had turned around to go back upstairs.

The dream woke her in the middle of the night. Her head ached, and her skin felt as though it would jump from fright. For some reason, she whispered out loud, "Truth is not proprietary." She spoke it aloud again, and then looked for a pen to write the phrase down. The room was dark as she patted her hand around the nightstand. She knocked her hand against the lamp. Finally giving up, she closed her eyes, chanting *Truth is not proprietary* over and over to take her back into sleep.

TUESDAY

It was cold the next morning. The cloud cover had gone, leaving a clear sky that rustled bitter Arctic winds blowing down from the north. Claire stood at the base of the stairs, staring into the candy machine. A package of miniature cookies would probably suffice for breakfast back in the room. She just needed some food in her stomach to find the strength to call Richard.

"Breakfast time, eh?" Tommy approached her from the side. It was as though he had been waiting for her. He looked more weathered in the daylight. The contrast of shadows deepened the crags in his face and brought out the artifice of the red in his hair. "You know there's a donut shop right up the street a bit, and just over the bridge is one those fancy coffee places. Don't have to cook out of a vending machine." He looked back to the window inches behind him. She turned around, following his glance, but only saw rustling curtains through the partially open glass.

She was fine, she said, hoping he would be on his way. He seemed shiftier than before, looking at her cockeyed and strange.

As if reading her mind, Tommy gestured to leave. "Oh," he said stopping. "You might like to know this. Old Mikey called."

She said, "Is that right?" She wanted to move this along quickly. "That's great."

"First he was in Knoxville, Tennessee, and then on to Asheville, North Carolina, but then he ended up following that girl all the way up to Chicago. Said he wanted me to tell you that he was spending a lot of time at the Art Institute there." He paused and looked as if he were fighting for memory. "He said to tell you that he saw the *Self-Portrait* there yesterday. Said you would know what that means. The *Self-Portrait*, I mean. Seeing it there."

She didn't know what to say. She started to fumble a response but swallowed back her words.

Tommy stepped to the side, leaving her feeling exposed. "What made you come back, Miss Andrews? And why are you sneaking into a motel just miles from your house?"

"It's more complicated than you—"

"You hiding from something? Something you trying to keep from view?"

"I don't need to—"

"You must have an answer."

Tommy looked back once more. Again, Claire followed his eyes. This time she saw the chrome reflection of a video camera being operated by a large woman silhouetted behind the curtain, who quickly tried to hide. "You son of a—" she said.

"Oh, come on now," he blurted out. "We all need to make a buck. Just give me something I can sell to the TV news or one of those true crime shows. Come on now. Have a little heart. Just trying to earn a little something extra here to make up for all these empty rooms. You must be able to appreciate that."

Claire stormed away. She stumbled on the first step and took hold of the railing. Pulling herself up felt as though it took minutes between each stair. She didn't break her focus long enough in order to hear Tommy saying, "Come on now, it's not going to hurt you just to give me a little something. Times are tough these days." She slammed the door behind her and bolted the lock. Then she drew the curtains and squatted down in front of the desk. She could still hear Tommy calling out to her. "So I guess you're not hungry for breakfast anymore, are you, Miss Andrews?"

♕ ♕ ♕

RICHARD SOUNDED MUCH CALMER THAN she had expected. There was no reaction to not being called the moment she had landed in Providence. In fact, he sounded as relieved by her voice as she was by his. "Don't worry," he said matter-of-factly. "I'll come get you right now, with Cocoa. But for the meanwhile, turn on the TV set. Pack your clothes. Don't give them anything to talk about. I can't imagine there is really any money for him in calling the press, but if he does . . . And if they get there before I do . . . Don't give them anything to talk about." On the way over he would call Ron Bernard to alert him to everything, and see if they needed to meet right away. Bernard had been engaged in legal maneuvering that Richard did not quite understand, only that Bernard felt hamstrung without her here. "I guess I'll bring you home after that?" he asked, stumbling a bit on the word *home*.

"I am just having a hard time, Richard." She paused for a moment. "A really difficult time."

He was silent.

"Can you just make all the plans for me, Richard? Just tell me and I'll be there. Because I swear to God . . . I just need you to tell me, Richard. I thought I could handle this. Thought it would all work toward . . . meaning, resolution, but . . . It's just . . . I can't . . . Because I have to wake up again tomorrow and have a whole new day full of thoughts that all just bring me back to the same place. Please just tell me what to do, Richard."

Claire didn't realize how loud she had been until she stopped talking, similar to her apologia to the class about Van Gogh on the afternoon of the accident. Her words rang off the white motel walls, chiming and metallic, vibrating in place against a dead stillness in the room. It was as though she had hit a shrill note that quietly destroyed everything in its path. She wasn't even sure that Richard was still on the other end. She didn't even hear breathing. "Richard, are you there?"

He swallowed while muttering a perfunctory reply, the kind that does little other than to dispel concerns of mortality.

Claire bit down on her upper lip, drawing in a long breath through her nose, while her chest heaved, fighting for air and stability. She hated crying. She hated the loss of control and the misdirected emotion that broke loose as though an impatient stowaway. She never felt good after crying. For her whole life she'd heard girlfriends talk about needing a good cry to purge overwhelming emotions, but for Claire it was only a letdown. It was as though her entire sense of being would surrender itself empty-handed to an outburst that offered no conclusion. Whatever she cried about today, she knew she would likely be crying about tomorrow.

Following his advice, she flicked on the television with the remote. Then she sat herself up on the edge of the bed, below the seascape portrait, swallowing her words, digging her nails into her thigh. Praying that Richard would start talking so she wouldn't have to speak, because even the uttering of more than a single syllable would break her apart.

Q   Q   Q

IN THE PIT OF HER stomach, where things that have no anatomical names swirl and churn, Claire is always complicit. It is the stirring of the guilty, the conscience personified. She feels it sitting in this motel room, baggaged by the silence of the phone, her fingers edging the document, guarded by a vigilantly loyal desk clerk who stands at his post with his own brand of guilt over keeping the secret. In Richard's voice she senses an ally but now wonders if he is not out to protect the innocent, but rather committed to freeing the guilty. He doesn't say that. He would never say that. But his manners suggest that he is trying to safeguard her instead of assist her.

Less than twenty-four hours of being home has shamed her. From the way that Tommy talked about her when he didn't know it was she, to the greedy deception once he did know. It is the true model of the behaviorists. Treat somebody a certain way long enough with the appropriate amount of reinforcers, and she will become that person.

From a legal and intellectual standpoint, Claire understands how she can be innocent. She knows that she is part of a collision in a moving target of chance. Where billions of moments are always crossing and intersecting with an equal number of variables. But no system is perfect. It is percentages. A gamble. The random chance that two autonomous moments may slam into each other. Sometimes it advances the species. Other times it destroys it. But isn't it that miracle of chaos that created the world?

Still Claire sensed that there always must be fault. And in her most emotional state she will believe it. The feeling will continue to build and balloon inside her. The battle will be with her cognitive side. She understands the truths. She can intellectualize the context. But she also understands that emotions almost always reign as the victor. Isn't that the heart of both murder and passion?

Q   Q   Q

CLAIRE MANAGED TO KEEP FROM crying. Richard instructed her that he would be there as soon as possible, and she mustered enough strength to tell him that he should park at the bottom of the stairs near the vending machine. A quick honk, and she would come running down the stairs.

She lay down on the bed and stared up at the ceiling, a strange moment of unaffected peace, the way that soldiers must feel the night before they prepare to leave for battle. She felt too paralyzed to move. The white noise of the television played low in the background.

She might have been floating.

She wished she were.

She listened for noises around the room, trying to hear if there were footsteps treading along the landing, or whispers outside her window. Every car from the freeway sounded as if it were idling beneath her room.

Then she recognized the Accord's horn blaring.

How did he get there so quickly? She wasn't even packed.

The engine rumbled at the bottom of the stairs. Claire could imagine Richard stretching his neck in all directions, trying to guess from which door she would emerge. Claire scooped up the stray clothes from the floor and shoved them into her bag, sadly confusing the dirty with the clean.

Richard beeped again. She thought she heard the car door open, followed by the subtle ticking of FM radio drums. His panic slowed her down, as though he had taken the bulk of the weight. Knowing Richard was there already reduced her anxiety.

In the bathroom, while she gathered her toothbrush and toothpaste and dumped them into her makeup bag, she stopped for a moment to take out her brush. She stood before the mirror, combing the bristles through her hair, strangely compelled to primp for Richard. She slowed herself down. Light gentle strokes that would bring some shape to the tresses, as well as a sense of life and body. She watched herself in the mirror as though the reflection were another person. She admired the poise and delicacy in which she comported herself, a graceful yet confident femininity. She smiled once, only to have the smile returned. Then she stuck out her tongue, and followed it with an exaggerated face that feigned shock and surprise.

After one last swoop along the bangs, she jammed her brush into her case, grabbed her bag near the door, and rushed out to meet him.

He shouldn't have looked any different. Standing at the bottom of the stairs as she had suspected, he was glancing around, seemingly unaware that she was coming down toward him. Although only one week had passed, Richard did look brighter. Yes, he still had the same lanky frame that was covered by layers of thrift store jackets hunkering down atop one another, and yes he still moved in contradictory patterns between jittery and languid, and yes his hair was still graying in the same spots with the same hapless locks sticking out in fashionable apprehension, but there was a grace about him that she hadn't noticed since they had first met at that Somerville party. A way in which he seemed to surf the gravitational pull of the earth and keep balance while the ball spun slightly off center. She wanted to just stand and ingest that, because in a matter of minutes it would all fall victim to the practicalities. Richard's frantic nature to minimize conflict would soon take over, as would her visceral reactions—again spinning them into the minutiae that made it so hard for them to remember that they had once only loved each other so simply.

Richard looked up, startled. "Oh Jesus," he said. "I didn't even see you there." He walked toward her as though to hug her, shoulders hunched. She let herself fall against him, so fragile that even the slightest bit of muscle might crush her.

So far, there was no sign of anybody else in the parking lot.

"Let me help you with your bag," he said. "Here. Let me, now."

"I'm fine, Richard." She waved him back, afraid of tears. "Just go open the trunk, please."

He surveyed the area in a deliberate manner, and then walked over to the driver's-side door to unlatch the trunk. He heaved her suitcase into the back, instructing her to get into the car quickly. "Anything else?" he asked.

"Where is Cocoa?"

"I left her home to guard the house."

"Cocoa?"

Once they drove out of the parking lot she would learn that a reporter had stopped Richard outside of the home just as Cocoa was shitting on the neighbor's lawn, asking if it was true that Claire was back in town. That was the word from a source at the airport. The goddamn reporter even bent over with Richard as he scooped the crap into the orange plastic bag from the reporter's own paper. "They are vicious," Richard told Claire. He wouldn't put it past a single one to trail him all over town.

Within three miles of the motel, two different cars had pulled side by side with them. Both times she slumped down, feeling her heart stop until she saw the chrome reflection pass by from the corner of her eye.

They drove for about fifteen minutes on a frontage road, trying to avoid a backup on the freeway. "Can you believe that asshole?" Claire said. "Can you believe the fucking nerve?"

"It's what everybody is talking about here, Claire. The story has really blown up."

"But the goddamn nerve of him to try to tape me . . . Is that even legal? You can't just go around secretly taping a person. You can't just do that."

"I am telling you, Claire. There has been a camera pointed at the house at any given moment for the past day and a half. They even snapped photos of Cocoa."

"Turn around," she said.

"Claire—"

"Turn around . . . This isn't right . . . Turn around!"

"Claire." He was visibly nervous. "Don't bring unnecessary attention to—"

"Richard, please."

"Okay . . . All right . . . But we leave immediately if there is any sign of a reporter around."

"Fine . . . This is still my home!"

He pulled off the road without a blinker and made a quick U-turn just before the on ramp. He had always been quick to acquiesce. The sudden turning was exhilarating in a way, lending a definitive air to the supposed cat-and-mouse chase. And there might have been a sense of victory had another car been present for miles in either direction, or even the caricature of a reporter left along the roadside, shaking his fist doggonnit as he disappeared into the rearview mirror. Instead, theirs was only one more car turning around because of some unfinished business.

They pulled back into the Ocean Front's empty parking lot. From the fresh perspective it looked more desolate, in the same way that returning to the scene of a grand childhood experience only finds it smaller and more dilapidated than in the memory.

Richard parked by the stairs. Claire asked him where the hell was he going. "The office is over there," she pointed.

He backed the car out and moved it down five spaces.

Claire said, "I'll be right back." She left the car door partway open.

The office was locked. Claire pushed at the door three times, barely rattling the frame. "Son of a bitch," she yelled, and then looked back to the car, hoping Richard hadn't heard her. She wanted to appear collected around him. Claire took a deep breath in order to keep her body from exploding. She was infuriated by the whole series of circumstances that had brought her to this moment standing helplessly in the parking lot of the Ocean Front

Motel at the mercy of a crusty career desk clerk named Tommy. This should have been just another normal winter break where she is relieved temporarily from the pressures of the classroom, and fully engaged in the writing and research that she loves. Instead she has been turned into a haunted wrecking ball.

She glanced back to Richard again. His eyes were glued to the rear-view mirror as he patrolled the entrance and the exit behind him. She looked over toward the steps, and let her eyes follow up each stair. It was as vacant as she had left it. Other than a couple of truckers, she had to have been the only other person who had stayed at the motel last night. Maybe in the last month. Tommy did say he needed the money. But why was she supposed to understand and then comply?

Claire tried the door once more. She pressed the night buzzer several times in a row, to no avail. Richard caught her eye, and raised his hands. He wasn't gesturing resignation, he just wanted to know what was going on.

Claire ignored him and pushed the buzzer once more. A woman nearly three times the width of Tommy stumbled out from a door behind the desk. Almost certainly the woman with the camera. She was bleary eyed, with her lips drawn into a scowl. She rubbed the corners of her mouth, as though wiping off uncontrollable sleep drool, and then pushed back her hair, which didn't move. She wore a long muumuu that appeared to be thrown on just prior to coming out, with her feet jammed into flip-flops. She pushed open the door uninvitingly. "Help you?" she spoke, partly blocking the entrance.

Claire said, "I need to talk to Tommy." Did that actually role off her lips so easily?

"Not available."

"Look . . ."

The woman shrugged. "Not available. Just missed him by about five minutes."

"You know what the hell this is about. I want that videotape you took, and any other pictures that *Tommy* might have. It's against the law. You can't just go filming people without them knowing it."

The woman considered the statement. Looked at Claire. Then back to the room behind the desk. There was the faint chatter of the television seeping out, along with the smell of stale smoke. "Why don't you write down your name and number, and Tommy will call when he's available."

Claire sucked in a deep breath, hoping to calm herself. She tried to sound rational. "Please." Her eyes started to well. "It's just not right," she said. "I just want the tape. It's my life. You must understand. I just want the tape."

The woman looked at her, nodding her head. "So, you going to leave a message or not?"

Claire could hardly speak.

"Suit yourself." The woman turned around and walked back, as disinterested as when she had entered.

Claire headed slowly to the car. She slumped into the seat. "Let's go," she said.

"No luck?"

"Can we just go?"

Richard knew better than to speak. Claire stared out the window at the decaying roadside, made even more desperate by winter's extinguishment of nearly all plant life. Her stomach was knotted. She tried to keep thinking in order to keep from crying. She wished they could drive around forever. Head up north like they did in the early days. Drive and talk and forget about what brought them together. Keep moving until it was safe enough to stop. And one thing she knew was that it would never be in Providence. That would never feel safe again.

🜍   🜍   🜍

RICHARD TOOK I-95, bypassing downtown. "Didn't you say that we needed to go to Ron Bernard's?" Claire asked. "I thought you said that. On the phone, you said that."

"I spoke with him by phone. That's why I was late."

"You were late?"

"Because I was on the phone I was late. With Bernard. That was what made me late."

Richard looked over his shoulder to change lanes. Then he switched back again.

Claire said, "So we don't need to go?"

"He said there was no reason to come in, just to know that he is most worried about the huge public interest in this situation. Fletcher Kennealy has managed to pull every string he has left in this town in order to make this case a public issue, blowing Bernard's strategy ass-back against the fence."

"Did he say what to do? What does he suggest?"

"He thinks that there is very little that can be done without further fanning the flames. Any reaction only gives the story life. As he pointed out, not reacting even fanned the flames. He made that point. 'Vintage Kennealy,' Bernard kept saying. 'Vintage Kennealy.'"

She wasn't completely sure what "vintage Kennealy" implied.

Richard looked over at her. "He said to call him if you think of anything new. He needs to anticipate. Anything will help. Is there?"

Claire tried to remain staid. She had told the police all there was to tell, and they had all the facts. It was all a blur anyway. A blink of the eye, in which certain images were captured like shadows or distant conversations. There was the woman in the Delta 88. The accountant who helped her in the car. But it all had the odd paradox of an eternal split second, where the same blurred images played over and over but without detail and precision. As unsatisfying as it must have been, she could only relay disconnected tropes. And they were no different from the ones she had already told the police, the investigators, the insurance men, and Bernard, who all tried their best to believe that someone who takes the life of another *can* be innocent because it is written into law that way.

Richard stared hard at her. "Nothing?" His tone seemed to nudge. He took his hand away.

She watched out the window. Head shaking, no. "Nothing."

Bernard also had advised to sit tight, that there was really nothing much to do until a complaint was filed. Next would be answering, discovery, and depositions. Until then, ignore the reports, no matter how painful it will seem at times, and act like everything is normal, and please oh please, don't say the words *no comment*; they have become too associated with the obviously guilty, and Kennealy is banking on you making yourself look guiltier, it only strengthens his play with the sympathy card, especially in the public eye. Let Bernard handle the press.

"So that's pretty much it," Richard said. "That's it for now."

Claire nodded that she understood. She looked away. She felt as though she might throw up.

In those final months in Auvers, Vincent might have remembered May 1889, when, after confining himself to the institution in Saint-Rémy, he wrote that he wished "to remain shut up as much for my own peace of mind as for other people's." He had sliced his ear in Arles, potentially decimated his relationship with Gauguin and the town and whoever else heard about his behavior, and consistently kept one hand on a bottle and the other holding a cigarette. It must have been more a moment of submission rather than resignation. He had failed in the outside world, and unwilling to give up his vices, decided to confine himself to a supervised life free from the world's harm. He would be managed and treated with the care of a child. He would paint furiously until, like a child, he tried to ingest the paint, at which point the professional parents removed it from his articles, and relegated him only to sketching. It is strange the deception that the calm eventually brought. The illusion that the crutches didn't exist and that he had been showing the promise to walk on his own. Perhaps it is not a marker of illusory hubris but rather the sadly compelling desire for Vincent to try to function in the world again. Maybe there is always a Gachet waiting out there, tempting you with the promise that you can lead a regular life. Craftily filling your head not with grandeur, but with one of a normalized ideal. The temptation must be extraordinary to give up peace of mind for what you believe peace of mind to be.

Cocoa looked different to her. The shape of her face strangely seemed longer and more distinct, almost as though the dog was a crafted replication that brought out the details in heroic realism. Cocoa circled Claire, sniffing at pant legs and cuffs, and then sulked into the living room with feigned disinterest, as though punishing Claire for leaving her alone for the first time. Cocoa flopped down on the rug, held her snout up high for poise, and as quickly lowered her head into her pillowed paws.

Walking into her house made Claire feel as though she were trapped in someone else's shadow, a tropism bent toward the familiar, but unable to touch anything beyond the silhouette's hard edges. She paused for a moment, admiring her home, taken by the delicacy of the early-twentieth-century moldings and the strongly seductive curvature of the archways. There was a flow through her house that ran even and balanced. No single room bore the weight of the interior; instead there was a great equanimity that gave a presence to every room, creating what felt like a living, breathing structure.

Richard was still outside. When they had approached her street, he decided to circle the block once to scout for reporters. Determining it was clear, Richard pulled into the driveway. They had both gotten out of the car feeling lucky. Then a red car appeared, commandeered by a reporter and his photographer. Claire had managed to move swiftly through the front door before they could spring into action. Richard was caught standing in the driveway, the literal version of the man left holding the bag. As she had closed the front door, Claire could hear him saying "Go away"— "Not now"—"Please let me through," and then tongue knotting the phrase *no comment*, forcing himself to comply with Bernard's specific instructions.

She walked over to where Cocoa lay at the kitchen's entrance, and knelt down to stroke the dog's head in a tender but respectably brief manner. "I'm glad to see you girl," she whispered. Claire couldn't move, leashed by Cocoa's gaze.

The kitchen still looked clean but tired. The outdated appliances, paying homage to another era, stood as a testament to the intangible relationship between inertia and adaptation. Although she had been gone for only a week, Claire was still awed by the museum quality of her kitchen. The sponge streak that had been the only prominent sign of life on that night of the accident was still pronounced in a square swirl on the countertop, as though the time had never passed.

She was jarred from thought when Richard bounded through the door. "Damn it," he declared, his voice animated in agitation. "Those guys are just impossible. Just badger the crap out of you. It's like they are trying to just wear you down, to break you until you finally cave." He stopped talking, perhaps realizing that Cocoa was his only audience member. "Claire," he called.

She heard his footsteps coming toward her.

Then she heard Cocoa rise and sniff toward Richard. Her nails tapped against the hardwoods.

"Oh, there you are," he said to Claire, impervious to any experience she might be having. "These reporters are out for their story come hell or high water. We're going to need to lay low for a day or two."

"Or just get out of this place altogether." She was still staring into the kitchen.

"I don't think that's an option right now."

A month ago he would have put his hands on her shoulders,

and excused his concerns as no measure for the poignancy of her experience. He would have deferred. Been hyperaware about her state, and reacted accordingly. But now he had become part of the experience. He no longer was the outsider who charmed compassionate sympathies. As a full-fledged member of the tragedy, his relationship to her had turned empathic, as though they now were wobbly pillared comrades who needed to brace each other to stand.

"The reporter out there—he's from the *Herald*, I think—he told me that a TV crew was on the way. He wanted an exclusive. I'll bet they are going to hound the neighbors too. The Wallers will be going crazy."

Neighbors. It seemed as though she were a million miles away from other people, the walls a numbing and isolating barrier from the rest of the world. But, that aside, Richard needn't worry. The surrounding houses were only neighbors in the most literal sense of the word. This was no real community. Other than the show of unanimity with luminarias on Halloween, these were not people who forged relationships or concerns about one another unless there was some sort of easement dispute. It was all part of the illusion of a unified earth in which everybody links arms and circles the globe twice. In truth, one could really only plan to face the world by herself. And if she were really lucky, alongside a dedicated companion.

Richard continued on about the reporters, the neighbors, and the lawyers. Claire wasn't able to hear him anymore. She only watched his face, weathered in its conviction. It was the face to fall in love with, the one that mirrors your hopes and fears but complements them with its own heart and thoughts. Why hadn't she recognized it before? Had they both just been skipping the surface so tangentially that they never even stopped to look at the other—even when they had fallen and the masks had slipped off? Claire hoped that it was due to some maturity on both their parts. She hated to think it had taken the accident for them finally to see each other.

They say that dogs recognize the natural disaster before it is about to strike, and it is through that same instinct that they dedicate themselves to the comfort of those who guide them. Cocoa jumped up on Claire's leg and licked her hand. A soft tender slurp to emulate a human kiss, so selflessly administered. Perhaps Cocoa sensed the need to be a nursemaid to her mistress. Or maybe the dog had given up the grudge and had come to forgive her. Either way Claire could not manage her tears.

"Don't worry," she barely said. "The neighbors will fend for themselves."

She just stood there, letting Cocoa lick her hand.

She desperately wanted to collapse into Richard's arms, to let herself feel weightless and protected.

Instead she stared at him. Still burdened by her sense of fragility. But also fearful of the comfort of his touch, and the possibility of relying on something that she understood could just as easily be gone tomorrow.

THE FOLLOWING MONDAY

A week of relative quiet passed following a mid-season blizzard. In a period of forty-eight hours nearly two and a half feet of snow fell on the region. The roads were thickened into a frozen paste. Each morning found them coated with a fresh layer, as nightly flurries struck in low-grade versions, much as the aftershocks following an earthquake. Coupled with the fear and drama of being out on the roads, people retreated into their houses, children stayed home from school, and businesses operated in barebones fashion, only attending to the necessities.

This unexpected lull brought a false sense of normalcy to the Andrews home. Apparently bored by the facade of the house, the neighborhood reticence, and the overall lack of drama, the local news reporters had gone on temporary hiatus until something meatier was poised to strike (plus it seemed that every available reporter was being called back for blizzard reports). Richard had had a few back-and-forths with Ron Bernard, but in concert with the rest of the city, most everything on the legal end had shut down for a while—including any progress or news on the case. Bernard felt cautiously satisfied that the Kennealy public relations blitz had thankfully subsided. Now they could get back to managing the case based on the standards of the law. Unless Jack DiMallo made some kind of legal move in the next few days, Bernard said he would be working at home until the weather cleared. Again, he emphasized that any new revelations about that night of the accident would only help. Richard conveyed that to Claire. She didn't respond.

Without so much as a discussion, Richard had retreated back to the upstairs guest room, sleeping on the daybed in his makeshift studio. His subletter was due to vacate the Cambridge apartment at the end of the week, and although he hadn't said anything, it was assumed that Richard would leave then. It was probably easier that way for both. He would still stay involved with the case and come back up as needed, but it was hard to find a reason for him to live here any longer. She almost brought it up once. But she had been sitting on the couch at the time. The same couch where she had sat the last time he delivered his commentary on the future.

♧   ♧   ♧

RICHARD WAS STILL WORKING ON the series of the muscles of the face, having finally settled on the details and angles, but still not fully comfortable with the presence behind the drawings. In order to keep his place among the digital biomedical artists, his work had to call out a passion or experience that was not possible through the coldness of pixilated perfection. For the most part, Richard had confined himself to his room, only coming out to stretch or inquire about meals, and then quickly returning to his work, also avoiding the conversations that might spring up about the legal case, or the state of their relationship.

Claire didn't mind the quiet. If asked, she would have said that she liked the feeling of having an invisible presence in the house while maintaining a sense of solace and privacy. For better or worse, it felt comfortable having Richard there. She sat in front of the fire in her long underwear, bundled by two pairs of wool socks, and curled into her overstuffed chair that matched the couch, dedicating most of her days to sorting through her transcripts from Auvers. She still hadn't considered how she was willing to handle the information she had gathered. She hoped that her notes and interpretations would be enough to support the theory without having to involve Dan Gould anymore.

Bill Harrison had encouraged her to center the book on the revelation of Gould's discovery. He envisioned it as not only revealing Claire's theories about Gachet and his manipulations of Vincent, but also riding a thematic undercurrent that exposed the greed of the art market and the illusion of value. The structural ideas did not bother her. They made sense. But she was reluctant to poach Dan Gould's private world, despite the impact of the discovery. She was still unable to convince herself that she had the right to intrude. Bill had assured her again and again that there were no legal issues to be concerned about. He had checked with Legal. As long as she didn't name anybody directly, or make blanket allegations, she could write as freely as she wanted. Sure, it might piss a few people off, ruffle a few feathers. "But," Bill had said during their last conversation, "can you think of any artist that you truly admire that didn't piss somebody off?"

Her notebook sat on her lap, loaded with blank pages that held hardly a single sentence. She stared at the embers popping off the logs.

Her train of thought was broken when she heard Richard stumble off the last step. She turned around to see him combing his fingers through his hair and looking out the window. "Has it stopped snowing at all today?" he asked.

Claire kicked her legs off the chair. The pen rolled from her lap. "I just assumed it never stops . . . How is the drawing coming along?"

He swatted his hand through the air. "It will come along . . . I suppose." Richard held his stare out the window, as though puzzled by the notion of snow. "And your work? Freeing the *Gachet* from the deception?"

"You know what I was thinking?" she said a bit louder than she intended.

"I don't ever know what you think."

"Well, I'll tell you what I'm thinking."

"Here it comes."

"Here it comes is right." She abruptly stood, fluttering her notepad to the floor. "Let's get the hell out of here. Just take a walk through the snow. Maybe go get a cup of coffee. Anything. Let's break from this house arrest. I haven't been out of the house since I came home."

"It might not be—"

"It will be fine. We just bundle up, and nobody knows the difference through the parkas and scarves and hats. I need the fresh air, Richard. I need it. Any reporter trying to hassle us is likely at the airport interviewing stranded passengers about being stranded passengers. And you know the neighbors are all in front of their TVs. Let's just go out and kick up some snow or something. For a few minutes let's forget lawyers, facial muscles, and dead painters and their antagonists. Twenty minutes of fun is what I ask for. Twenty little minutes." She clasped her hands together, as though making a plea before the court. "Please, Your Honor, please. Twenty minutes."

Soon Richard was focusing his anxieties on finding the only scarf that was long enough to wrap his neck *and* cover his face, and within minutes they were bundled and on the front walk, ankle deep in the snow.

Outside, a sense of liberation overtook Claire. The overcast sky that normally felt trapping now opened up. The empty streets, whose only signs of life were the smoke curling out of the chimneys. Roads with nary a tire mark. Small cavernous walkways dug out of the snowdrifts were absent of footprints. Shapeless trees.

Faceless houses. The familiar all mutated and abandoned under the whitewash. It was as though it were her world alone. One with no history, or even more precise, with no definition. Unlike in Auvers-sur-Oise, there were no cultural signifiers to dissect and interpret. It was the clean canvas, of which the world she would paint would become the only world she would know.

"Man alive, it's cold," Richard said. "I swear to God that my breath is freezing up before you can even see it. Icicle words." He shook his gloved hands, trying to bring warmth to them. "It is no wonder that old people end up going to Florida. Who needs this after a while."

" 'Old people'? That's you and me in just a few years."

They had to walk single file between the snow piles. She could hear Richard prattling on about the cold and the winter. As with the often-quoted myth that the Inuits have a thousand different words for snow, Richard seemed to have an equal amount of takes on the brutality of winter. His aversion to the climate was strange, consider-ing that he had lived in it all his life, and really didn't know anything different. Claire stopped paying attention, partly from not being able to distinguish his words through his scarf and her earmuffs, but mostly from marital familiarity. It was a seasonal rant with the same predictable effects as the first snowfall that it came with.

Claire proceeded down the sidewalk, thinking cinematically about stepping out of this monochromatic purity and into the trop-ically brilliant colors of the South. It was no wonder that Van Gogh had practically pleaded with Gauguin to come down to Arles to set up the Studio of the South. He must have felt as though he had stepped into a painter's paradise, seeing colors that he probably hadn't even known existed. She was deep into imagining that transition of black-and-white to color when she felt her feet slip out from under her. It was a hopeless feeling that left her body weight-less, as though its only ability was to float up in the air just long enough before belatedly realizing it had played the fool to gravity.

Although she had landed on her hip, it was her knee that hurt. She hadn't winged out her hands enough; her torso it seemed had broken the fall. She was laid out flat along the sidewalk's trail. Snow had pushed under her shirt, numbing her lower back. Some-where she had lost a mitten, leaving her right hand stiff and brittle in the tentative but desperate search of the near-blind looking for his glasses.

Richard, who had remained a few paces behind while still jaw-ing about the injustice of winter, ran up quickly. His feet slipped side to side as he managed to keep his balance. He had her mitten in his hand and was shaking the snow dust off. He knelt down in an unpredictably calm manner and slipped the glove onto her hand. Her fingers were still freezing but grateful for the shelter. Claire, helpless and in pain, looked up. "Son of a bitch" was all she could bring herself to say. She thought she saw the face of a small boy watching her through a window across the street. When she looked again Claire did not see anything but her fallen frame reflected.

The street now revealed its true self—deceptive and brutal.

"Okay, let's get you up," he said. "What hurts right now?"

"It's my right knee. The same one as from that night." She tried to extend it, but the kneecap shot out in pain with the slightest movement. "And my left elbow doesn't feel so great either. Where are the news reporters and lawyers now?"

Richard moved in front of her, skating along the ice patch that had taken Claire down. He reached both arms across her chest, bracing his hug just beneath her armpits. "All right," he instructed. "On three I am going to lift up, and I want you to throw your full weight into me."

"I don't think I can stand on the knee."

"Just put your weight against me."

Richard steadied his heels against the snowbank. With an exhalation he burst out three, and heaved up. Claire's body pulled upward as though devoid of muscle and bodily control. She felt herself fall side to side in tandem with Richard's slipping feet, until at once she collapsed into him, feeling his heavy breath against her ear, from lungs still warm and moist.

"We made it," he whispered, between breaths. A sense of victory coated his voice. "Now let's get you back to the house."

Claire yelped, wounded as she planted her right foot, retreating it quickly. Pain shot through her knee, and up into her pelvis.

"Where does it hurt?" Richard asked.

"All I know is that the pain is blasting up and down my leg and that I can't stand on it."

"Hopefully it is not a torn calf muscle. Once those snap, the ligament just bunches into a purpled mush that just sits there . . . A pulp the size of your fist. The swelling is a painfully slow reduction that takes forever to heal."

"How on earth do you know that?"

"Do you have any idea of how many knees I have drawn over the years?"

"I think I need a carriage now, not a doctor's textbook."

She draped an arm around Richard's shoulder. Following the balance of his instructions, she leaned her full weight into him and used his body as her second leg. They turned their bodies sideways as he guided her limping gait through the small trail dug out through the sidewalk. After about ten feet Claire told him to stop. "This is ridiculous," she said. "Stupid. I can't get there like this. Hopping all the way."

Richard looked at her. Considered. Then without pause he reached down and scooped her into his arms, holding on to her like the brave soldier carrying his wounded comrade off the battlefield. He moved at a brisk pace, ignoring her pleas to put her down, that now they were both going to end up lame.

The intense cold burned her cheeks. Her nose ran just enough to form small icicles. An icy wind blew up her cuff, and if she weren't a half block from her house, she would have seen herself as the hubristically tragic protagonist in an Arctic wilderness adventure.

Richard's strength was fading. She could feel herself slipping down a bit. He jockeyed to hoist her up. "For God's sake, Richard."

He finally replied as they neared the house. Each word barely fell between breaths. When they reached the porch, he told her, he was going to have to put her down in order to open the door. "If it hurts, it will only hurt for a minute. Give me just that minute, and then we get you to the couch. Okay?"

She didn't answer. She assumed her affirmation was implied.

"Okay?" he repeated.

"Yes," Claire said. And then she enunciated louder over Richard's panting, "Yes."

Once he set her down on the couch, Richard helped her remove her wet pants. The right pant leg had stuck midthigh, the cotton refusing to move another inch past the swelling injury. In wriggling her hips side to side, Claire felt the full extent of the fall through her bottom and lower back. With her pants finally off, she felt a rush of warmth that was momentarily soothing. There was no visible bruise around her knee, but it did look double its usual size. She rolled to the side and tugged down at her panties to see her hip. It looked slightly discolored, as if in the early stages of bruising. Mostly it was her knee that was still throbbing. She wondered if she should have walked on it at all out there. Maybe it was like trying to drive on the rim when you have a flat tire. Stupidly increasing a damage that you can't take back.

Richard propped up her leg, and draped a blanket over her. He stood there, holding the sopping wet pants in his hands. Chewing on his lip. The droplets fell on his socks. "I guess this is what it takes to get your pants off again."

She tried not to smile.

"I guess this means I'll need to stay a little longer," he said.

They stared at each other.

§   §   §

SO THIS IS WHAT HAPPENS to little girls who don't eat their broccoli. As a child Claire would sit at the table, pushing the florets from one side of the plate to the other, dabbing at the fish sticks crumbs before touching a single green stem. The nightly ritual infuriated her mother, who would stand behind her, lecturing that little girls who do not eat their greens don't grow the kind of muscles that make girls pretty. Her mother's voice would be in a modulated cadence of parental importance but almost always ended up on the edge of anger. Meanwhile Claire's father would sit at the table, engaged in his own meal and the evening newspaper. She used to think he was just too tired to involve himself in the battle. Teaching high school science and coaching the boys' volleyball team up until dinnertime extracted a noticeable physical exhaustion. When she became a teenager, Claire would make the assumption that it was not exhaustion that stymied his participation, rather it was that he just didn't care about her. She would swing back to the exhaustion theory as an adult when she watched him tumble through real estate licensure and a host of other certificate programs, all in the measured cause to ease the strain of his life. Her mother never relented. Every miscalculation on Claire's part was a sign of weakness, and as her mother was so fond of saying, "Weakness is so unattractive."

Maybe that had been the attraction to Vincent. A man whose frailty not only produced beauty, but also emoted strength. But either way, it was always her own face she saw in the mirror. A hollow, delicate expression, starved into weakness, bound to fragility.

If her mother were still alive to see her now. Laid out on the couch, handing the telephone back to Richard, relaying the advice from Dr. Heddeman, who said that it sounded as if Claire had fractured the knee joint or broken the kneecap, either of which he would likely treat the same way—namely, bandaging the injured area with a strap that would hold her knee as an immobile hostage until the damage could repair itself over the next month or more. It likely was further damage to the knee she had jammed in the car accident. Don't come in to the hospital today. Driving in these weather conditions would be more cause for harm than waiting it out on the couch. Dr. Heddeman said he would phone in an order of codeine to the pharmacy on Hope Street, as the pain would likely increase with the swelling. That druggist is like the post office when it comes to doing business in all kinds of weather, and Claire should send her husband out on foot, as the roads were messy. Heddeman wanted her in within the week to check her over, maybe take some films, and fix her up, but she shouldn't consider it an emergency. A little rest certainly isn't going to harm it.

Claire lowered her head back on the throw pillow. She draped her arm to the floor, where Cocoa licked her fingertips. Her hip throbbed in opposing rhythm to the painful pulsing in her knee. She felt the invalid that she was, knowing that she would have to rely on Richard even more, but privately thankful that he was not going to leave. It was all only temporary. She knew that. There was no way that she was even going to be staying in New England after this all wrapped up. How could she? Her own street, masked in all its beauty, was no longer safe. She needed to go someplace far away. Where the sky was higher. Where she didn't have to live in shame or hiding. But until then, she was glad Richard was going to be here a little longer.

She thought she might even be able to forgive his infamous outburst.

And she thought she might even be able to forgive her reaction.

TWO MONDAYS LATER

Claire spent her time on the couch. At night she watched videos of old movies, and then read a little before bed. Richard would work all day, dash to the video store, pick up some takeout, and sit beside Claire, manning the remotes. Then he would put her to bed, help her back onto the couch in the morning, and head upstairs, not to be seen until evening. They didn't talk much. But that was okay.

The Cambridge apartment was now empty, and at one point the other day Richard had made reference to possibly staying there for one night after a scheduled meeting at Harvard. He never did. But now the possibilities really hung out there. They were best treated with silence.

Initially the codeine had made her head cloudy, but as though she had conditioned the blood brain barrier, her mind started to clear, and it was only her body that seemed to go light, giving her the illusion of normalcy. Her notebook rested on her lap. On the coffee table sat four sharpened pencils, one schoolboy eraser, and her laptop. She looked at the knee brace that Dr. Heddeman had placed there, once she finally had been able to get to his office. It was surgical green, and the thick spongy texture against her skin looked so foreign. In a way her whole body looked foreign. But soon she started to look at the wrap as though that was the only real part of her. It was her flesh that was the miracle of modern science. It occurred to her that she might not ever walk right again, forever burdened by an awkward limp, or at the very least a painful reminder when she tried to push herself beyond normal existence. Somehow it seemed fitting that her physical body should be as permanently wounded as her mind.

There wasn't anywhere for her to walk anyway. Once the storm had passed, the reporters came back. The neighbors avoided them—even the Wallers ignored Richard when they passed at the grocery store. One pizza delivery boy just stared at her, sort of dumb and angry, and the next night the kid delivering Italian food tried to snap her picture, even more blatantly than Tommy. She felt more imprisoned than ever. Afraid to pass by the window. Afraid to answer the phone. And now being immobile made her feel even more vulnerable. The need to move away and start over was that much more pressing.

She tried to pass time by working on the book. The previous week, she again had raised the issue with Bill Harrison about citing Gould's findings. Bill, trying to put her at ease, suggested that she try to contact Gould. Some weeks had passed, and maybe wiser minds would have prevailed. "See what he has to say," Bill had said. "Tell him you have thought about it, and that you are going ahead with the book, and that he can put his two cents into it if he wants. That this is his chance. If he still maintains his vigilance, then we'll talk about how to handle that. But first, see what he has to say now." Taking that advice, Claire had looked up the BCE Web site and found Dan Gould's extension and e-mail, against his wishes. She composed the rationale in her head and had then dialed the number, punched in his extension, and had even let it ring one time before she hung up, her throat parched and her forehead suddenly cold. Instead she transposed her speech into an e-mail, and sucked in a deep breath and clicked the send button. She checked her e-mail hourly for the next seven days. He never replied.

"So there you go," Bill lobbied over the phone. "I guess that is your guy's way of telling you to go ahead. He'd be blasting the shit out of you if he didn't want you to continue. You told him it would stay anonymous, RSVP with any and all concerns, et cetera, et cetera. Well, here you have it. The silent stamp of approval. Now go to it, kid. The world deserves to know this."

It still didn't make it right. The loyalty still felt abused. Yet Claire could not find a logical counterargument to halt the project. Plus Bill was right. This was about showing a truth that was bigger than any of the people involved. Herself included.

❦   ❦   ❦

WELL BEFORE DINNERTIME, RICHARD CAME down the stairs in slow modulated steps. He stood at the foot of the couch. The late afternoon sun framed him in flagrant orange. Claire completed the sentence she was writing before looking up. Partly she wanted to finish the thought, but mostly it was for the dramatics of how she would acknowledge Richard—casually surprised, treating his sudden presence as more of a draft that ruffled the edges of her notebook pages, instead of the constant state of alert she was in every time he came downstairs.

His expression looked rehearsed, as though he had been contemplating something drastic all afternoon. It was an expression that she knew.

"It looks like you have something you want to say," Claire said, as though having to give permission for Richard to speak. She braced herself, prepared that he would announce he was returning to Cambridge.

He drew in a breath. "I just got off the phone with Bernard."

"Yes?" Oddly, this came as a relief. She felt her shoulders drop.

Richard stared at her, as though her reaction was not dramatic enough. "He was served by Kennealy's lawyers. They have filed with the court, and are ready to proceed with the civil case."

"I guess now that the roads have been cleared everybody is back to work."

"The complaint is requesting one point five million dollars in damages."

"From me?"

"Mental and emotional distress."

She dropped her head into her hands. She laughed in incredulity at the figure. "They can't possibly think . . . I'd have to work the rest of my life . . ."

Richard's throat lumped as he swallowed. Claire could see there was more. Maybe this would be the point when he leaves. "Apparently there is a statement from some driver that DiMallo dug up." Richard was almost whispering. It appeared as if he might cry. "Bernard doesn't think it's much. But he wants you to look at it. He says you never know with a case like this. He's going to fax it over. He says you never know."

"They think taking money will change things? I don't under-stand this, Richard. I just don't know why they . . ."

Richard dug his hands into his pockets. He turned as if to leave but stayed in place. Shifting, uncertain of his role.

"Can you sit with me?" Claire asked. She moved her good leg over, leaving her injured knee propped on the pillow. She took his hand, and stared up at the ceiling. She turned light-headed, almost sick.

Claire dropped her head into Richard's lap. She unleashed a cry that erupted from her gut, and heaved through her chest. The one that contained all the tears gone stale from years of being pushed down and rationalized out of sight.

♧   ♧   ♧

LATELY SHE HAS FOUND HERSELF going over the accident. It is every night. Always as she is about to fall asleep. Claire reviews it, blurred frame by blurred frame. Sometimes it is hard to know if she is seeing it as it happened, or if, like a persistent storyteller, she has chosen to believe the exaggerations and missing details by accepting them as truth. She does not know anymore. She sees the untended dark, still strange from the clock being reset. The traffic. Endless pairs of red lights. There must be hundreds of houses along Route 111, but she only remembers a single Colonial. The shadow of the boy stupidly playing with his skateboard too close to the street. The traffic breaks, the stoplight hovers on yellow, and her last chance to go, but the Delta 88 tries to muscle its way in, and when Claire refuses her the driver mouths off something. There is no memory of accelerating to make the light. How long could she have taken her eyes off the road? A second? Maybe two? Isn't this *anybody's* story? There is only the quick glance at the woman in the opposing car, who has taken Claire's attention through the anger of the challenge. Even still, it is the same quick glance that taken a moment later might have saved the boy's life. The traffic investigators confirm that she is not at fault; has done nothing wrong. Nothing wrong except take the life of a child.

TUESDAY

The morning edition of the *Herald* ran a front-page feature with the headline "Two Sides of Grief." In a rare interview, Fletcher Kennealy spoke of how the news of his grandson's death had stripped him of the remaining strength that he had in a body already being eaten by age and its diseases. He had danced around some of the worst this town had to offer, seen the greats fall, and even compromised his family at times, but none of that came even close to the level of mutilation that he said he felt when his daughter-in-law had called with the news that horrible night. And he spoke of his son, Dave, and their once publicized estrangement.

How over the past four or five years he and Dave had worked hard to mend their relationship. He was proud of his son, he said. Sure the kid had gone a different path than his father had hoped for, but Dave was now running one of the most lucrative businesses in Carver, where he specialized in refurbishing antique bathtubs that could sell easily at up to five grand a pop, and he did it nearly all by himself, save for some hired muscle from a recently immigrated Guatemalan man who cared for his seven-year-old daughter while trying to earn an honest American dollar. Fletcher's point was that his son had done well, and in turn had done well for others. He said that hearts were breaking all up and down that family right now.

Following some biographical information, the story proceeded into the background of the accident, primarily drawing on the police report for details. Speaking on behalf of Claire and Freedom-Safe, Ron Bernard spoke cautiously, saying that it would be imprudent for him to discuss the details of the case, but he did indicate that his client had no reason to challenge any details of the police report. The evidence, in accordance with the laws of Rhode Island, was clearly on her side. Bernard spoke of the obvious emotional difficulty that his client was experiencing, and added that knowing she was innocent of any wrongdoing still didn't make this any easier. It was a case in which there could be no winners, despite what a verdict may read.

The article ended on a jump to a back page with Fletcher Kennealy saying that the family mostly looked forward to this being over, to a moment where the grief does not obsess them. He had been in law long enough to know that you can't close a chapter until the full conclusion is written, sealed, and filed. The piece ended with a quote from Fletcher saying that he hoped that "every

mother and father makes sure to stop what seems so damn important every day for just one minute to tell their kids *I love you.*" The
neatly stacked columns were surrounded by a story in photos: a
classic Fletcher pose on the steps of City Hall in the days when his
blood supposedly ran cold; a family photo circa 1975; a private
snapshot of grandfather and grandson smiling at each other in startled wonderment; an author photo of Claire; two of her book jackets; and the roadside memorial on Route 111.

      ☘   ☘   ☘

THE SMELL OF MORNING COFFEE spirited down the hallway toward the living room. Claire lay in her now standard recuperative
position on the couch, in spite of Richard's earlier insistence that
she needed to be up and about, negotiating some way to return to
normal. "It is curious that you would define normal for me," she
had commented. "Spending your days cooped up in the guest
room." He had smiled, and then turned grim, delivering a daily
lecture where he encouraged her to follow Dr. Heddeman's advice
about using the knee in small doses in order to keep it fluid, and
getting back to her work. She needed to take control of her life,
both physically and mentally. It was tender how much he wanted
things to be normal for her again. She wondered if in Richard she
had loved two different men, or two parts of the same man. And
the secret truth was that maybe she wasn't in a hurry to get everything back in order, because once she was better, he would be free
to leave.

It should have felt like a happier day. Bill Harrison had
e-mailed earlier saying that based on their conversations, he was
going to move the book up on the list, to a year from next spring.

He just wanted to make sure that she felt comfortable with that deadline, if she could please just let him know by tomorrow morning. Dan Gould never had written back. Maybe Bill had been right. That was Gould's way of giving his blessing. Still she couldn't stop the nagging feeling that she was about to destroy his life. Was that the only thing she was capable of doing to anybody she encountered these days?

The fax with the new witness statement sat on the kitchen table. She had not read it yet. Although her avoidance would be perceived as stubborn pride or even childish indolence, the matter went deeper for Claire. Reading that statement would take her into the night of the accident from another angle, through a different pair of eyes. In reentering that moment on the road, where indeed pride and elitism had taken over, she would see herself reflected ugly in the mirror. The human characteristics that she most despised had overtaken her for a lightning flash of a moment. The very behaviors by which she had condemned others in judgment, were the same acts that found her in search of contrition. But it was more than just facing herself, it was the idea that her secrets could be shared. The renowned, well-mannered scholar of Vincent van Gogh could have the same level of ugliness that everybody has. The same proclivity to misjudgments and prejudices as the next person. And in those secrets lay the heart of the real fear: that once the socioeconomic indicators were stripped away, Claire, in that moment on the road, was really no different from the Delta 88 woman.

When the phone rang Richard yelled from upstairs that he would get it.

Claire heard him stumble across his drawing equipment to try to catch the receiver before the answering machine. His voice was muffled coming through the ceiling. Still it was possible to make out the intonation of the conversation. It was news being delivered without the intent of celebration or despair, only the unnerving flow of information.

He came rushing down the stairs, lacing his arms into his overcoat. Rummaging through the hallway closet, Richard grabbed a coat for Claire, along with her boots. "We have to go" was all he said.

Claire sat upright. She pushed her laptop computer to the side. Since they had given up on the local media, the Internet had become her only source for news of the world.

Richard was kneeling down, slipping her boots onto her to feet.

"Richard? That wasn't Bill Harrison, was it?"

"We need to go right now."

He did not seem very celebratory. "Can you explain, please?"

"Bernard will tell us everything."

Claire stood, placing a hand on Richard's shoulder for balance. She followed his lead, starting to tense with the same nervousness that he exuded. Once her coat was on, they made their way to the door, where upon opening it, Claire realized that it was the first taste of fresh air that she had known since the ice incident. While it was in part refreshing, there was a sense of deterioration that frightened her.

❦　　❦　　❦

RON BERNARD WAS PACING WHEN they entered his office. Upon seeing them he reached over to his desk and grabbed the front page of the paper. "This has been a pure horseshit case from the start," he said, pushing the *Herald* toward them. "Pure horseshit."

Richard shrugged.

"You haven't seen this yet? My word." Bernard delivered a brief summary of the article, and then sat down in his chair, his sizeable frame melting into the plush leather. It was as though he absorbed the padded hide, rather than the expected opposite. In his younger days he could have played college football, maybe one of those big lugs on the line who crouch down and sink all their might into the field, forming a wall that momentarily exchanges flesh and blood for bricks. Perhaps a back injury had steered him into law. Or maybe the realization that the competitive nature to stand his ground in order to protect the ball had a better place in a reliable vocation, not one steeped in high risk. "Well, Mrs. Andrews, what a difference a week makes, wouldn't you say? And what the hell happened to your leg?"

A year ago she would have made a clever remark that combined the irony of timing with the self-deprecation of one's own luck. But that was a different Claire Andrews. One who had known her place in the world. "Broken kneecap," she said. "A slip on the ice."

"So now you'll appear reckless too. And I'm sure the doctors have given you painkillers, so add a drug history into the mix as well." Bernard picked up the *Herald*, and then slammed it atop his desk. "I have told you. The dirty little secret of any case involving the death of a child is sympathy. Once the jury makes incontrovertible fusion with the family, it makes a defense almost impossible unless there is irrefutable evidence to the contrary. And now this horseshit of an article is the final piece of the puzzle."

Richard interrupted. "Can you please tell us what is going on? Beside the *Herald* article."

"DiMallo contacted me with a settlement offer this morning. They finally put their offer on the table."

"Do they really think I have money for them to take?" Claire asked, her voice wearied.

"It's not money they want from you, Mrs. Andrews. They want an admission of guilt. Bullshit, I know. But bullshit is how it goes in my business . . . One last hurrah for Fletcher Kennealy in the name of his grandson."

"Excuse me?"

"DiMallo called me first thing this morning. He said the family is willing to not proceed to trial if, along with the recovered legal fees, you publicly acknowledge complicity for the death of the boy. Those are their settlement terms. Simple. Otherwise, they go to trial to seek the one and a half million dollars."

"But I didn't—"

Richard said, "We have the police report."

"Jack DiMallo will have a thousand and one ways to show that it is all a question of one man's judgment."

"What are the realities?" Richard asked.

"*The* reality is that a case is supposed to be determined on the rules of evidence—the facts of the case and the law are intended to be presented to the jury without prejudice. Still we know that the sympathy card is the cornerstone that makes the case. Kennealy and DiMallo are fully aware that it will only take a sprinkling of nonprejudicial evidence—some witness statements, a kink in the investigation, something about your character—to the allow them to introduce sympathy and emotion under the cloak of integrity.

You've seen the statement . . . And based on the precedent from Connecticut regarding 'the failure to keep a proper lookout'— what we talked about the other day . . . If you role that in with a jury's sympathy for the family—which was only further tainted by today's paper . . . Well you see where this is going."

Richard crossed and then uncrossed his legs. He reached for Claire's hand. She let him hold it. It was a strange gesture. His fingers clasped slightly over hers, prepared to move with the slightest indicator of rejection. Claire used all her might not to flinch. Richard's hand provided her with a sense of grounding, as though comforted by the grace of a strange angel whose touch feels familiar but is totally unrecognizable.

"I guarantee that DiMallo knows that we are meeting at this very minute," Bernard mused. "He's used to playing tough . . . I don't mean to be crass, Mrs. Andrews, but you hit the wrong kid."

"What do we do?" Richard asked, ignoring the last comment.

"I don't think there is a choice, do you?" Bernard ran his hand through his hair, leaving a single shock of black hair standing. "We're in a stranglehold. The good news is that you are dealing with a rich family—meaning, this is not about assets. I believe that all they are really after is a public acknowledgment and apology."

Richard asked, "And if we don't settle?"

"We could try to fight it, but I don't think we have a chance, for the reasons I have already laid out. Then your wife risks losing everything she owns, and then some. Plus the case becomes broadcast anyway; and as you have already found out, the public has already judged her guilty, even without any real evidence having been presented. From where I stand, the end result is the same. Either road you take will expose you. It can't be avoided. Accepting that, you have to ask yourself is your pride worth one and a half million dollars? That's the only real difference."

Claire finally spoke. "The only difference?" She instinctively tried to stand, but the shooting pain in her knee forced her right back down again. "This isn't right. You know it isn't right. Can you imagine what this will . . . The university is already distancing itself from me . . . My neighbors . . . Colleagues . . . This isn't right. Of course, I'd give everything if I could wake up and . . . But giving up my name doesn't change anything. The *real difference?* The *real difference* is that it's not right."

The bottom line was that DiMallo had given them twenty-four hours to make a decision. After that he was raging forward toward the courthouse. Again, Bernard summarized the basic truth that they had been outmaneuvered by the best and most powerful, and they should all feel lucky and relieved that the Kennealys were really only after an apology. It could all end tomorrow, the disruption and destruction complete, and everybody's lives could proceed as normal as possible. As far as Bernard was concerned, there was nothing to consider, plus it was more than likely that FreedomSafe Insurance would not allow him to go forward at this point anyway, especially with a reasonable settlement on the table. That was another reality. But still, he said, Richard and Claire should talk it over and come to terms with it on their own.

By 8:30 A.M. tomorrow.

❦   ❦   ❦

IT WAS A SILENT CAR ride home. Claire stared out the window. A light rain had begun to fall, leaving distorted streaks along the glass. The streets were blackened. A thin woman under a blue umbrella scurried over the bridge toward College Hill, hunching her shoulders and pressing her chin down into her collar, too distracted to notice the swirl of the river below. Claire envied the way the woman seemed to float up the hill. Weightless and undistracted.

Her knee was throbbing. Too much time had passed between pain pills, and quickly the hurt was unmasking. She tried stretching her leg out, but that only seemed to complicate matters. The simple movement of withdrawing her leg to the original position was almost enough to make her scream. She just wanted to be back on her couch. A painkiller falling down her throat, a pillow propped beneath the knee, and her notebooks on her lap. She wanted to close the door, lock and seal it tight, all in an effort to keep the world from spilling in.

♧   ♧   ♧

"SHOULD WE TALK ABOUT IT?" Richard asked. He stood over the couch where Claire had landed instinctively, her arms crossed over her chest.

"No." She stared at the ceiling. "This whole place has just grown so miserable."

"I wonder if we should get a new lawyer. I'm not sure Bernard's right for this. They have been bullying him from the start. He's never once been willing to take these guys on. To call them on their—"

"He works for the insurance company, Richard."

"Maybe we need someone who represents us, is all I'm saying. That's all, I mean. Look at how he came across in that article." He shook his head. "I just don't know what to do."

"I do. I need to move, Richard. Far away from here. I just need to move."

He sat down beside her. He placed his hands flat on his lap.

"Maybe west. Someplace expansive. Montana, maybe. Or Wyoming, even. A little house with a lot of land around it. A lot of land. Big wide fields for Cocoa to run around in. I think Montana, Richard. Nobody there will know anything. It will all be fresh. Someplace expansive."

Richard just looked at her. He spoke slowly, almost matching her dreamy quality. "Maybe I could come also, Claire. Maybe being away from everything familiar would be good for—"

"I couldn't ask that, Richard. I don't know that I could ask that."

"But if you did . . ."

"Montana, Richard. That will be the place. Montana. Away from this depressing area and the way people are . . . The Wallers with their sad pitiful smiles, and all the others gawkers looking down at the bumper, like they are going to see . . . The university, which would pressure me to resign the minute I'd admit to . . . And where does that leave . . . Out of this stinking town is where it takes me. Someplace expansive, Richard. And then where are you in that, Richard? Where are you, really?"

"Claire, of course I am—"

"Don't answer, Richard. Don't answer anything until you know what you really mean to say. Because you can't take it back again this time. You can't . . ."

"But I—"

"No, don't answer. Please."

Richard unleashed a long breath. "Then what do I do?"

"How about if you go upstairs and work, or something. I just need to be by myself for a while. I need some quiet."

He stood up. "Eight-thirty tomorrow morning. I'll look forward to this all being over once and for all . . . Finally."

"Even when there are no choices?"

"Claire."

"Okay." She nodded her head. "Okay. Just go work on your face muscles, or whatever it is." She tried to smile. "Then we'll talk."

When he left to go upstairs, Claire tried to clear her mind of what "this all being over once and for all" would really mean. She closed her eyes to see the painting of *Crows over the Wheatfield*. She saw an amalgamation, the print above her office desk and the actual site in Auvers. It was almost as though they were two distinct images, both on clear paper, and laid over each other. And in her single image, the painted crows darken the sky, while the heavy mud compresses her step. There are the deep blues of the impasto sky, contrasting the fragrances of breaking straw. She stands at the convergence of the paths, waiting, contemplating her first step. It is a perfect moment of peace, one that should be preserved forever, because it will never be again.

Van Gogh knew that.

Gachet knew it too.

Opening her eyes to her living room, where a burst of sunlight streaked through the window, and the ears of her dog peeked in attention to her movement, and the phone rang nonstop from reporters hoping for a story, and her husband, or whatever he was, sat upstairs drawing her a picture, and her leg ached while her stomach churned, and the true beauty of this moment is that she is neither innocent nor guilty, Claire knew it too.

Vincent did the only possible thing to preserve the moment. He captured it into an immortal space, and then to ensure his sense of permanence he removed himself from the picture. And in the parlance of modern psychology, perhaps he had displaced the difficult process of reasoning with the illusion that choosing suicide was a logical decision.

In the effort to foster dependence, Gachet would have reinforced the notion that any road was treacherous. No matter how bright they appeared, he would say, all of Vincent's paths eventually would lead to darkness.

But what Gachet had failed to consider was that his dire predictions cast the illusion of an idyllic present to his patient. Coming to Auvers and escaping the swirled dreams that told the story of the South had all shone brightly on the painter. Vincent would not have seen this as a moment that he needed to progress from, but a place where he wanted to be.

Now here comes the good doctor telling Vincent that he inevitably will be forced to step forward into the dark.

For Vincent, who must have felt himself slipping away under his relentless trust in Gachet, there would only be one way to cling to the purity he envisioned. As for Gachet, he would have smiled as he took one more step up the evolutionary ladder.

Although Ron Bernard seemed certain that there was no choice to the settlement offer, Claire had become more and more convinced that she was not willing to be pressed into a public revelation of her private guilt. She will always hate herself for being the woman in the car that night. For the stupidity of judgment, for the imperfection of her life, and mostly for her helplessness. But as she lay back on the couch, a head medicated just enough to detach from a throbbing knee, she considered that she should not take the settlement. It is her own truths that she must have to live with, not those imposed by everybody else. And in this moment she is willing to stand by them. And die with them too. Because there really are truths that transcend the individuals who tell them.

Ω   Ω   Ω

SHE THREW HER NOTEBOOK TO the floor. Bill Harrison had just left her a message checking in to make sure that he got her previous message, and to see if she had any thoughts on it. He *really needed* to have this settled by tomorrow morning. She tried to grab for her notebook, but it was just out of reach. She had wanted to throw it again. Maybe this time out the door. She was about to commit to selling out Dan Gould.

Her initial tendency was to get up and storm around the house, calming herself through the energy of movement. But due to her immobility, Claire instead reached for her laptop, hoping to lose herself to the computer world. She scanned the news headlines. The state of the world only further riled her, sickened by the helpless reality that the educated middle class will never rise from the ashes of elitist embers.

She checked her e-mail. When all was said and deleted, there was left a lone correspondence. Claire didn't recognize the address, nor did it have any of the nominal indicators, such as a name or an organization. It was a jumble of letters, followed by a random numerical sequence. She clicked it hesitantly, remembering the virus warnings of the university IT squad. But with the subject line reading *Auvers*, Claire felt a degree of safety. The moment that she clicked it, the thought occurred to her that *Auvers* might be something related to Dan Gould or Paul Chambers. The idea temporarily startled her until she came to the conclusion that she should have known from the beginning: if there was concern about what she wrote, then what she wrote must matter.

The letter started off with the strikingly formal but personal *Dear Claire*. She quickly scrolled to the bottom of what was turning out to be a lengthy e-mail. Lauren Morris was the signatory. A former student? A colleague from a past conference? It sounded so familiar, yet she couldn't place it. She scrolled back to the top. Had she just read the first line prior to the chase for the name, it would have clicked instantly. "It was awesome meeting you in Auvers a few weeks ago, and having you show us around all the sites." Immediately she drew the picture of the girl and her boyfriend— Lauren and Bobby. Claire could see the soft brown hair, hanging slightly unstrung in the carelessness of the traveler. Her blue eyes. A girl's face on the verge of becoming womanly yet still having the softness and ease of a child. She couldn't recall much of Bobby, other than a mood of impatience that swelled as a dark green blot. It was as though he were a story that Lauren had told over and over again, a trailing familiar presence without any distinct sense of being.

In the e-mail, Lauren told Claire that she was writing from a little Internet café in Barcelona, and that she could see Gaudi's cathedral. Bobby had gone on to Madrid solo. After they had left Auvers for Paris, she and Bobby had started drifting apart. "You inspired me to take more interest in the art and history of what we were seeing," the letter said, "while B just wanted to hang out during the day and party at night. You saw how he was in Auvers. A quick look to say he'd been there, and then gone." They had spent an unhappy week in Paris before they caught the train south, "right on schedule, as you are probably imagining." Lauren had done the unthinkable by altering their schedule to stop for the day in Figueres to visit the Dalí museum, a little more than an hour from Barcelona. She even had made the train arrangement. "B literally flipped out of his mind. He couldn't believe that the town was so boring, and that I had dragged him here b/c of this art that he tried to say wasn't even art." They hardly were talking by the time they got to Barcelona later that night. And when Lauren had said the Picasso museum was top on her list of sites for the city, Bobby had just "thrown up his hands whatever." It was late in the evening by that point, and he stormed out to a club and wasn't even back by the time she left for the Picasso the next morning. "I guess I don't have to tell you that it seems that we were seeing things differently." After another blowup that sounded to Claire as if it were more obligatory than passionate, Bobby left for Madrid, with no real plan on reconvening for the rest of the trip. "He said something lame like he hoped I enjoyed my egghead trip, or something like that. And then he was out of there. I went off to look at La Pedrera."

It was a strange communiqué, one that carried the tone of old friends who have promised to keep in touch, but only remember to do so on occasion when the odd reminder cajoles them. Although a little puzzled, Claire was happy she'd gotten the note. It was an antidote to all the temporarily intimate relationships formed while traveling, or even the counterbalance to most of her former students, who quietly disembarked out into the world as though evaporating. The ending of the note touched Claire the most. Lauren had said that she didn't know when she would be checking her e-mail again, and that

> *I don't think that I really expect a reply. And maybe you and I will never talk again, I don't know. But sometimes, you know, you walk around all dreamy, thinking that things are the way they are b/c that's the way they are, and b/c that's the only way they are supposed to be (I hope that makes sense). And then something steps right out in front of you and startles you, and wakes you up into a better place. I think that's pretty cool. It kind of makes me sick thinking that I could have just gone on with B as before. If I hadn't crossed into your path in Auvers I would probably still be following B around, too foggy to know the difference of how miserable I was. Anyway, that's about it until next time—whenever that may be.*

For the first time in months, Claire had the feeling that she had given life to someone. From Ronnie Kennealy to Paul-Ferdinand Gachet to Dan Gould, and even, to some extent, Richard and Vincent van Gogh, it seemed as though Claire had been razing something at every turn. But finally here was a collision that resulted in Claire being able to help someone feel alive. A rainstorm doesn't always produce a flood.

Claire would reply later. She would fill in Lauren when there was a complete story to tell. Perhaps they would continue the correspondence. And perhaps once the gap in their ages started to close they would find themselves as friends, forever amazed by the coincidence that had brought them together. But for now she relished being the perfect stranger who had no history other than having appeared at just the right second.

The upstairs floorboards were creaking from Richard's endless pacing. "This is shit," he yelled down the staircase, after a pause.

Claire kept her eyes closed. She laid the computer on the floor after rereading the e-mail a last time. The chenille blanket was pulled up to her neck. The soft nubs tickled below her chin. In order to avoid getting too hot, she had pulled out her left arm and let it drape along the couch top. She stretched her bum leg out of the covers, hoping to ease the stiffness. "Just keep going," Claire yelled back.

"What did you say?"

"I said that you need to keep going."

She could hear Richard walking down the upstairs hall. The top stair squealed its unique cry that can only be avoided by gripping the banister and putting your full weight on the left. Claire forever had held the idea that the unequal distribution would eventually eliminate the creak. Richard stopped after only one step down. "What did you say again?" he said. "What did you say?"

Although she didn't open her eyes, Claire could feel him looking directly at her. "You need to keep going." She spoke slowly, as though on the verge of sleep. "You just have to draw yourself out of this," to which she laughed quietly at her own pun.

"Right," he mumbled. "Right."

In the natural rhythm of the situation there would have been a slight pause before the stair creaked several times, with Richard heading back to the makeshift studio. But a stillness held the moment. Only the sound of his hand rubbing back and forth along the handrail could be heard. It was as though he were absent of breath.

"Richard?" she called out.

His palm continued to stroke the wood.

"Richard, is everything okay? What has happened?" She could see the whole thing. She was going to have to kick off the covers, use the same strength that allows fragile grandmothers to lift up their Pontiacs to save trapped grandchildren, and bound up the stairs to his rescue, with one hand on the receiver to 911, and the other pumping his chest between respirations. She pictured it clearly. Most telling, though, was the sense of urgency that she felt. She would have no idea how to manage without him.

He said, "I'm fine." He spoke as though snapping out of a dream. "I was only thinking for a minute . . . Yes, I am fine." Then Claire heard the proper order of sounds, and Richard was back in the bedroom, his footsteps as markers.

    ❦   ❦   ❦

SHE MUST HAVE FALLEN ASLEEP. There was no sense that she had been dreaming. No feeling of rest. Or even the murky perceptions of a world come back into focus. Still she knew that she had been awoken when Richard stood over her, saying her name at least three times in a room that suddenly seemed too small.

    ❦   ❦   ❦

A RUSTY DARKNESS SETTLED OUTSIDE. Upon waking, Claire was glad to figure out that it was night, far away from tomorrow morning. There was still time before any decisions were to be made about books, lawsuits, or even relationships, for that matter. The moment, as awful as it was, was a comfortable place for her to be. It may have been surrounded by terror, but at least it was known terror.

Richard knelt down. His face looked bright, eyes crinkling at the corners, biting down into his lower lip. It was the look he had when trying to control excitement or anticipation. "I've got it," he whispered, as if any rise in volume would wake them from a mutual dream of a long life of simple companionship.

"Got what?" The medication parched her throat, making it hard to talk.

"The drawing."

Claire rubbed her eyes. She straightened herself up a bit. Her cheekbones felt weighted. She pushed her fingers against her sinuses, hoping to relieve some of the pressure.

"It's not quite finished, but it is finished enough."

"Okay then." She began to turn. "You'll have to help me upstairs."

"It's down here already. On the easel."

Claire craned her head to the left to see Richard's easel blocking the staircase. A red flannel sheet hung over the top for the grand unveiling. She must have been sound asleep, because she didn't hear even the slightest disturbance while he must have been setting it up. "Why the big presentation?"

Richard didn't move, still kneeling beside her. His right foot tapped furiously.

"Well, let's see it already," she said.

He stood up and walked over to the easel. "Before I show you," he said, "please remember that it is not fully finished. In fact it is still probably more of a draft."

"Richard, don't apologize."

"But first, I just want to tell you what it is called."

Claire nodded. "Fair enough."

"Remember it is still a work in progress . . ."

"For God's sake, Richard."

"It is called, *Claire as the Wheatfield*," and with that he pulled off the flannel sheet.

It was primarily a black-and-white sketch, with subtle hints of deep yellows and patches of sky blue shaded into the background. While Richard's medical illustrations reflected his proclivity toward the control and rigidity of the pencil, the lines in this sketch captured the fluid motion of his entire arm, as though it were a boneless, free-flowing conduit, acting in sway with the grace of a body in dance.

It took a moment for Claire to focus on the piece. Initially the drawing appeared as a mass of strokes. Chaos spiraled in multiple directions, the blues and yellows calling out in homage to the patterns and hues from Vincent's wheat fields. It took full commitment to believe there was any sense of order. But as Claire looked beyond the obvious, the randomness of the lines began to take shape. What had at first seemed so disordered and arbitrary now took its form in the literal.

The sketch portrayed Claire lying on the couch. Her injured leg was splayed out to the floor. It kicked out straight, and disappeared off the corner of the paper. The opposite arm, healthy but wearied, rested languidly on the top of the couch, a slight bend at the elbow, with piano-length fingers hanging down, their tips touching the brash yellow pasture that was the fabric. Her blanketed body spired down the center of the drawing, with only the texture of indiscriminate shapes to indicate human form. The picture was, as Richard had so obviously titled it, Claire as Vincent's wheat field. Three paths. In one direction went the injured leg. The weariness of her draped arm represented a second path. And the third path, the lost staid valley, was her reclined body. Beyond the theme, most fascinating was the technique. Through the riptide of structure, Richard brilliantly had alternated the force of his strokes to show the incongruity of rationality and irrationality. In many respects, technically, the piece was as Claire initially had seen it: the perfect blend of calm and chaos.

Richard stood beside the easel. His chest billowed in and out. He glanced at Claire, and then to the floor, over to her, and then out the windows where the night temporarily had stained even the stars. This was a familiar posture for Richard. One in which Claire imagined he took comfort. It was the Richard of every one of his openings. Fussing about in the gallery hours before the show. Going home to model a dozen different sport coats that were as ratty as the next. Gathering his poise. Rehearsing faces in the mirror as he mussed his hair and then combed it back. Arriving at the gallery in time to ensure that people had already gathered, and then seeing his bravado shrink into the awkwardness of a teenage boy who finds himself emotionally exposed and the center of attention. As painful as it might have felt to him, Richard would know that feeling as the measure of his success. And in that he must have taken great comfort.

"It's really good," Claire said.

"It is still unfinished . . . The fields. It's also supposed to represent Montana. *Someplace expansive.*"

"I don't know what to say." Looking at it, she could picture them living out west. And it would not be a holiday, a project, or even a quick escape. It would be a new life, one in which they were willing to live with everything being unfamiliar and new. They would exist solely in the future—someone else's future—without any past to call on.

Richard grabbed at the flannel sheet as if he were going to cover up the picture again. He let the flannel fall to the floor. He bit down on his lip again. "Now what?"

Claire sat upright. "You might get bored with me in Montana, Richard. *That's* what. Away from all this. With no drama. No craziness. Just us, Richard. It would be just us. You'd have swear to me—your Scouting medals, your whatever—that you will not get bored with me, Richard."

He didn't react much except to nod his head. But that was to be expected. He was not one for dramatic speeches. Still even his expression, as flaccid as it was, implied a promise of compliance and commitment.

"I am tired," Claire said. "And the morning of decisions is not far away." They lay in her bed through the night, holding each other. There were no inferences of lust, nor intentions of sex. Just the kind of passion that has no form or expression. A gift that cannot be defined.

On that warm July 27 night in 1890, Vincent lugged his easel and painting supplies up to the wheat fields. Somewhere he tucked the revolver onto his person. The analogy cannot be assumed that Vincent had agonized about this decision the night before. That he had watched the clock, knowing that the following day he would be forced into the definitive decision that he had likely contemplated in many temperamental moments

throughout the past. Likely, it was some impending expecta-
tion on the twenty-sixth that troubled Vincent in that impetu-
ous moment. This is where conjecture takes over. It is the
missing step in the proof. The equation is laid out, with the an-
swer gleaming proudly under the answer bar; but there is a de-
pendent variable missing that, despite the presence of a logical
conclusion, renders the theorem useless by the absence of a
completed logic. And that is where Gachet lies hidden. He has
tried to burden Vincent with dependency. He has woven the
cure into the sickness. Gachet has trained his patient to fear any
step he might take alone. He has convinced Vincent that be-
sides the drugs, the path to wellness lies on the easel, subject to
his medical translation (and, not surprisingly, also subject to
the doctor's possession of many of the canvases—greed and
power being the underlying motive to all manipulations).

On that warm July 27 night in 1890, Vincent might have
looked out at the terrain, and then back to the easel. For the
first time in all the years of frantic artistic explosion he had
nothing to say. The next day he would be expected to walk over
to the good doctor's house to show off his new work and talk of
the good health his painting brought, while drinking a toast to
lucidity and the doctor's benevolent generosity. But there would
be no work. The painter, despite Gachet's intentions, would
have seen himself as cured. In his first real moment of objective
clarity, Vincent would conclude that he was no longer subjected
to the need to produce art as his means of coping. Now, instead
of rushing to show off his newest creation to Gachet, Vincent
would awake in the Auberge Raveaux beside an empty canvas.

Intrinsically he would know that the truth of the cure would disappoint the doctor. Gachet might turn in disgust from Vincent, causing the painter to leave Auvers disgraced and potentially broken, yet again, and having to seek out his brother's assistance for another in a series of fresh starts. Or Gachet might summon up the rueful gaze of the surrogate father and tell Vincent that categorically there was no living end for this depression without him as therapist, the so-called proof of the empty canvas only representing deterioration, not progress. Even with Vincent's suspicions about the doctor's mental health, Gachet's manipulations still would prove successful. Vincent, knowing that he had reached the point where he had to choose a path, would still find it impossible to believe that he was capable of making the right choice, courtesy of the good doctor.

It is no wonder that on that warm July 27 night in 1890, standing in the wheat field before those three disparate roads, Vincent put down his brush and reached for the revolver.

To paraphrase what the Cheshire cat said to Alice, If you don't know where you are going, then any road will do.

WEDNESDAY

Surprisingly, Richard was still sound asleep at eight-fifteen. The night had passed rather quickly, dissolving into a morning disguised under a low cloud cover. Claire had suspected that Richard would have been up pacing between the bedroom and the living room, anxious to wake her in anticipation of Fletcher Kennealy and Jack DiMallo's deadline. Instead, with only fifteen minutes to spare, Richard lay curled on his old side of the bed, still wearing the sweats that he laid down in, lost in restful slumber.

Claire limped out of the bedroom, steadying herself along the wall. She took a careful step over Cocoa, whose snoring and twitching were the only signs of life from an otherwise flaccid carcass. In the living room, Claire sat down on the couch. She gripped the cordless phone. Stared at the numbers on the keypad, and then looked up at Richard's drawing to see herself reflected back at her.

She began to dial Bernard's office.

She had decided that there was no such thing as good and bad. They were merely the markers of a cultural relativism. It was a fallacy of alternatives in which something that is bad cannot be good, and even more so, the communal jurisprudence that the holder of a bad action cannot be a good person. In truth, that fallacy was what the Kennealys wanted reaffirmed. Without the distinctions, there could be no logic for them.

She punched the last number. Her stomach tightened. It only rang once.

"Tell him it is Mrs. Andrews," she said to the receptionist. "He'll be expecting my call. Tell him it's Mrs. Andrews."

She waited for Bernard, listening to the rhythmic silence of the hold. He answered with stuttered anticipation. "Mrs. Andrews," was all he said. Then Bernard repeated her name again, this time as a question.

"I just can't accept this offer," she said. "I guess I'll go to trial, if I have to. Just tell me what . . . What needs to be signed and I'll sign it. What needs to be done and I'll do it. It's just that I can't . . . I'm sorry, but . . . I just can't."

And later she will call Bill Harrison and apologize for wasting his time, knowing that the only clean path is one that does not trample over Dan Gould. She knows it will sicken her to say that. That she will forever be tongue-tied by the secret of the painting, but that she will rest easier knowing that she has spared a man, based merely on his word. She will tell Bill that she will write the book when Dan Gould is ready. After all, like him, she has to live with herself.

PART FOUR

One

Spring

Morning

MONDAY

Claire and Richard went out the back door of their Sunset District apartment, and quietly looked for the Golden Gate Bridge against the San Francisco horizon. When perched on tiptoes in the rear corner of their backyard, halfway up the slope on Sixth Avenue, the uppermost pillars of the bridge could be seen, its red peaks cutting through the oaks and liquid ambers, a strong sight against a blue sky paled by fog. Richard stood behind Claire, peering over her shoulder. It had been nearly a year since the legal nightmare had ended. He watched her back rise and fall in steady breaths. Cocoa ran anxiously along the fence line, sniffing all possible spots, before she finally squatted near a patch of wild calla lilies, and then resumed her search, leaving behind a trail of steam. "It seems impossible," Richard said. She didn't need to ask him to clarify what he meant. "Yes," she replied. "Completely impossible."

They never did go to Montana. As the case had appeared to be heading to trial, Claire had taken a leave from the university with the intent of never coming back—a mutually satisfactory decision—and Richard had sublet his Cambridge apartment for the balance of the year, anticipating that they would be hunkered down in Providence for many stressful months to come. After a lot of deliberating, they decided to fire Ron Bernard and in his place hired a lawyer named Porter Smyth; he came down from Boston with a reputation, and an hourly fee that matched. Smyth spoke with a slight tick in his left eye, and he drummed his fingers against his thighs while he thought. He was not afraid to go to trial, something that Jack DiMallo didn't need to be told—any lawyer in town could tell you stories during cocktail hour about Porter Smyth's love of the courtroom—and all interested parties knew that the last thing Kennealy and DiMallo wanted was to actually go to trial with a case that lacked substantial evidence. He was willing to call their bluff. DiMallo initially had countered by trying to paper Claire to death, hoping to induce her into their settlement terms by increasing her financial burden with Smyth's legendary fees. Smyth threatened a countersuit of harassment, and then barked at DiMallo that he hoped the judge saw past the obvious lack of evidence that the Kennealy case had, because he just wanted to go to court for the thrill of proving them wrong. What followed was a stressful month of give-and-take negotiations, resulting with Smyth finally convincing DiMallo to drop this whole thing, agreeing that he would broker a settlement with FreedomSafe to close the case for its nuisance value, coupled with a binding agreement that would allow everyone to walk away as though these negotiations had never happened. It ended up being a little more complex, with Claire owing a significant amount of out-of-pocket fees. But just like that, the case was over. Nearly eight months after the first brief was filed. And barely a story appeared in the newspaper.

Standing in the backyard, as the fog started to burn off, Claire could still remember the moment when Smyth had called to say that the legal battle officially had ended. She and Richard had just stared at each other. They hadn't smiled or sighed, or even broken down into tears. They only looked at each other as if they were lost. And finally Richard had reached down and taken Claire's hands. They were cold and sticky, and as he tried to grip them tighter, they only went limp. He asked her if she was glad that it was finally over, and she coughed, clearing her throat and looking for words, and then asked him if he honestly believed it really was all over. Richard tried to smile at her, as though implying something along the lines of a new beginning, but it came off cockeyed and awkward, and he stammered out "I mean" a few times before he stopped trying, and neither of them made any gesture toward the future. At the moment when they might have ordered an AAA travel plan to eagerly plan their escape to Montana, they stood motionless, as though encased in thin glass and overly cautious of the slightest movement. The idea of Montana had become as ridiculous as it should have been all along. The illusion of either of them living the outback life simply was laughable. These were two people who thrived on the energy of crowded streets, who were given purpose by trying to seek solace from the chaos. They would be out of their minds within days in rural Montana, perhaps only briefly comforted by the sight of watching Cocoa run freely (assuming that was what *she* wanted). They had dreamt up their whole sentimental fantasy of the wide open when they believed there was nothing left to dream, when they both believed that they would be ensconced in everlasting legal battles, anchored to New England until the last drop of blood had been spilled. When they had hired Porter Smyth, Richard bought a bottle of champagne in hopes of a victory celebration. A month after the case ended, it still lay on its side in the refrigerator, pushed to the back of the bottom shelf, and layered with Tupperware and cheeses in plastic wrap. Together, Richard and Claire had been wandering around Providence feeling lost. There no longer had been anything for them to hope for anymore. Richard found the bottle when they were packing to leave for San Francisco, nearly three long months later. When he opened it, the champagne had gone flat.

"It is amazing how quiet this city can be sometimes," she said to Richard. Cocoa ran up and smelled her leg, and then scampered away, as though it was a game. "You can almost hear the fog rolling. It whispers."

He just nodded, staring out as the sun started breaking in toward the top of the bridge. "We are lucky to be able to live here," he said. "We are lucky."

It had been more than two years since the accident. And the roads that Claire drove were different, and the air that she breathed smelled different (even tasted different, with a salty edge), and the history of where she lived was different—this dollhouse of a city that once was ravaged and destroyed, since reconstructed in elegance, and even expanded, where some of its most scenic points are built on top of the ruins of that very devastation, bringing to it a false sense of foundation. And yet there was still not a moment when Claire did not lose her breath when a shadow fell across the windshield, nor when she felt a sense of panic while reaching over to turn up the car radio or passing the boys who cheated into the crosswalk on Market and Castro as she veered up Seventeenth Street toward the Avenues. She considered that it was not as though every one of these moments served as a reminder, but rather that they were an extension of that moment on Route 111—a bubble that had trapped her, stretching with no dimension.

"I can just see part of it," Claire said. She pointed. "Right there. Just the tip. Through the fog. Where the sun is breaking through."

Richard stepped beside her, crouched a bit, and swayed some to his left. "Yes," he said. "Yes."

Aware of the time, they rushed back into the apartment, gathered their things set in the long narrow hall, and left through the front door. The furniture was laid out the same as in the Providence house, just more compactly.

Parnassus Avenue was busy this time of morning. The hospital staff and medical students and visitors and the infirm all made their way up the hill to the medical campus, as though the business of illness could be set to a clock. Richard had an interview with a neurologist who was coauthoring a textbook on the spine, and still not sure if he wanted traditional illustration or if he wanted to give in to the digital age. It had been harder here on the West Coast for Richard to sell his skills, since the proximity to Silicon Valley had pushed everybody's expectations toward computerized images. But this doctor had seemed to value tradition, and based on the phone conversation they had had a week earlier, Richard felt confident about getting this job.

Claire was going to catch the 6, and then transfer downtown onto the BART train to get across the bay to Berkeley. She did this twice a week, where she taught two back-to-back classes at Cal as a distinguished visiting professor. There she could stand in front of her class in 308B Doe with no other identity than as a scholar of art history. Her only backstory was the research she had conducted and the books she had published. Her future was only presumed by the research she would continue on *Crows over the Wheatfield*, and its subsequent publication. (However her research still sat in an unpacked box with the illusion that she needed some distance on it before returning to the project.) Claire looked forward to her teaching days. She was able to leave the overwhelming ennui that was recalled when she sat alone in the quiet of their flat. Taking the train to the East Bay gave her a reason to venture out—minus the anxiety of having to be behind the wheel—and have the sensation that she was leading a different life. But sometimes when the train would be underground, Claire would catch her reflection in the darkened window, and for a moment startle at her face, as though she were seeing a long-ago acquaintance who she couldn't quite place, but nevertheless had once held some level of intimacy. And it would just hang there, framed in the black, like a backlit museum mask whose aloneness is both haunting and powerful.

"Look back," Richard said. He turned around and walked backward up the hill. "Turn around," he said. "Come on, Claire, turn around."

She kept walking forward, her satchel pulling down on her shoulder. The wind kicked up, as it always does going up the hill, and the air felt more damp and clinging. She pulled her collar up, and hunched a little, looking down at the ground to quicken her pace. Barriers blocked off the intersection at Third Avenue. Plastic sawhorses with calico stripes. The city was tearing up the street. It seemed as though they were always tearing up the streets around here.

"Claire. Just look. Right behind you. Turn around to look behind you."

"I don't need to see anything back there right now, Richard. I need to get to my bus, and you need to get to your meeting."

Richard still did not give in. He took large backward steps up the hill, occasionally glancing behind to make sure that he was staying straight. "If we get up above the fog line you won't be able to see what I'm seeing. Come on, Claire, turn around."

But she didn't turn around, and Richard walked backward for a few more steps before finally righting himself. Then he reached down and took her hand, and she held it. He didn't tell her that from the side of this hill one could follow Parnassus as it descended the short distance down the hill where it turned into Judah, and then ran out its course for another mile or so until it dead-ended into Ocean Beach. There, the water was shining in its blueness, infinite as though there was no horizon—only the rise of the Farallon Islands breaking up the expanse—and that off to the right, if they kept going up and into the parking lot at the top of the hill, the entire span of the Golden Gate Bridge would be visible. He really wished she would turn around, and look to see the boundless beauty and the potential that was always available. Had the conversation taken place, Claire would have said that she didn't need to see the whole bridge. Just a speck of it was good; enough to know that it was there.

They held hands as they walked onward, always aware of keeping forward because that was the only place that the past could never really be. His hand felt good in hers, it felt strong, and it somehow felt impossible. And sometimes she had to catch herself. She needed to turn off her mind, and feel the love that came from Richard for what it was. Because even three thousand miles away, where their histories were anonymous and they could walk as quietly as they wanted through the noise of the living, over a terrain that was as foreign as anything either had ever known, and where all should've been forgotten or at least forgiven, Claire could not help but link all the incidents in her life as though it was a collection of framed events, separated by thin white borders. It would be absurd to take Richard's hand without thinking that this moment—walking up Parnassus Avenue in San Francisco, her legal troubles behind her, on her way to teach at Berkeley, deeply and unconditionally loved—was not possible without the tragedy. But she knew this thought would pass. Claire now lived fully aware that every day brought collisions of split-second decisions that could alter the course of your life forever. Most of the time they were barely noticeable. It was only the unlucky times when they made themselves aware.

And tonight, when the sun has set over the bridge, and the city turns even quieter, and Richard has turned in early when she wasn't quite ready for sleep for another few hours, she will step over Cocoa, finally on the way to the bedroom. She will lie down next to Richard. His breath will float like the atmosphere. No matter what the consequences, she will know that together they are the keepers of the truth. What they know exceeds books and jobs and paintings and commercial ventures. They are the art. Both the exposition and expression of truth.

Claire will place her hand on Richard's back and close her eyes. Let herself drift down this road. Willing to accept wherever they are going. But when she closes her eyes, Claire knows that she will see Ronnie Kennealy staring at her, peaceful and passionate, just as he had through her windshield. He is still there every now and then. Maybe one day, she hopes, he won't be.

ACKNOWLEDGMENTS

As always, thanks to family, friends, and colleagues. I am grateful for the support of Michael Morrison, Henry Ferris, Lisa Gallagher, Sharyn Rosenblum, Peter Hubbard, and everybody else at William Morrow/HarperCollins who lends their expertise to my writing in ways I barely know about. Thanks to those who helped with the various stages of research: Emilie Benoit, Richard Lefebvre, Tara O'Neil, Mel Yoken, Roger Williams University Center for Global & International Programs, the town of Auvers-sur-Oise, and others I know I'll be embarrassed later for neglecting. Rhea Wilson for her close and thoughtful reading, and Dr. Roy J. Nirschel for his encouragement. And of course, Alisson and Addison, without whom little would be possible.